Garibaldi's Overcoat

DAI BLATCHFORD

Iponymous Edition

First Published in 2015

By Iponymous publishing Limited Iponymous Swansea United Kingdom
SA6 6BP

A CIP record for this book
is available from the British Library

(EBook) ISBN 978-1-908773-90-6
(Physical Book) ISBN 978-1-908773-91-3

www.iponymous.com

DAI BLATCHFORD

Dai Blatchford has lived in Wales and Cornwall. He has been variously a Police Cadet, Local Government Clerk, Civil Servant, and Careers Adviser. He received his higher education at Oxford and Swansea. At Oxford he was fortunate to be tutored by Terry Eagleton and it was as a student there that he published his first poetry in an anthology called 'Doves for the Seventies.' Once upon a time he was a lecturer and subsequently a Senior Tutor at an F.E. college in Cornwall. On retirement he returned to Wales and settled in Mumbles where he became a freelance journalist writing for a series of magazines. His first novel 'A Touch of Pigskin' took a while to write and was well received. The sequel, 'Garibaldi's Overcoat' is the book you are now holding and there is another project in the pipeline. He is married to Rosie and has two grown up children, two granddaughters and a grandson.

1

GARIBALDI'S OVERCOAT

Garibaldi's Overcoat was one of those harbour bars that got darker when the lights were turned on. Mostly they stayed off.

The sun outside could shine as much as it liked. Inside the bar it was always night. Lighting was by way of candles and not the popular scented ones either. This bar smelled of tallow. It was the way that Marco Spinelli, the owner, liked it. Visitors who happened upon the place tended to sit at the few ageing tables just outside the front door which was the only point of access to the place. They could talk of the original atmosphere, and of meeting the real Italians when they returned home. Few would have realised that this was the roughest bar on the Villa Novello seafront.

Marco ruled with a rod of iron. He kept it under the scrubbed whitewood bar that he spent most days and nights behind. Many a drunken sailor had spent the night in the local ospedale having been laid low by Marco's peacemaker for stepping out of line. He had broken more than his share of heads when things became a little feisty round about closing time. As he was fond of saying he was big enough to look after himself.

Marco was not a member of any sinister local grouping but came from a large and very tight family. His five brothers all carried the family stamp: they were all giants. Not one weighed less than sixteen stone and all earned money through fishing supplemented by a range of other activities, mostly legal. They spent their days fishing whenever they could and their nights drinking. When trouble did start, as it occasionally did, Marco had his own private army dotted around the candlelit gloom of Garibaldi's Overcoat. Into this waxy gloom stepped Bones and Prideaux both thankful to get out of the strong Italian sun and into a drink or two.

"Don't look now Bonesie but if this place had a piano player he would have already stopped playing."

"Don't be such a softie Piers. Look behind the bar. That's Marco. It's his bar and he's a friend from way back. I haven't seen him for a while. He'll look after us. Don't you worry your pretty little head about it."

"Never mind him. What about that table of monsters playing cards at the corner table and those sailors over there looking like they've just stepped off the ship of fools for a bit of light mayhem?"

"Not a problem old fruit. The toughies over there are Marco's brothers. And the sailors will be there for just as long as they behave themselves. Now pull up a stool and I'll introduce you to Marco."

Piers did as he was told. Both men sat facing the bar and the back of the man who Bones insisted was an old friend.

"If he's an old friend, why doesn't he turn around," whispered Prideaux behind his hand.

"You can see he's busy preparing those bar snacks. He'll turn around when he's ready. Marco does everything when he's ready. He's part Italian and part Cornish. There is no rushing him."

The man behind the bar finished filleting the tiny fish and arranging them in earthenware dishes. He put down the filleting knife and wiped it and his hands on an old rag. He turned round to face the bar with a big grin on his weather-beaten face.

"Well now my handsomes. Bonesie you old wastrel!" He vaulted the bar, making light of his years. Beaming, he enveloped Bones in a bear hug sweeping him off his feet as he did so. Bones struggled ineffectively as Marco swung him around the bar as though he were a rag doll.

"Steady on old chap. You'll have me seasick. And anyway this is very unseemly behaviour. People are looking."

"I'm delighted to see someone from the old country," said Marco as he placed Bones carefully back on the stool he had just vacated. "How goes old Cornwall? Have they turned it into a theme park yet? Is the battle lost, or are the boys still fighting?"

"To be honest things could be better. It is becoming a playground for upcountry folk. But you know the Cornish. It's their special patch of ground and they'll defend it to the end. By the way I'd quite like a drink and perhaps then you can tell me a little about what you've been doing since I saw you last?" Marco's eyes flickered as he turned to look Prideaux up and down. "Who is your friend, Bonesie?"

"This quiet chap next to me is my pal from Oxford days, Piers Prideaux. He has a bit of an aversion to dark bars unless he knows everyone present. He's a little shy really. He is, however, one of us." Bones's wink was exaggerated but chimed with the longstanding relationship between the two men. 'One of us' meant something significant to the Cornish and that included the Italian Cornish.

"Any friend of yours Bonesie. Pleased to meet you Piers." This time the greeting was a much more restrained handshake. Niceties over Marco poured all three men large glasses of deep, dark Puglian wine. If the sea was wine-dark in these parts the wine was darker still. It was the legendary black wine of Ostuni. Essentially red wine from the Negroamaro grape poured from a jug rather than a bottle and served slightly chilled. It was also made locally and could blow your head off at 16%. The three men toasted old Cornwall and even older Puglia before descending into reminiscing loudly about old times in both countries.

Prideaux was sidelined as he found it hard to join the conversation having met Marco for the first time. Accordingly, his attention wandered. He looked around the bar. The sailors were becoming more and more raucous. Occasionally he noticed one of Marco's brothers shoot a warning glance in their direction. The menace was palpable. Prideaux was no fan of violence and the bar crackled with violent potential. His mind full of unpleasant possibilities he looked desperately around for something to focus on.

The woman who caught his attention was seated with her back to the open area of the bar. There was something about her. Prideaux couldn't swear to it but he half thought he had seen her somewhere before. Could she have been the one helped into the car by those characters back in Ostuni? The woman was huddled over a scarred and stained side table that had been pushed back against the wall. She was drinking black coffee, constantly refilling her cup from an old ceramic pot. Her headscarf ensured that she looked like an Italian peasant woman. Yet there was something about her body language that didn't fit. More than that when she turned round as she frequently did she seemed always to be looking directly at him. It made him distinctly uncomfortable.

It was only then that Prideaux remembered why they had come into the bar in the first place. The ambience and the business between Marco and Bones had banished it from his mind. Bones and Marco were irrecoverably lost in reminiscence. The men had kept in touch over the years. They obviously remained close it was a strong relationship that had stood the test of time. And Marco had information for Bones that went beyond poring over old times. He had been in touch with Bones about a strange Englishman who had taken up with the Olive Pickers. Nobody seemed to know who the man was but Marco was fairly sure that he was the one that local gossip was currently focusing on. There was another Englishman whom Marco had asked to leave the bar. He had seemed oddly obsessed with the other Englishman they were all talking about to the extent that he had annoyed Marco's regulars. He had left an envelope telling Marco that it should be kept safe and handed to Bones when he next saw him. "He knew you, Bonesie so I took the envelope even though I kicked him out of the bar. I have it now in the safe in the back of the bar. Trust me I have not opened it. But it seemed important."

The bar was getting noisier, particularly the sailors one of whom had approached the woman in the headdress. He leaned over her and said something. The noise in the bar masked his comment. The woman seemed not to respond. He turned to his shipmates then seemed to think better of it. This time he put his hand on her shoulder and forcibly turned her around. She spat in the man's face. Without attempting to clean the spittle from his face he hit her with the back of his hand. She reeled from the blow. Shaking her head she readjusted her headdress, then simply picked up the chair and sat in exactly the same way she had previously been sitting. The sailor's face twisted and darkened. He had hurt her and he knew it. She continued to ignore him as if he counted for nothing.

All this had been in front of his group of drinking friends and of Marco's brothers who by now had all turned to face him. He had lost face and some form of retribution was inevitable. The only people in the bar unaware of what was unfolding were Bones and Marco who were lost in memory of times past and just starting to wobble with the effect of the black wine that took no prisoners. Suddenly, Garibaldi's Overcoat was the last place in the world that Prideaux wanted to be. It is at times like these that the world seems to move seamlessly into slow motion. What followed was not the bar room brawl that was already established to be imminent, at least in Prideaux's head. It was far more sinister than that.

Marco broke the spell. He turned away from Bones to face the sailor. He shouted at the man who stopped and glared back at him. Marco had the sort of voice that would stop a charging elephant and it had the intended effect. To Prideaux this was edging even closer to the sort of brawl he would have paid good money to be a long way away from. The sailor took a step towards Marco quickly clocking the short metal bar he now held in his left hand. Marco indicated with a nod of his head that the man should sit down. Now thoroughly discomfited the sailor looked towards his erstwhile companions only to see them getting slowly to their feet and heading for the exit. They left without a word or a sign of any sort to him. He was left completely isolated. Marco held him with his stare. His brothers had not moved an inch from their table. The woman adjusted her headscarf and stood up. The sailor was swaying slightly cutting off the woman's only access to the door. She seemed a very minor player in the drama that was gradually unfolding. Her only way out of the bar was to pass the man who had just assaulted her. Her prospects did not look good as she walked towards him. The sailor's gaze was flickering from her to Marco. He seemed confused. This was a grave mistake.

As the woman came within reach of the sailor Prideaux noticed yet again something about her gait. She looked to be an elderly woman. There was something not right though. Her posture was that of a much younger woman. Her shoulders were not hunched and her stance was confident and balanced. She stopped. Standing in front of the sailor he at last realised how close she was and it forced his concentration away from Marco. The woman faced him making the sign of the cross. He took a step forward grabbing at her headscarf. She lithely ducked under his hand and made a swift upward motion. The sailor had a look of confusion on his face. His legs started to buckle and he crashed to the bar floor to lie face down without voicing a sound.

One of the brothers rushed to the man but it was already too late. The other brothers had already disappeared through the bar door in pursuit of the rest of the crew. The woman's face was contorted in fury as she rushed across the bar towards Prideaux. It was Marco who reacted first stepping across to catch her arm as she attempted the same manoeuvre as with the sailor. He twisted her wrist viciously forcing her to drop a second stiletto that had appeared as if by magic from her headscarf. She screamed in pain and shaking herself free made a break for the exit. She was gone in a moment.

The sailor lay where he had fallen, the handle of a stiletto protruding from his rib cage. He was stone dead. There was very little blood except from his nose which had broken as he hit the stone floor of the bar. Fresh blood in a small trickle ran down from the knife that had penetrated the chest wall and severed his aorta. He died without even knowing what had happened. It was Prideaux who pointed out the engravings of olives that decorated the handle of the first weapon used by the woman.

The Spinelli brothers returned in a bunch sweating with their efforts. With standard Italian sign language and shoulder shrugs they indicated that the sailors and whoever the woman was had got away. They crossed themselves in a synchronised blessing and looked towards Marco for guidance. Marco looked as confused as anyone else. If this had been a planned hit it could not have been better executed. And executed is the word. The sailor lay dead – with the killer a little old lady possessed of a rare talent with the stiletto. Except that she wasn't an old lady. Her movements were not those of one weighed down by misery and stilted by arthritis in old bones. She had known exactly what she was doing. The sailor paid the price of underestimating her speed and brutality. She had all the attributes of an assassin. Perhaps unwittingly the two friends had found what they were looking for. It seemed that the old nightmare was returning only this time they were not on their own ground. A post mortem on the events was quickly underway. Marco was able to tell Bones that the sailor who lay dead had come to the bar as he claimed he had information on the shady Englishman who had become involved with the Olive Pickers. He had agreed to talk to Marco about the man's whereabouts if he was paid enough. That was why Marco had sent for Bones to come to Garibaldi's Overcoat.

The arrival of the Job twins proved a welcome distraction. They were not expected but for Prideaux at least they brought some reassurance. Their first task was to establish who the dead man was. He was obviously a sailor and one who had met his match unexpectedly. All Marco knew is that he was prepared to sell what information he had, provided the money was good enough. Perhaps he was one who had been involved with the olive tree scam. At any rate this was not the type of area where mindless violence was a regular visitor. Most people knew each other in the port. This was not tourist Italy after all. Not much had changed here over the centuries. Like most real villages and towns it had its own pace and the outside world rarely penetrated. What was happening now was somehow of a different order.

This wasn't the first violent death in the immediate area within the past months. There had been others and so far nobody had made a connection. There was some speculation that perhaps some form of turf war might be brewing but that was all. Marco had a business to run and blood stains on the bar floor were not a good advertisement for the bar. Local colour has its place as long as it is not too frequently dark red with a tendency to coagulate when spilled.

What might have been merely a pleasant afternoon of drinking and reminiscing had taken a wrong turn. Marco knew the local chief of police so removal of the unfortunate sailor was easily arranged.

With the blood washed away and normality restored Marco insisted on closing the bar and getting some fresh air. In Villa Novello that meant only one thing, a promenade to the castle at the end of the breakwater. Marco took the lead and marched them along to the 16th century castle. "Come on you lot," he ordered. "There is something I want to show you. For once it does not involve alcohol, and I say that as a bar owner who knows of what he speaks."

"The bloody man's gone totally berkers," muttered Bones in his practised stage whisper. "He's dragging us off to a bloody museum or something. A touch of the sun if you ask me. That's what you get for not wearing a hat in these parts."

"Here you go Bonesie; we have arrived. Now tell me what you see."

"This is just what we need round about now. A nice little quiz. Never mind that we have just witnessed a murder. Or that there is a possibility that the scrote Slope and bitch Bennett are alive and killing in this lovely scrap of Italy. We have a quiz. Well Marco, the short answer is a castle. The slightly longer answer is that it is a castle built hundreds of years ago to subjugate the masses to the will of a few robber barons. Ask Bonesie the same question and he will doubtless give you the opposite and completely wrong headed interpretation. But then the truth is always relative."

It took Marco a while to realise that Bonesie and Prideaux between them represented polar opposites when it came to political viewpoints. He wasn't unfamiliar with such a situation. After all in this part of Italy friends could hold two extremist viewpoints yet still be friends. In short the communist mayor could drink with the mafia clan chief in relative harmony. That was a distraction. Marco had brought them to the castle to show them his latest venture. What he could do without was a discussion of the opposing forces of capitalism and Marxism. Marco was looking to open one of the towers as an upmarket restaurant. Puglia was gradually being discovered by the British and Marco had every intention of introducing the increasing hordes of visitors to the best of Puglian cuisine. At a price of course. Marco had regularly received Bones's correspondence charting the success of The Hand of God. In reality he was boasting outrageously. No matter. This would be his chance to pick his old friend's brains about the best way to ensure similar success for his latest venture. He wanted to move beyond the harbour bar and become a respected restaurateur. Stranger things have happened.

A tall red-haired man hailed the group from the foot of the tower nearest the sea where Marco planned to open his restaurant. The central tower still operated as a lighthouse and the one nearest to land was now derelict. Marco waved his hand in greeting to the local immobiliare. The group worked their way around the volcanic rock that typified this section of the Italian coast. There was plenty of grumbling from the British contingent while Marco moved like a mountain goat.

Finally the group assembled around the immobiliare who was smartly dressed in the sharpest of Italian suits. Introductions were completed. Vito was a senior partner in the largest estate agency in the area. He was in Villa Novello to give a second showing of the property to Marco. The two men left the still squabbling group in their wake as they reached the ancient door opening into the castle. From his briefcase he produced a comedy key. It was the largest key any of the men had ever seen and provided a contrast with the wonderfully sharp suiting of the Italian estate agent. The contrast was so acute that it started the Job twins giggling. They were inveterate gigglers at the best of times and the present situation was so absurd as to agitate their twin funny bones. Laughter of such a kind is infectious and in seconds the group was helpless with laughter.

Vito did not take kindly to such a display. He was convinced they were laughing at him. The flush on his face showed his displeasure as he desperately tried to turn the key in the ancient lock. Eventually, a small shower of mediaeval rust indicated that the key had turned successfully. Marco followed Vito through into the courtyard without a backward glance at their four companions.

"Come on then lads. Shape up," urged Robert Job who was doing his best to adopt a serious face. "We seem to have upset an estate agent. They are not a humorous bunch at the best of times and Vito is bound to think we were laughing at him."

"Now we don't want any stereotyping here," answered Prideaux with a controlled smile. "It is equally offensive whether it is nationality or employment based. Perhaps we had better stay outside until Marco has conducted his business. I don't think he'd thank us for screwing things up." And that's how things would have stayed had Marco not stuck his head round the castle door shouting, "Avanti, you likely lads, come and see what I'm looking at."

The 'what' that had attracted Marco's attention was not immediately obvious as the group squeezed through the entrance door and into the courtyard. The place had been empty for a good while and looked like it. Airborne sea salt had done its destructive work on the metalwork. Neglect had allowed a wide variety of weeds to establish themselves and lizards abounded.

"Take a look at this," shouted Marco from a precarious looking balcony that ran along the courtyard facing side of the castle. From that angle the balcony gave a clear view of the sea and this seems to have been what had perked Marco's interest. He was a man clearly locked in a dream of what might be rather than what was. His entrancement made things easier than they would have otherwise been. One man's disaster is another's opportunity. That is one equation in human progress that never changes. In his mind's eye Marco could see the balcony renovated with tables along it to get the full benefit of the stunning view of the Adriatic. He could see himself at the gate welcoming the great and the good of Ostuni, Alberobello, Locorotondo and perhaps as far afield as Lecce pouring through the door desperate for the cachet of being seen at Ristorante Garibaldi's Cornishman. Sometimes dreams can come true. Sometimes.

"This is all well and good," opined Bones as the four climbed the stairs to the balcony. "All I am thinking is that it will depend a lot on what sort of rent they are looking for. It is sure as hell going to need a lot spent on it to turn it into anything attractive."

"True enough Bonesie, but just for once let us look on the bright side. Marco is already running a successful bar and he has plenty of family to help him out. If you are looking for positives the fresh fish his brothers catch coupled with some of the wild herbs and vegetables growing around here could allow him to move up to the gourmet restaurant end of things. I don't think he is thinking about burger and chips. Puglia is finally being discovered by the travelling classes and an upmarket restaurant could make a fortune in this area."

Inside the building was in dire condition with weeds everywhere and evidence of graffiti covering the walls. A really competent builder could make something of it in short order. There was of course the small matter of the dearth of competent builders in this area. This didn't bother Marco unduly as his brothers all had multiple talents and would set to as and when required. In any case what mattered was not decor. That might hold sway in the more fashion conscious parts of northern Italy. What counted here was the quality of the food. Two things only really counted in Puglia, freshness of food and quality of cooking. Marco's brother Pietro would argue that there was a third issue and that was quality wine but as he ran his own vineyard that would be hardly a surprise to anyone. To succeed it would need to be a family affair. In this area that was par for the course.

Marco's enthusiasm was contagious and the mood within the castle rooms lightened as the group followed the immobiliare through the connecting series of rooms. The rooms led to a central banqueting suite that had avoided most of the depredations found elsewhere within the castle.

Prideaux and Bones watched Marco and Vito in animated conversation. It was clear that Marco was more than interested. What remained seemed to be settling the commitment on equitable terms. After a prolonged bout of arm waving and pointing the two shook hands and the deal appeared to be closed. Both appeared satisfied and Vito left the castle for the short drive back to his main office in Ostuni. "You look a bit like il gatto who got the crema Marco," Prideaux said.

"You may well be right Piers. The deal is fine. I talked him down to a manageable monthly rent and he knows enough about my family to understand that there will be no room for interference once we are up and running."

To Bones this suggested that Marco was raising the spectre of local gangsters having some involvement. "Marco you are not getting involved with anything dangerous here I hope. It's just that when I hear the word 'family' in these parts I get these visions of a fat bloke with a mouth full of cotton wool and half a horse lying amongst silk sheets. I wouldn't want an old mate to end up sharing a watery duvet with the fishes. You understand my concern."

"Concern duly noted Billy. Be assured there is nothing to worry about. My family grew up around here without alliance to any of the groups you have in mind. We have respect borne of a refusal to bend to any threats. And if you need any further reassurance I can tell you that I really do know where the bodies are buried."

"That's good enough for me. Now whereabouts is this vineyard of Pietro's I've heard so much about?"

They could not have known it at the time but Prideaux and Bones were about to be launched on yet another complex adventure where death lurked around every corner. It had all seemed so different back in the Welsh winter when the first indication that the reaper was treading in their footmarks appeared.

Seasons might not fear the reaper but Bones and Prideaux would have every reason to do so.

2

ZEBEDEE

Simon Rush had joined MI7 direct from university. It seemed like a reasonable career. The rewards were good and the job not too onerous. He had mapped out a career path that would allow him to retire in comfort in his early fifties. Promotion, if it came, would be a huge bonus.

It was not something Rush was expecting at an early stage. The promotion itself had come as a welcome but daunting surprise. Joining the section was by invitation only and he had not expected that to come until much later in his career. Rejecting the honour was not an option or was at least a risky one. Stories were whispered of those who had attempted refusal. Of course it could have been coincidence. He knew at least two of his contemporaries at Oxford who had died in mundane circumstances shortly after boasting a little too loudly that they had refused the call to serve. One car crash and a drug overdose later and nothing remained of two bright young things who had badly overestimated their worth to the section.

He was not so foolish. It had been three weeks now and another summons had arrived as if by magic. If magic were involved then sure as hell its colour would have been of the blackest kind. The summons had come from his section head. It was to meet him precisely at 6pm at his club in Pall Mall. He had never met the man. He believed that he had been at Eton and Oxford with his father but so too had a lot of people.

He didn't even know the name of his superior. Just about all he knew was that the summons came through an intermediary and was non-negotiable. He hurried across the road and walked quickly past the Institute of Directors building at 116 stopping shortly afterwards at the designated address. The club looked much as one would expect. It had the sort of façade that looked comfortable in this part of the capital city of England. What lurked behind its ancient doors God alone knew. Simon Rush was about to find out.

Once inside the club two brawny men, both dressed entirely in black, materialised to either side of him. Without a word of acknowledgement they became his escort. The club itself was more or less what he had expected. Bertie Wooster would have been right at home here: Simon Rush was most definitely not. It wasn't that he was outside his comfort zone. Eton and Oxford had prepared him for such surroundings. It was simply that he did not regard himself as a clubbable man. He preferred his own company and the sight of leather armchairs, obsequious waiters and pink gins did not stir his juices. Neither did the braying conversations of the great the good and their demented ideas of the return of empire in his sharper than average mind. Still the money was good, the perks were outrageous and whereas he was not particularly proud of his easy ride on the gravy train he was not about to trade his ticket for a stinking bedsit somewhere. In any case he was well aware that at this level one did not leave the organisation unless invited to do so. The goons either side of him escorted him up the imposing staircase to the third floor.

They stopped outside a room towards the rear of the club. With a curt order of, "in there and be sure to knock first," his escorts turned on their heels leaving a bewildered civil servant feeling less civil than usual.

"Ah well. In for a penny and all that nonsense," he mused as he tapped tentatively on the heavy oak door. The door opened slowly with a creaking sound that mirrored the finest hour of the old dark castle scenes from Hammer's back catalogue. Rush was almost tempted to voice a deep, "you rang," response before remembering where he was. The door opened and what could only be described as an old and faithful retainer beckoned him inside. Whether the old retainer had retained much in the late winter of his life was a moot point, but obediently he followed the crooked finger into the room. There was nobody there, nobody he could see anyway.

The windows were heavily curtained, with one exception and the only electric light came from one of those green hooded lamps favoured by bankers and gamblers. "Little difference between those grubby occupations really," thought the newly promoted spy. The sound of the door closing behind him as the club servant left jerked him back to reality from his reverie. Now was not the time. He was here to meet his boss. It was important that he showed that he was up to the job or God knows what the outcome might be.

Rush had enjoyed a smooth passage almost from birth. A military family with a father who for years operated in a section so secret that nobody could ever give it a name meant that he was raised by a nanny. This was fine by him. His mother was a lush who spent the majority of her time drunk. He saw his father occasionally, mostly when he was home recovering from some wound or other. It seemed that he was in action most of the time in one war or other. Like all men in such organisations he never discussed his work. The times when he was at home were great even if they were infrequent. Often his father was recuperating rather than in a position to play with an introverted son.

It was his father who had pulled the strings to get him into the section at a basic level. The rest, a climb up a very slippery ladder, had been down to the deep seated cunning that was his basic nature. The ability to cope and to accumulate any form of power over others is what tended to drive this only child. He gained no real pleasure from his climb to the heights but he enjoyed the material benefits and had no intention of relinquishing them.

"Sit down then young man, over there, over there." The voice was male, he thought, but high pitched with the extended syllables of a Kenneth Williams impersonator. He stifled a laugh as he looked around for the source of the voice.

Slowly a large high backed leather chair revolved to reveal a small man immaculately dressed in a pinstripe suit and striped shirt with a blue silk spotted handkerchief. He was perfectly in proportion, just small, that's all.

"Before you say anything that could harm your career I am well aware that I am a small man. It has not hampered my career. I could, if I chose, hamper your very existence. Let me explain. Physical stature has no relevance in this game. I'll say to you what I say to all those promoted to the level where you are invited to visit this room. Just remember what Hobbes wrote about human life. Do you remember, Gabriel?"

"I think he wrote that human life was 'nasty, brutish and short'."

"And so am I," squeaked the small man. "That is why I am so successful in my chosen career. That is also why I have chosen you to replace Cornelius in charge of Unit S. You are no towering figure either but I think you have sufficient low cunning to be useful. I am aware that you have been acclimatising yourself for a few weeks. I have called you in to see how you are progressing. I could show you on screen if you like. Over the past weeks you have not even taken a shit without being recorded on our monitors. And if you'd like a record of your sad masturbations, then I'm your man. So don't lie about anything or you'll regret it."

"I have made some progress with the team, I think," answered Rush with a blush. "It's early days yet but I think I have something to offer. But why did you call me Gabriel just now? You seem to know everything; you must know my name is Simon Rush."

"Not any more. You are now Gabriel. That's all. Single name. My choice and that is how you will be known henceforth. Here, catch." With an effort his new boss threw a thick file of documents in his direction. It fell at his feet. Gabriel picked it up and walked across to sit next to the man who would direct his every waking moment from this time onward.

"Now listen, Gabriel. Don't ask any questions and I'll tell you all you need to know. You have been selected to fill one of the most powerful posts in this country. I appreciate that you are essentially still wet behind the ears. Reminds me old boy, were you a Wet Bob or a Dry Bob at Eton? No matter. The point is you are of the right stuff. I knew your father of course. Stout fellow, was with him when he died don't you know. Classified of course. Can't tell you a thing. Point is old darling, bloody good egg your old dad. Pity he's not with us now, could jolly well do with him. Still you'll have to do. Thin rations compared with your old man but beggars and choosers and all that."

The waffle came thick and fast. The newly minted Gabriel allowed his eyes to roll back in his head. He had heard all this before. It rarely led anywhere. Everything seemed to revolve around what a stout fellow, good egg, outstanding badger and diamond of the first water his father had been. That was it. A surfeit of eulogies and not one of the old buffers troubled with a single piece of information concerning his father's demise. The catch all of 'classified old boy', was the answer that never changed. All he knew, or thought he knew, is that his father had been killed in the service of his country. As a result he had been brought up, once he had grown too old for his nanny, by a maiden aunt who lived near Swansea in the wild west of Wales. In his darker moments he mused endlessly on finding whoever had killed his father or at least how the old man had died. It didn't seem likely as he was never regarded as soldier material. He was, however, very much regarded as a thinker and better still a meticulous planner with just the right soupçon of cunning to make him a difficult opponent to outwit.

There were those who needed such men: one of whom sat opposite him now. It looked as if he had nodded off but Tarquin Trudgeon frequently played the failing old buffer to great effect. He was probably around ten years younger than he looked and dressed and was a great deal sharper than he appeared. It was a well honed act. "Keeps the enemy on their nasty little toes my old corncrake," he would burble. "Never hurts for them to think I'm a bit on the slow and desiccated side. Lures the blighters into a bit of a lion trap, don't you know. They think old buffer and never even see the golf ball in the sock until it catches them a good one in the back of the neck. Lights out and one up to the chaps."

He remained in a seemingly passive state observing Gabriel as he twisted uncomfortably in his club chair. "Well then, where the devil was I? He sat suddenly upright and attentive fixing his guest with a hard stare. Come along man, pay bloody attention. Where was I?"

"You were telling me what a fine fellow my father was, sir. And you seemed to have an interest in whether or not I rowed when at Eton."

"Well did you? Were you a rower at Eton?" Struggling to contain himself Gabriel answered in the negative.

"Bloody good show, young man. Nasty lot rowers. Can't stand the fellows myself. Not natural floating around in bloody canoes, bad lot all together. Do me a favour, would you. Bloody inconvenience but I seem to have mislaid my glass eye. It'll have rolled over there under the desk. That's what usually happens. Be a fine fellow and crawl under there and fetch it for me. Don't feel properly dressed without it."

A reluctant Gabriel did as he was asked muttering under his breath as he did so. After much stretching and twisting while lying prone on some very expensive carpeting he located the missing item. Dusting himself off he regained his feet and walked across to return the object to its owner.

"No that's not mine. Must belong to some other blighter. Looks to me like a cheap piece of bloody tat." As he said this he threw the offending article over his shoulder through the only open window to land several storeys lower down on a Pall Mall pavement. The pavement artist who had just finished his rendition of Dante's seventh circle of hell was extremely put out. He was unused to flying eyes arriving unannounced in the centre. "No bloody respect for culture," muttered a low-rent Banksy as he moved off to start work on his version of Munch's Scream.

"Now where were we, young fellow me lad? Ah yes I remember. Cornelius is the rub one might say." Zebedee grinned effortlessly asserting his authority.

The man clearly had two perfectly good eyes. What sort of madhouse was this he had landed in? What followed did not entirely reassure a now troubled newly promoted servant of the crown.

"From now on you will refer to me only as Zebedee," explained the curious old man in the leather chair. "You, as I have already explained will be referred henceforth as Gabriel. You look to me far too young to remember The Magic Roundabout. Perhaps for your benefit I should explain that Zebedee was the father of the disciples James and John and that Gabriel was the bringer of the word of God to the specially chosen. I am one of those and as my disciple you will bring me, if not the word of God, then certainly the information I need to allocate my considerable resources to the protection of this country and its people. We live in interesting times, young fellow. I wish to God we didn't but it appears we no longer even own a gunboat never mind the balls to send one anywhere. Be lucky to have a bloody canoe the way things are going."

Seemingly exhausted by this effort the old man leaned back in his chair as if to gather his strength for a fuller briefing.

Strangely, given the initial impression cultivated by the old man his outline briefing was concise and for once he stuck to the point rather than meandering between the centuries. All was preceded with a warning that any mention of the briefing outside the Blue Room would result in a painful but absolutely certain death.

The essence of the briefing was to detail Slope's return to action after a long period of quietude. As in everything to do with Slope, information was sketchy. This time it revolved around the resurrection of an old Mafia scam. Fact will beat fiction every time they meet and the old saw was never better expressed than in this unlikely set up. The briefing mixed fact with apparent fantasy but in the intelligence business to be expected to digest several unlikely happenings before luncheon was par for the course.

"There are about sixty million olive trees in Puglia way down in Italy's south," began Zebedee. "Some of these are hundreds of years old and are so revered that they are not allowed to die. If a productive branch looks likely to fall it will be shored up and looked after like a wounded bambino or bambina. That much is attestable fact." The newly christened Gabriel correctly surmised that his section head was whipping up a head of steam and this briefing might take some considerable time, he decided to help himself to a cup of tea. There was a small occasional table to his left with a steaming china tea pot and some ridiculously small cups and saucers.

"The value of such trees is incalculable to the farmers who tend them. The scam originated because a member of the Puglian Mafia realised that they may well have a considerable monetary value to Italians in the much richer north of the country. In conjunction with Mafioso from the Naples area the scam ran for several years back in the 1950s. Basically it consisted of a nocturnal visit to an olive grove with a digger and transporter. The trees were then taken to the north and sold to wealthy Italians. Many of these men pined for their young days in the south and lusted after ancient olive trees with which to adorn their designer gardens.

"The scam eventually petered out as the transporters used were just too easy for the carabinieri to track. It became clear that a new generation of enriched Italians in the north were happy to deal with anybody capable of resurrecting the scheme. There was a difference though. This time the organisation involved appeared to be one totally independent of mafia organisations both Puglian and Neapolitan. It was known that a group identified as the Olive Pickers, rumoured to be led by an Englishman, was involved. That man bore a remarkable resemblance to one Sebastian Slope."

Gabriel sipped at the tea and examined the whisky cake that looked as if it had been hewn from granite. Small black currants dotted it resembling dead blue bottles. He decided to take a pass on the cake.

"You paying attention young man?" barked a suddenly animated Zebedee. "You will be aware of the existence of the vile Slope and his equally vile consort Elizabeth Bennett. What you may not yet know is that your predecessor, Cornelius, has just stuck a shitty stick into the hornet's nest that is the world of Slope and wiggled it about like a conductor on speed. Result one pissed off Slope and one irritated Zebedee. Cornelius, damn his foreskin has only gone and siphoned off almost all the cash the blighter Slope had stashed away from his myriad unlawful scams. Now if that isn't enough to piss off a card carrying psychopath I don't know what is. We now have one angry Slope on our hands and a miserable forcibly retired Cornelius." Gabriel nodded he had read the section reports on both individuals with increasing alarm.

"It was like trying to prise a six foot limpet off a comfortable rock getting rid of him. And now there is more shit flying around than you'd expect if you were attending a choreographed bungee jump by the sewer cleaners of old London Town. I hope you are absorbing all this Gabriel. In case you have not yet noticed you are in the direct flight path of all this low flying shit. Now this is not a case of whether you choose to accept your mission or not, you have no bloody choice old boy so bloody well pay attention."

"I think you'll find me more than up to the job, sir."

"As if all this wasn't enough," the old man paused for extra emphasis fixing him with a stern stare, "Cornelius has stolen something from the tied vault that cannot be replaced. You do not need to know the contents but it is something that could shake the country to its core should it become generally known. It is in the form of an old leather bound book with parchment pages. The royal seal is on the cover. If you can locate such an item then you will acquire it and return it to me here. I cannot stress sufficiently how important it is that the item is returned. There are also three sections of a gold medallion that clearly fit together into a single piece. The best minds in the department and a few old sweats from the mediaeval history department at Oxford have failed to identify its purpose. Best they have managed is that it could be some sort of key. Bloody marvellous. I could have come up with that. Would help if we knew a key to what."

The newly minted Gabriel had been listening to the old man for long enough to recognise that things were even more serious than he had imagined. "Two men you need to be aware of are Piers Prideaux and the third Earl of Mount Charles, generally referred to as Bones. They are a bloody nuisance but useful on occasions. Be wary of them." Zebedee deliberately glossed over the fact that Prideaux and Bones would likely end up as collateral damage when Slope eventually cornered them. Besides that they were expendable. The two men attracted almost universal dislike from the security services. They had got in the way before and there was general disapproval in the service of the way they had profited financially from the murder of their oldest friends Mark and Ginny Williams.

"Here's the clincher my old fruit pie. Having nicked the bastard's life savings Cornelius has only gone and used a very large chunk of it to employ the Canadian." The former Simon Rush, forever more Gabriel, spat out a mouthful of curdled tea. "You do not interrupt when I am speaking; first rule of the department. Yes, the Canadian – that seven foot madman that they threw out of Canadian ice hockey for being too violent. Short step to becoming the world's highest paid hit man, don't you think?"

"To be honest I'm not sure what to think?"

"Well you'd better be sure a bit swiftly old son. This chaos has landed fairly and squarely on your desk like a cowpat from the great big cow of confusion who grazes in her heavenly pastures. A crinkly-titted old cow at the best of times and these, the last time I looked, are the worst of times.

"Cornelius has appropriated just about every last ill-gotten groat that Slope managed to amass. He was warned to leave it alone but it seems that he took it to heart when some young filly he had been involved with got bumped off in Paris. Decided to hit the bastard Slope where it hurt most, in the old pocket book. That would have been bad enough but splurging the lion's share of four billion in euros, whatever that is in real money, was a bit like pulling the tiger's tail. If we know that the Canadian has been approached then the rest of the loonies that make up the Assassins' Fellowship will also be on the trail. It will be like a fruit loop party for the coldest killers on God's earth. You see my…I mean your problem."

As Zebedee droned on Gabriel tried to keep pace with his ramblings. He had a vague knowledge of the AF. It was a loose association of hit men and women, women only recently having been admitted. In past weeks their committee had been culled. It seemed the AF felt it their duty to freshen the committee on a fairly regular basis. Rather than remain hamstrung for years by democratic principles they preferred direct action when there was a groundswell of feeling. They were professional killers after all.

It was following a pretty heated debate on the way forward for the association that several committee members were found dead in unusual circumstances. Chief suspects were those who had previously stood for election against them but had been considered too dangerous even for an association of murderers. There was, of course, no evidence of their involvement but the officers of the committee had all been found dead before the annual general meeting took place.

The chairman, Hans Kneebone, known as Idle Hans since he was a lazy bastard, had been found floating in a vat of maturing lager in his brewery. Given his usual intake there was every chance that he could have drunk his way out. He hadn't. Tests showed that he had drowned and there was a minor scandal when the entire vat of first class lager had to be poured away. The AF did not appreciate senseless waste. And there was a good profit margin in lager.

Conchita Lopez, secretary and specialist poisoner had been mixing a batch of her famous poisoned guacamole in her third floor flat. It was a pleasant day and she had no pressing engagements so she decided to use her time in preparing a batch of her favourite murder weapon. It was her custom to add the poison lovingly derived from the deadly corn cockle flower to the mix before finishing the dish.

Lopez was thorough and had a habit, left over from her days as a chef, of tasting the guacamole to ensure it was top quality before adding the poison. She was found face down in a plate of lovingly prepared top quality guacamole. Someone had added a pinch of corn cockle seed to the pepper grinder. A pinch was enough to kill a hippopotamus. By the time she was found the guacamole had congealed into green concrete and it took a long time to chip the mix of vomit and guacamole away from her face so that she could be identified.

The treasurer, Ernest Fringe a man who specialised in animal related murders was found in his laboratory. He was well known to experiment with all types of animals and insects in discovering ways to use them in carrying out some of the lucrative contracts he undertook. He was so dedicated to his craft that he often slept in his lab on a sofa bed kept there for the purpose. When eventually his body was discovered it was covered with thousands of Guatemalan singing cockroaches that had somehow escaped from their secure cages. There wasn't much of Fringe left to identify, and nothing at all for Ernest Fringe to sing about.

All of this left the way clear for a new committee: Francois Meurtrier (aka The Canadian), Elizabeth Bennett and Sebastian Slope. Whereas this was no good thing for the AF Cornelius had made it even worse by nailing his bounty details to Slope's ugly head. This meant that members of the AF were more than likely to be at each other's throats, even more so than usual. Gabriel thought admiringly of the irony implicit in the ultimate scenario of setting a thief to catch one simply delicious.

He was now beginning to recognise that he had inherited the especially shitty end of a very shitty stick. It had been made very plain to him that he was in the box seat and it was threatening to be something of a baptism of fire. For a first case surely something a little lighter could have been sent winging his way. Just when you think life is beginning to acknowledge your existence along comes the devil and pisses down your drainpipe. It was ever thus. Time for a little judicious laying off of the odds, thought the new head of Section S within MI7. As poison chalices go it was a pretty grim prospect.

"Surely the expertise exists to replace the funds Cornelius siphoned off. I mean that might placate Slope for a while at least. There must be a fund. There's always a fund. I know that Slope is a difficult person to deal with but returning his money would surely go some way to putting things right."

"I thought I heard you refer to Slope as a difficult person but it must have been the wind. Plays tricks on a chap you know. Slope is not a difficult person, he is bloody impossible. He will never quit. He will make sure that Cornelius dies in agony along with those two old busters Bones and Prideaux. He does not do forgiveness. And in case you didn't get the smell of the man through the files I had delivered to your desk he doesn't simply kill, he enjoys the process. He gets some sort of perverted thrill through making someone who was once alive no longer so. There is no shortcut young Gabriel. Consider yourself about to be tested in the fiery furnace. Do not be found wanting."

Gabriel was left in no doubt of the task at this point. A worthy adversary and victory, once his, would ensure his status, a decent income and a healthy pension. Surely worth a bit of effort. He needed to show willing. He'd worry about how to do it at a later date. For now looking the part was essential.

"I appreciate the trust you are showing in me, and I intend to repay it," said a now energised Gabriel. "Starters then. Do we have intelligence of Slope's current exact whereabouts?"

"Latest says that the ghastly oik is trundling around the deep dark south of Italy. As I explained earlier we are aware that he is pissing about with some group of characters known as the Olive Pickers which means he is in Puglia and somewhere near the White City. Ostuni to you. No info on the whereabouts of the loathsome Bennett but wherever Slope is Bennett is never far away."

"It seems to me that if Slope is there and Cornelius is at his trullo which is just outside the city then I might as well take a trip over there and see what is happening on the ground."

"Sound thinking young man. Pull the old legs from under the desk and give the jolly old piles a bit of an airing. Hands-on spooking, one might say. That would be just the badger."

"Might I make a suggestion? Gabriel asked. "I wondered whether there would be any profit in dangling those idiots Bones and Prideaux in front of Slope's nose. If he hates the pair as much as you say then surely he will break cover to get a clear shot at them."

"Sound thinking. That would be one less thing to keep a fellow awake at night. Off you jolly well go then and the very best of British luck. You could stay for the big bird, old chap?"

A lifelong vegetarian Gabriel blenched at the invitation. He knew the meat holocaust to which Zebedee referred. The club was probably the last place in Britain that the big bird in anything like its original form was still on the menu. It comprised a veritable Russian doll of whatever birdlife the hunters and shooters of the club had done to death in recent weeks. The only concession to civilised eating was that swans had been expressly banned from the meat mountain. Although it would be hastily restored to the menu should a fossil from Buck House be enticed to dine at the club. These days even a Bullingdon bully could influence the standard menu. In the ordinary run of things grouse, pheasant, blackbird, lark, peacock all either freshish or defrosted would be stuffed one inside the other to form the ultimate feast. When cooked it would be set before top table and carved by a government minister before being put before the great and good of the land. In time honoured fashion Gabriel made his excuses and left.

As he stepped out onto a rainy Pall Mall he reflected that he would rather eat his own head than indulge in the carnivorous festival of the 'downing of the big bird'. He had work to do.

3

HUNTERS IN THE SNOW

Winter and the weather has turned round. In Wales you can scent the snow in the air. January, usually wet and dull, suddenly sparkles whitely. In and around the hamlet of Skenfrith the snow lies deep and crisp and decidedly uneven.

Strong swirling winds have driven the snow metres deep into asymmetric studies in white. It is cold enough to cut a man's throat. Scarves are worn in an old style, bunched up to protect the delicate skin around the neck. Any form of headgear is deemed acceptable providing it is well anchored against the capricious and taunting wind. It has recently swept in and is brooking no resistance. Animals are dying in fields. Birds are dropping from trees like so many dead leaves. Only the lonely, the mad and the lost venture out. It is conversation-stoppingly cold and no respite is envisioned.

Piers Prideaux and William Radleigh de Beaune are neither lonely nor mad and though once lost now are found. Instead of battling the elements the joint owners of The Hand of God are warmly ensconced in the long bar of this 14th century tavern. The huge fireplace is stacked with logs that are giving out enough heat to smelt iron. The bar is bustling with snowy locals. Some have struggled across fields deeply swaddled in drifts like elegant stacks of sleeping giant babies. They retain a hunted look. That hunted look though is gradually fading as the white heat of the bar takes hold creating glowing faces and peaceful souls. Nobody has been foolish enough to drive to the village local. Not even the four by fours would get far in these conditions. And Italy seems a very long way away. Despite the weather things are going well for Bones and Prideaux. Now is the worrying time. All things must pass and the shadow on the stairs sometimes turns out to be that of the reaper. It is probably for the best that we know not when the time will come.

It is twelve noon on a Saturday and there is an increasing air of naughtiness in the bar. Grown men and women more used to the powerful locally brewed real ale are turning to the local Welsh whisky, Penderyn Red Flag delivered weekly from a few miles away. Fortunately, in this part of the world weather forecasts are accurate, they have to be. Locals knew this blizzard was on the way. They knew in the way their ancestors knew. They knew because they have remained rooted in their surroundings.

No flamboyant presenter windmilling around an arty set is required to tell the people of this area what the weather is going to do. They know what they have always known. It is the disconnected folk of the towns and cities that need climactic conditions distilled into sound bites before they dare to open the front door. Country folk despise the faux sophisticates of the cities, with good reason.

There is enough Penderyn whisky in The Hand of God to fuel an uprising. Dic Penderyn you should be living at this hour. In another time perhaps such a thing was a possibility. For now it is enough that the silky smooth spirit is smoothing out local animosities and loosening recalcitrant tongues. It is beginning to look and sound like a school disco from times gone by except that Prideaux is in charge of the music. Billy Bones as the third Earl of Mount Charles is familiarly known or more often simply as Bones minds the wine and spirits, of course.

It is Prideaux who minds the music. He minds so much that he maps out a week at a time what will be playing and when in the bar. It will depend on what mood he finds himself in at the start of the day. On this Saturday he is having an Everley Brothers sort of day. He has been playing songs by the melodic if fractious brothers from early in the morning. He has already recalled, for those in the bar sober enough to listen, the concert he once attended when only one Everley bothered to turn up. Fair play to Phil though he put on a storming performance as the Everley Brother. In a later time and in another place he also witnessed a performance by the whole band. This time Phil stood at one side of the stage, Don on the other. They arrived and left separately and never once looked at or spoke to one another. Again, it was a mesmerising masterclass in close harmony singing, from a distance.

At midday he has brought things up to date by switching to Songs the Brothers Sang an Everley Brothers retrospective featuring Dawn McCarthy & Bonnie 'Prince' Billy. The music and the whisky are both going down equally well judging by the raucous chorus of Somebody Help Me currently rattling glasses behind the bar. Tomorrow it could be a Bowie retrospective and so it goes. It goes until Bones digs his heels in and insists that it is his turn and the Devil's music can take a day off. Dear loveable and completely unreconstructed Bones. Couple his music, by which he means classical, and nothing else with a bottle or two of Nuits St George and Bones is as happy as the legendary Larry. He will no longer touch Petrus since the unseemly death of Petroc Trethewey but that was in another country and besides the bastard's dead.

As the day wears on the bonhomie increases and village life becomes livelier than ever. It's as if the village pub is haunted by all the goodtime ghosts who had ever lived and prospered in this border area. It is a force that harnessed could move mountains but like all forces, positive or negative, eventually it will begin to dissipate.

The snow still fills the air flittering down exactly like down. The wind has died and a cold sun reflects light icily off the accumulations clogging up roads and lanes in the village. The fire burns as brightly as ever, the stock of well seasoned firewood producing heat, light and the unmistakable scent of a proper fire. There are homes that need to be returned to. There are dinners that need to be cooked and domestic animals that need to be reassured. This is a caring society. An initial slow drift away becomes a flurry, this time it is of villagers rather than snow. It is still mid afternoon but might just as well be evening. The light is beginning to fade and soon the pub will close anyway.

Bones and Prideaux have already decided not to open for the evening session. Accumulated wisdom says that this is the storm before the calm before the storm. It is preternaturally quiet and the Everley Brothers have moved on to songs like So Sad as the mood begins to dip. It has been a great afternoon but that tide in the affairs of men is about to come roaring around the corner in the very real natural incarnation of 70mph winds playing tricks with a sky full of snow. Jack Frost has not yet had his fill. Home is probably best in such circumstances. Hatches need to be battened and there is at least the prospect of a let up over the next few days. Bones and Prideaux will relish the break and if anyone feels lost and lonely enough to seek succour in the evening they know that the door will not be barred. There is always room at this inn.

It is a time for reflection. With glasses washed, bar tops cleaned and floors swept there is a quietus inside The Hand of God. Not even Prideaux's music punctures the peace though Bones's thoughtful voice does.

"Once this present blizzard has passed things should start looking up a bit Piers," he opines in his, I really don't believe it but I am getting bored with these constant snow storms mode.

"I yield to no man in my appreciation of the transformational effects of snow sweet snow," continues the old aristo, "but it is becoming a little tiresome now.

"Before you say anything I am well aware that the village looks as if it has recently been peeled off a giant box of chocolates and jolly nice it is too. That's fine for those with nowhere to go and a lovely window to look out of but I'm beginning to feel a bit claustrophobic. I feel as if I have not seen the outside world for months and we are still only in January. We've hardly touched the year yet and my regular walking regime has taken a back seat for the first time I can remember."

"If I remember correctly my old pal your much vaunted walking regime only ever involved a quiet stroll over the packhorse bridge as far as widow Samuel's cottage. A stay which would eventually lead to a stagger home and a prolonged snoring session in your room. Not exactly Olympic standard. Although I imagine the snoring might get you a podium finish if snoring ever gets included in the games."

"You can be a snarky bastard at times Piers. You know full well that my visits to the widow were solely for the sharing of intellectual interests and not some mere sordid roll in the hay. In any case the merry widow spends most of her time with that corduroy clown who pretends that he is a farmer, when we all know he only has a ratty smallholding. If it wasn't for the regular shoots where he charges his erstwhile chums silly money to slaughter a few pheasants he'd be queuing up to sign on. It's just that much as I love this place fresh air is essential even to a superannuated barfly like me. I miss it Piers."

Such talk was unlike the Billy Bones that Prideaux knew and loved. His natural habitat was the bar. He had the complexion, the slightly beaten air and unkempt appearance typical of the friends of Bacchus. His youthful roistering was well behind him but just as older ball game players compensate for loss of natural pace with knowledge so Bones made up for his physical decline with a coruscating wit that could fillet the most aggressive bar room lawyer.

If Bonesie felt trapped then it could be serious. Previous events had conspired to give both men more from life than they could have ever hoped. The Hand of God was more than handsome compensation for both of them: Prideaux for a thwarted academic career and Bones for the millstone of a fading estate. In a couple of years Prideaux and Bones had elevated the restaurant to its current enviable position. Under their direction The Hand of God had acquired Michelin Star status. The two were making good money in a place that they loved. They had established their business as the leading place in Wales and all points east for those who prided themselves on the sophistication of their palates.

Bones had raised the status of the wine cellar to stand comparison with well established wine merchants internationally. Experts came to consult William Radleigh de Beaune. His wine tastings were legendary and bookings needed to be made a year in advance. He was in a place where all was light and airy yet a dark cloud was beginning to intrude. Prideaux hoped that this was to be a temporary blip in the upward trajectory of the only aristocrat he had not wished to see hanging from a handy lamppost. As for Prideaux he could never forget that it took the death of two of his oldest friends to put him in his current happy position.

He could never forget, nor could he forgive. His nemesis, Slope had made no appearance in his consciousness for many months. Memories of Mark and Ginny Williams and the cruel manner of their deaths at the hands of Slope could not be fully expunged. It was a qualified happiness, but welcome nevertheless. He owed them the memory and now that he had some space where creditors never needed to venture he had the head space to remember them in print. His current lifestyle allowed him the time to write. He had the experience gained from years writing pieces for the Oxford Record. He could write, he could meet deadlines and sure as hell had a story to tell. His problem was not the story, it was the ending.

One thing bothered him. He was sure that the story he had to tell wasn't finished yet. Worse than that he didn't know who would write the ending. His gift to Mark and Ginny was to record their part in the story that he and Bones had lived through. He could do no more for them than to record the manner of their deaths and the evil that had led them to those deaths. As gifts go it wasn't much but for him it was some form of cleansing.

So much bollocks is talked about that nebulous thing called closure by those who should know better. There could be no such thing whatever the quacks chose to call it, not for him. Not for anyone who had been involved with the pure evil that was Sebastian Slope. He had no wish to open that particularly toxic Pandora's Box in reality. Fiction could perhaps expiate the whole thing in the writing. At the moment life was good and Bones would surely come all one way once the daffodils were out and shining. As a Celt Prideaux knew that a time of hope was the time to be more concerned than any other. No true Celt ever relaxed: when spring threatened its renewal was the time when the sky was at its most likely to fall. That was in the blood, it could never be ignored. The present was the time to cheer up Bones, the waiting spring would have to take care of itself. Neither man had the remotest idea that their cosy little idyll was about to be disturbed by the very nemesis that had almost done for them both in the past. A rough beast was at this moment shuffling its way towards The Hand of God.

"Listen Bonesie," said Prideaux. "It seems to me that you need a bit of cheering up. What say we go down to the cellar and start cataloguing that last wine order of yours? I know you still haven't taken any of it out of the boxes. It might take your mind off being cooped up here. I could do with some exercise myself and there's a fair bit to do down there."

"As ideas go my old fruit pie that's not the worst one you have ever had Piers. Let me just finish replying to these emails. I've been meaning to do so for months. You know how it is. I'm down to the last couple. I've had one from Rosie down there in Truro. She seems to be expanding her empire. Opening up a deli apparently. She sends her regards and hopes to see us both soon. She's thinking of a walking tour in these parts later this year. I've told her she can stay here any time she likes."

"I'm surprised you can send anything anywhere using that archaic laptop you are so fond of. The computer manufacturers will never make a living out of the likes of you. That thing must be around ten years old."

"So what, Piers? It's a little slow. But if it ain't broke why fix it? Does the job, that's all that counts. Hey up. Here's another email from good old Marco down there in the black heart of southern Italy. I sent him a long missive a while back telling him how well things were going here in The Hand of God. He sent a short one back yesterday telling me I was a bullshitter and a blusterer. I think he's interested though or he wouldn't be in touch again so quickly. You know the Italians always mañana with them."

"I think that's Spanish rather than Italian Bonesie."

"Well whatever it is Marco's half Cornish so that means he does everything 'dreckly' anyway. And as you know 'dreckly' is similar to mañana but without the same sense of urgency."

Bones guffawed over the old Cornish joke. But his face darkened almost immediately as he opened the email and began to read its contents.

"Piers come over and have a look at this. Marco says that some old buffer was in his bar recently throwing his weight about and being generally rude to his regulars. He kept asking them about a sinister Englishman who was mixed up with one of the gangs locally. He says he mentioned me and someone called Piers. Apparently Marco says he thought that piers were those bridges that the British like so much because they didn't ever go anywhere. I think that's meant to be a joke. But get this Piers, he says he threw the old buffer out but not before he had handed over a sealed envelope with strict instructions that he keeps it safely for me to collect. He's going to do some sniffing and see what else he can find out. What do you think of that?"

"Not a lot, if I'm honest," said Prideaux. "I don't even want to say the name but it feels to me like some kind of Slope alert. Did he say anything else?"

"The thought had occurred to me too Piers. I just didn't want to raise that particular spectre just when things are going so well. Oh! One thing he did mention is his new business venture and his wish to pick my brains about how to be as successful as I've been in this business. Yes I know its ours Piers but Marco doesn't know you. I tell you what let's put all this to the backs of our minds for now and do what we originally intended in the wine cellar. It will give me the opportunity to improve the parlous state of your knowledge of the drink of the gods apart from anything else. It would be a giant step for mankind if you learned a little more than constantly insisting that there is white wine on the one hand and red wine on the other. It will probably be as rewarding as trying to educate pork but roundabout now I could do with a challenge. One warning though: I know that blasted sound system of yours covers the entire pub but if I find out you have installed a speaker in my wine cellar I shall in all likelihood be forced to set fire to your head."

"It's a deal my old chum. No music, no singing not even the odd whistle or two, just a solid couple of hours of bottle arranging together with the odd bout of cobweb chasing. Come on the last one down the cellar makes dinner."

"Surely you jest Piers. We have a garlanded chef to cook our meals so why would a couple of culinary rabbits like us enter the unknown country that is the kitchen of The Hand of God? One does not keep a dog merely to bark oneself."

"You are of course as right as a trivet my old miserabilist. We do indeed have a top notch chef and I for one yield to nobody in my admiration for his culinary skills. If Camilleri's Inspector Montalbano were to unexpectedly come to life and leap from the pages of one of his novels it is to The Hand of God that he would head to satisfy his near permanent hunger. But when the snow lies all around and said chef lives just outside Crickhowell the fact that he is not here is hardly surprising. What is surprising is that he has not been here for the past three days, yet you have not so much as mentioned it."

"I can't keep track of everything Piers. I have my reputation as a wine expert to maintain and that takes up most of my time."

Anyway what is all this I've heard about sorting out the wine cellar? Come on you idle bastard or you'll have it dark."

The two men scuffled, pushed and pulled like teenagers overdosed on hormones as they made their way to the cellar door and precariously down the still rickety steps. Prideaux had been agitating for the removal of the lethal old steps but Bones would have none of it.

"Gives the place the proper sense of atmosphere," was all he would say whenever Prideaux broached the subject. Some constructive work was just what the two old friends needed to shake off the slight winter depression that was becoming hard to avoid. It might also help to keep two minds away from dwelling on unexpected thoughts of Slope and all that this could mean. At the best of times this part of the country could be a hard place to live. Winter came early and stayed late. Snow was a frequent visitor and because almost all the roads were little more than lanes they were rarely cleared. Four by fours could deal with all but the worst of it. This winter had tested the resolve of the hardiest villagers. It was on foot or nothing and most locals simply hunkered down in houses and cottages as they waited for a break in the weather.

Deep in the cellar work was proceeding at a fast lick and both men were enjoying the physical effort. It was a refreshing change from watching snow falling, helping unwary motorists out of snow drifts and speculating on when the weather would lift. Prideaux was running a sweep for regulars. The first person to predict the arrival of a thaw would pocket a three figure sum. The knowledge of the debilitating effect of the current cold snap made the echoing of the pub front door bell all the more surprising. Whoever was ringing the bell evidently meant it. Eventually realisation dawned that one of them should at least find out who was making such a fuss. Reluctantly Prideaux nodded to Bones as he turned and made his way back up the cellar steps to answer the persistent bell ringer.

Grumbling his way across the bar and out into the vestibule to open the door all sorts of thoughts set off on a wander through his mind. "What fresh hell is this," was the dominant thought as he turned the heavy ancient key that kept the heavy old door secured. It took some tugging as the door had swollen over the previous weeks of bad weather. It came loose suddenly and like some form of cartoon forced him backwards almost losing his balance. Peering around the door he was faced by what seemed to be a snowman with attitude.

"About fucking time you idle prat. I'm turning into a fucking icicle here," said the miserable snowman. "Come on man let me in before I bloody well freeze to death."

The snowman strode through the open door dropping snow all over the floor and Prideaux as he shook himself to gradually reveal a smartly dressed Gawain Cornelius beneath the snow line. As realisation dawned Prideaux simply stared as if confronted by the ghost of winters past.

"For God's sake shut your mouth Prideaux. You look like a stricken guppy. Shut the door man and stop gibbering. Warmth and whisky in that order. Come on let's get to the bar and get outside a couple of goodly slugs of a decent malt."

Prideaux did as instructed too shocked to be able to put together a comment, smart or otherwise. He would have given very long odds on the night caller being Cornelius of all people. In truth an ambulatory snowman would have got better odds. As far as Prideaux knew the man had retired and gone off to Italy or somewhere European to enjoy a sybaritic retirement. If he was here, never mind how the bastard had got here, it could not be good news. Bad memories had been more or less expunged, but Cornelius arriving had prompted them to start flowing back. Prideaux followed him meekly to the bar. Reaching over the counter he grabbed a bottle of 12 year old malt and three glasses.

"I assume that the third glass is for that ancient idler that will no doubt be around here somewhere. Well go on conjure him up. Rub on a lamp or spout a magical incantation whatever it is you do to cause him to materialise." This last stung Prideaux who had never been a man to react well to the sort of verbal bullying at which Cornelius was so adept.

"Listen Cornelius you oily bastard. I don't like you. As far as I'm concerned you are supposed to be retired and oiling around Italy or somewhere similarly not Wales. And in case you have conveniently forgotten you have no hold over me or over Bones any longer. I don't care if you have a posse of your highly educated thugs outside the pub, if you don't start explaining what the fuck you are here for I shall kick you from here to the front door and bury you in one of the many snowdrifts outside."

"It's not my job to get people to like me. It's my job to get the job done, if you see what I mean. I couldn't care less about your feelings for me as long as you don't get in my way. However, I take your point and I suggest we sit down as close to the fire as sensible."

"Yes, wouldn't want you getting chilblains, would we?" snarled Piers wishing quite the opposite. "Take those blasted Hunters off. Trust you to wear something suitable to a light snow shower. Marks you out right away as a tourist. Perhaps the combination of my log fire and my whisky might mellow your current mood. For your sake I bloody well hope it does. You are not looking well old chap. Dragging your leg like that either means you have recently pissed down it or perhaps caught it in a mangle."

"Not exactly that. I did get it stuck in one of those revolving doors though. I was on a promise and not concentrating. Somehow I got the bloody thing jammed when arriving at a rather swish West End hotel. Mashed up my lag and jammed the entire bloody system. They had to bring in an entire bloody team to dismantle the damned thing. I was lying there in full view for hours. By the time they got me out my promise had buggered off and I was en route to the nearest hospital. Damned embarrassing all round."

Prideaux did his best to stifle a smile. "I suggest you say nothing of this to Bonesie since he likes you even less than I do. He will rip the piss unmercifully if he finds out. I promise not to tell him until you are long gone. It might be a good idea, however, to take one of your humility pills and start treating us both with some respect."

"Of course. Sorry Prideaux. I forgot how sensitive you Celts can be. No offence intended. I suppose it's all the time I've been spending in Italy. The Italians can be a trifle sudden but in general they are the most delightfully laid back folk I have ever encountered. Probably the climate, don't you know. All those cloudless skies and that lovely bone warming sun does tend to lift the spirits a tad. Then you have this. Return to the Ice Age part two or whatever it is. No wonder you lot are so miserable most of the time. Anyway the point is I had retired but unfortunately our lot is not unlike the Mafia. You never actually retire. You can get retired but that usually means an anonymous hole in the ground following a nasty bullet hole in the head in some government owned chunk of land. Fact remains that I have been ordered back from Italy's lovely shores and temporarily reassigned to my old post. Go and fetch your chum and I'll reveal all. Pour out a couple of healthy fingers of this rather toothsome Scotch. Once I tell you why I'm really here you are sure as hell going to need it."

The need to ferret Bones out of his favourite cellar evaporated as the man himself appeared around the corner of the bar. If Cornelius had resembled a snowman then Bones was giving a fine impression of a cobwebbed ghost as he walked into the bar. Cobwebs hung from his tousled hair, dust dropped from his suit jacket as he shook himself vigorously.

"Bloody dusty down there Piers my handsome," he said as he turned towards the fireplace. His lugubrious expression turned to one of extreme distaste. "What is that snidey little wastrel doing here?" He was addressing Prideaux. It was Cornelius who answered. "Sit yourself down over here Bones you scruffy oik. I suggest you avail yourself of that rather tempting looking glass of whisky. You will need it I can assure you of that. When you have got yourself nice and comfortable I'll answer your question."

Bones for once did as he was instructed. Sitting down he drained the generous glass of whisky in one slug. "This had better be good, Cornelius."

☐

4

NEWS FROM SOMEWHERE

If there was one thing Gawain Cornelius liked better than an audience it was a captive audience. There was nowhere for Prideaux and Bones to go. They could have emulated Captain Oates and gone outside for a bit but that way madness most certainly lay. So they listened. The news was only partly softened by unlimited whisky and a roaring fire.

"I'm sorry to be the bearer of bad news," he began in his best civil service voice, "but I'm afraid it is unavoidable. And when I say that it is the last thing in the world I ever wanted, believe me that is the absolute truth. After the last debacle I vowed never to have anything to do with you two ever again. Sadly, it looks as if my decision has been overruled."

Cornelius continued to waffle on outlining scant details as both Prideaux and Bones began to look increasingly bored. Typically it wasn't at all clear exactly what Cornelius was attempting to tell them.

"Now I don't like this any more than you do," he droned. "There I was enjoying a well earned retirement in the depths of Italy when I get a knock on the door and there stand a couple of oiks from the Goon Squad with written orders telling me to temporarily suspend my golden years while I return home to receive some new orders. Some sort of little local difficulty it seems. There is no gainsaying such orders when it comes right from the top. As a last resort I have dragged myself along here through drifts of snow topping the houses and causing sheep in their fields to lose the will to live."

"I have absolutely no idea what you are talking about," replied a clearly needled Piers. "You'll appreciate how busy we've both been getting this place on its feet and then some. But there is something you're not telling me Gawain. Why on earth would someone of your level in the intelligence community give a stuff about two people who are not remotely interested in you or your undeserved retirement. I'm not exactly keen on the government agency you represent. To my mind they are just a bunch of murderous bastards. If they have dragged you kicking and screaming back from Italy then it's more than likely what you deserve. So come on for once let's have less civil service obfuscation and a teensy bit of clarity. In case you haven't noticed it continues to snow and I'm sure that if you mess us around Bonesie and I could manage to cart you out into the cold, cold snow and drop you in a drift. Try losing the usual arrogance and tell me the whole story."

"Not a bit of wonder that Slope hated you Piers. I shall correct myself, not a bit of wonder he continues to hate you. You are not exactly the most tactful of individuals. I have done you the favour of coming all this way to tell you of my concerns and all you do is threaten me with a violent ducking in a snow drift. The unvarnished truth is that we genuinely think that the bastard Slope has become active in Puglia. My original informant was adamant that something is afoot. There is at the moment no reason for immediate action but we are left with something of a mystery. And if there is one thing I hate it is a mystery.

"It all sounds spaghetti baloney, what a load of old tosh," snarled Piers.

"You have every right to be suspicious of my motives but they are of the purest kind. My briefing made it clear that there is intelligence to suggest that Slope has fetched up somewhere in southern Italy. If that intelligence is right and he is active again the chances are that he will have linked up with one of the lesser known secret societies in that area. My bet would be the Charcoal Burners or less likely the new mob the Olive Pickers but nothing is clear as yet. My immediate worry is that somehow Slope has become involved with some dangerous characters, even more dangerous than he that is. Given his record this could obviously have serious repercussions. Bottom line is that I am here in case either of you have heard anything."

"Not as such," replied Bones with the lie written all over his face.

"Come on Bonesie," insisted Cornelius. "What about that old pal of yours who runs a bar in Puglia. That Cornish Italian friend of yours, Marco. I know that you are in touch with him. After all you've known each other for years. The Spinelli brothers have their fingers on the pulse of that area. If anything is going on one of them would know. I did some ferreting of my own before the bastard threw me out. I left an envelope there for you too. Marco has it in his safe. I thought it safer there than to risk losing it in transit. As a last resort I thought that you might be able to shed some light on things but it appears my journey has proved to be a wasted one."

"What is it with you civil servants," exploded Bones when Cornelius had settled back into his chair as if all discussion was over and his work here was done. He had no intention of revealing any of his emails from his old friend to Cornelius. He had never like the bastard anyway. "All you had to tell us is that you think Slope might be involved in something again. That's it. A couple of sentences and you could have told us all you know which by the way sounds like bugger all. But no, we have to get the newspeak version. Now you are lounging about in that chair as if you are ensconced in the Drones Club and awaiting some mindless competition resembling cricket but played with bread rolls and rolled up copies of The Telegraph. You have an almighty nerve Cornelius and if my chum Piers would like me to assist him then I shall be first to volunteer for the snow drift detail for useless public servants."

His glance at Prideaux was chock full of meaning but his best friend's response confused him more than a little. Far from looking like a man shaping to debag an important intelligence agent he began to laugh. When he had recovered himself and with tears still streaming down his face he looked at Cornelius with something that approached indulgence.

"Gawain I realise it is not your way to come straight out with anything but I'd put money on the fact that you are building up to something here. I'll also stake my mortgage on the near certainty that you have to ask us to do something rather than tell us that we have to do something. I'm right aren't I?" Cornelius's face gave Prideaux the answer he sought.

"I thought so. Let me hazard a guess. I'm almost certain that the something you want from Bonesie and from me will involve a visit in the very near future to Italy. I also predict that the visit will not be to share your good fortune in having a trullo near Ostuni where we could spend many happy hours around the pool or strolling through the olive groves that you supposedly tend. The thought of you posing as a horny handed son of the soil gives me endless amusement in my darker times. What you really want, unless I miss my guess, is for us to come over to Italy and do our best to help you find out what Slope is up to."

"What, act as tethered goats?" a worried Bones couldn't resist asking the question before Prideaux continued:

"However, if it's not too much trouble I'd still like to hear you ask and please add the word please. I realise it will be unfamiliar to you but perhaps just this once."

"Oh for God's sake, Piers you just have to have your pound of flesh don't you. If it makes you happy then please will you and Bones come to Italy and help find out if Slope is involved with any of the ghastly gangsters that inhabit that lovely place. And yes, help draw the bastard out into the open. Nothing is more likely to tempt him into breaking cover than you two wastrels gallivanting around his lair."

"I knew it, tethered bloody goats," gulped Bones.

"And you were wrong about one thing Piers because the fact is that you can stay with me in my trullo. If you are prepared to do it I shall want the pair of you somewhere I can keep an eye on you. God alone knows the chaos you two could cause left to your own devices.

"All I want is a new perspective from you on what seems to be suspicious activity and, of course, your company while we run the fox to earth. I believe it was Mussolini who reached for a gun when he heard the word culture, or it might have been Thatcher, but whoever it was I think I know how they felt. It might be perfectly innocent but when I hear the word Slope I really do reach for my gun. So yes, you would be doing me a great favour. So what do you say?"

"Well I for one say Si, grazie mille old chap," interjected Prideaux sarcastically. "I'll just pop up to my room and start packing. I've always wanted to go to Italy. It stirs the juices just to think of it. Now which bathing trunks shall I pack? What about you, Bonesie?"

"Under no circumstances. I am happy here and there are more reasons for staying than going. For staying: everything. For going: too hot, been there, various mafia types, no decent ale. Need I proceed further? And if it is that important that I have access to your important envelope Cornelius then I can always get Marco to post it to me over here."

"Alright, alright," spat Cornelius. "Don't bloody milk it Bones. It should give me an opportunity to redeem myself after the debacle when Slope and Bennett escaped from the high security prisons I had shipped them to. It wasn't my fault but I was forced to fall on my sword. Blotting the old copybook like that doesn't sit well with me and let's face it if Slope is active again then any of us could be in a whole mess of trouble. And none of us would want that, would we?"

"We would not," chorused Bones and Prideaux not quite achieving the harmony of the Everley Brothers at their peak.

"Besides what about Mark and Ginny. Surely you want to avenge their deaths. Let's all have one last go at the bastard and bring the murderer to book."

Although there was an underlying seriousness to their response it was clear that Prideaux relished the idea of staying in Cornelius's trullo and Bones would travel reluctantly but spend time making Cornelius's life hell in the process.

A couple of whiskies later and Cornelius began to relax. He seemed preoccupied and as always where Bones, Prideaux and Cornelius foregathered the streams of whisky flowed like wine. In vino veritas, even if they were drinking whisky. Never had a Latin tag been more appropriate. The more Cornelius drank the more he told the truth. What had been an initial flirtation became a full blown affair, the truth flowing out as the whisky flowed in.

Cornelius wore his drink lightly and somehow managed to retain that still small centre of control even as the river of alcohol flowed through. Slurring a little and uncharacteristically emotional it took him a while to get there but eventually Cornelius began to explain the real situation. He had not retired at least not willingly but had been forcibly removed from the payroll. It was a perfect storm that had forced the hand of his superiors.

The Spriggans, that evil organisation Slope used to lead were now regarded as a fading threat without the top priority significance they had once been afforded. A little like UKIP without Farage, headless chickens. In this case the chickens are all looking for somewhere to hide. Cornelius was a shadow of the hunter he had once been, and his obsession with personal revenge following the brutal killing of Lola by Slope and Bennett had clouded whatever judgement he retained. There was no alternative, he had to go. A familiar old story but he had not gone until he had squeezed the last drop of opportunity from the vast resources at his disposal. Capturing or killing Slope was never going to be enough. He had to grind the bastard into the dust. He had to take away everything that he had. His revenge had to be the coldest dish ever served if he was ever to sleep easy again this was the way it was going to be. No man can serve two masters and revenge can be the cruellest of malign forces when it runs deep.

"I want you two to promise me that if anything happens to me you will make sure that the bastard Slope suffers for what he has done. Don't ask me how I did it but I managed to bankrupt the bastard and made sure that he knows it was me. The trouble is that now I am officially outside the ministry I have no protection. And there's more."

"Wouldn't you just bloody know it Prideaux," slurred Bones. "Here we go again. Let's have it then Cornelius you sad little soldier. What life-threatening nonsense have you visited on us now?"

"I'll leave it to your imagination what Slope will do to me if he ever tracks me down so I've covered myself pretty well. The thing is that Slope has declared open season on me through an encoded email to the AF. He can't offer any cash reward but he still has the power to terrify even some of those hard-bitten bastards in the Fellowship. And you know how competitive these killers can be.

They'll have a go just for the sake of being the person to do it. Do the world of good for their assassins' CV too."

Cornelius belched loudly without excusing himself as he made a pantomime of getting to his feet. He staggered and limped to the fireplace making a drunk's attempt at leaning on the mantelpiece. Turning to face his companions he managed to stammer, "I've already fixed the bastard. I bearded him in his den and cooked his goose." It was all Prideaux could do to keep his mouth shut as Cornelius mixed his metaphors. "I put up the bulk of money I relieved him of as a bounty on his head. It's all getting a bit complicated. The AF are after me and also after Slope. Bit ironic, don't you think? Set a thief to catch a thief and all that. Sad thing is we're dealing with professional killers. Thieves would be a piece of piss by comparison."

Suddenly, Cornelius began to look old and very tired. The whisky had done its job in mellowing a man who had seen it all he became more maudlin than Bones and Prideaux had ever seen him. Clearly, he needed to talk and he wanted them to understand. The talk quickly became arcane. A lover of crosswords, acrostics and all manner of word puzzles Cornelius possessed a steel trap of a brain and had used it to locate the devious trail of hiding places where Slope had salted away his ill gotten gains over many years.

By the introduction of his own byzantine system Cornelius had gradually drained Slope's wealth depositing hundreds of millions in his own carefully concealed accounts. He had also been careful to turn these assets into tangible possessions. He was aware of the fragility of the financial system and had circumvented it for his own purposes. Slope would never be able to trace the whereabouts of his erstwhile fortune Cornelius had seen to that. What was at issue was whether Cornelius had also concealed his actions from his own bosses.

"So what you really appear to be trying to tell us Cornelius is that you have robbed the robber. What you have made no attempt to explain is whether that makes you an equal opportunities crook or whether you have saved this country a significant sum." Prideaux had got straight to the nub.

Bones quickly followed suit. "Not only that my little tinker," he added with a smirk, "but you have most of the known world out for your blood in one way or another. Isn't that just peachy?

Chances are pretty good that you have led said assorted bastards right to our front door. Haven't you done well?"

"Well I do have a small confession to make. I have made it known, in the appropriate quarters, that you two are the paymasters in control of said bounty should anything messy happen to me. No, no. There's no need to thank me." He waved a drunken hand in the general direction of Bones and Prideaux.

"It's all in hand. The envelope in Marco's safe keeping will provide you with all the details. I'll issue you with everything you need to know when I see you in the morning. The thing is, it's complicated. And I'm finding it hard to focus at the moment. I hope you haven't spiked my drink or anything. Au revoir, my friends."

"Bloody cheek," blurted Bones marginally beating Prideaux to the punch. Both men stared slack jawed at the man who had just about written their death sentences. They resembled a pair of puppies who had just been asked a very difficult algebra question by an aggressive Cambridge don.

Cornelius continued to stare blearily at both men. It was clear he was finding it hard to focus but he finally managed to slur the words before dragging himself to his feet limping badly and staggering in the very general direction of his room. "Garibaldi's Overcoat," was all he managed to blurt out as he left two very confused hoteliers to sleep off their joint indulgence in the bar of The Hand of God. Before drifting off into the Land of Nod Bones reminisced briefly about his long friendship with Marco.

"He's a really good bloke is Marco," he slurred "I've known him for years. I met him out in Italy yonks ago. He didn't have a bar when I knew him first. I saw him playing water polo in Villa Novello. It was a big game back in those days. He was a star in those parts. Nobody messed with Marco. Apart from his brothers he could look after himself. He had moved from Cornwall out to join his family in Italy having already been a star for the Charlestown Water Polo Team. I'd lost touch. I used to watch him when he played water polo in Charlestown harbour. People forget what a big game it was in Cornwall. It was even bigger in Italy, of course, so he transferred to the Villa Novello team who were basically professionals. Pure coincidence. I was on a short break in Ostuni when I saw that there was a big water polo match scheduled in Villa Nova between the home team and Monopoli. Monopoli was a little way up the coast. It was a grudge match and there would be blood in the water. I caught the bus down to see the match. I couldn't believe my eyes when I saw him. He captained the side and they won what was a very bad tempered match. There was blood in the water and none of it was Marco's. I met up with him after the match and we have stayed in close touch ever since. Piers, Piers."

It took Bones a while to realise that his other close friend in this world had drifted off into a deep sleep. Bones was not far behind. Neither man could be bothered to climb the stairs to their respective rooms. There was still some heat in the fire and the leather chairs were very comfortable.

The morning after and breakfast in the restaurant. Still no sign of a chef so it falls to Prideaux to do the honours. The previous night had been a tricky one. As he performs small miracles with some dry cured bacon, and local pork sausages and organic eggs from nearby Owen's Farm.

Prideaux's mind is whirling. The mind whirl is not simply because the kitchen is not a place where he is comfortable. It is also because he has the generally gloomy outlook of the Celt. He knows that whenever consensus says that things cannot get any worse the statement always comes a nanosecond before things get much, much worse. That view of life is a given to one of mixed Welsh and Cornish descent.

It is exacerbated this particular morning by a vague feeling of concern. As if his state of mind needed a further tweak provided by the staggering arrogance of Cornelius. Words such as Cornelius and arrogance are comfortable bedfellows in any sentence but placing the order card with a request for breakfast in bed together with a copy of The Telegraph and the Do Not Disturb sign probably takes the biscuit. He will get neither breakfast nor newspaper. No breakfast because Prideaux is in uncooperative mood. No newspaper because none has been delivered within this area for the past week or so. He does his best to concentrate on the task in hand.

William Radleigh de Beaune is in much more positive mood. Dressed in typical three piece tweed suit with shirting from Jermyn Street and for the day a flamboyant spotted sky blue bow tie he sits at the restaurant table nearest to the window. This particular window looks out onto the organic vegetable plot. A steep hill rises behind. Both plot and hill are inches deep in overnight snow. The Third Earl of Mount Charles lets down his ensemble somewhat by his insistence on wearing wool mix dark brown full length walking socks and slippers. He sits and munches his way through the mountain of toast he has made using the restaurant multi toaster. Melted butter gives his chin a shiny appearance as he shouts, spraying crumbs over the immediate area as he does so, regular meteorological updates for Prideaux's benefit. "Not snowing yet, Piers. Looking a bit dark over Big Hill. I think I can smell snow, don't you know."

It is a litany that falls on deaf ears as Prideaux concentrates on producing a breakfast that will help to allay the biting cold that penetrates The Hand of God at this time in the morning. It is 7.30am. The fire in the bar has not been lit. Prideaux is cooking on gas and the reserves of logs to supplement the struggling heating system are being rationed. The kitchen is the warmest place to be.

Eventually, Prideaux emerges from the kitchen wreathed in smoke and a quiet smile of satisfaction. "Here you go Bones my lazy old friend. Here be bacon, eggs and some lovely sausages. One piece of advice for you before tucking in and that is do not criticise one single bloody thing or you can add a cooked breakfast to your apparel for the day. A bacon and egg waistcoat would neatly tone you down I imagine."

"You wound me sorely Piers. Here am I having cooked enough toast to choke a mountain lion and I am being accused of slacking. Aristocrats do not slack my little working class friend. It is simply that we, that is I, take the longer view to that taken by you impatient oiks. Now without going too deeply into politics that is the reason we are still here and still upholding all that is great and good about this country. Left to you and your revolutionary chums the country would have gone to hell in a handcart years ago. People like me would be hanging from lampposts all over the countryside. Now resume your proper position of servility and respect there's a good lad. Pass the HP and listen to your old friend and mentor."

There is something between old friends that allows them both to understand what is required in any given situation. Such was the relationship between these two that far from inflaming Prideaux's ever present left wing sympathies Bones had simply made him laugh. They had been through too much to forget that they had been best friends for a bucket full of years. Instead of erupting at his friend's insouciance Prideaux chuckled to himself as he brought over what would be a magnificent feast for a table of eight and placed it between him and Bones.

"If there's any left by the time that lazy bastard upstairs stirs himself then so be it. As far as I can see we need to fortify the inner man to keep out this bastard cold Piers. But there are more important things even than food and I'll bet that is a phrase I'll warrant you never thought to hear me say. Look, here is the problem we are facing as I see it. And what was all that talk of Garibaldi's overcoat?"

"Do you think Cornelius has lost his mind? Nice idea to spend some time in the south of Italy though, but what about the drawbacks? We can go out there and do some snooping around whilst staying at the trullo. Now I know that you have some knowledge of the Ostuni area but do you really think we ought to involve ourselves?"

"My Italian is non-existent and yours, at best, is rudimentary. Apart from all that we will have absolutely no support, no back up and if Slope is in that area small hope of getting back here alive. And for all those reasons we are going to go, aren't we? For Ginny and Mark."

"Bonesie my old darling I am not going to lie to you; I mean what would be the point? You are right to highlight all the reasons that a sensible person would go nowhere near Ostuni given what we already know. We will need to question that lazy bugger Cornelius and see if we can get some assurances from him. If he ever manages to unstick himself from his pit that is. It's nearly nine now. Look out of the window. It looks as if at least a mini thaw might be setting in. We could even get out and about a bit later on. Let's just finish this. If he isn't down by then I'll go and bang on his door and never mind any Do Not Disturb notices."

"You can kick him for me Piers, that'll rouse the bugger."

"What are we going to do Bonesie? We've batted all this about for too long already. We need to agree on whether we are going to get involved yet again in something we don't really understand. I can't help thinking that we owe it to Mark and Ginny. If we hadn't involved them in the first place they'd still be with us. Most of the time I put it to the back of my mind but sometimes, like now, it comes flooding back."

"You say sooth old pal. The sensible thing would be to ignore everything and carry on as normal. Not really an option though is it? Half the world's loonies are probably on our trail as we speak. If we are to go down the least we can do is go down fighting. If we can take the bastard Slope down, however we manage it, then at least we will have gone some way towards avenging two good old friends.

"We are Celts after all and it is our way to take bloody revenge on those who offend. Perhaps we should start collecting severed heads again as our ancestors did. Anyway, look on the bright side if we get the chance to sample some fine Italian cuisine and some top-hole vino in the process then so much the better."

The two continued to plough their way through the mountainous breakfast that Prideaux had managed to produce. By 9.30 they were both loosening belts and finishing up the second pot of coffee and generally feeling like a lie down in a warm room.

"I tell you what Bonesie. I'll just pop out into the snow and bring in a few logs then I'll light the fire in the bar. That'll start to warm the place up anyway. In the meantime you go up and give our honoured guest a knock and we can then see if we can get some sense out of him."

"Off you go then my intrepid little polar explorer. Go on. Chop, chop get a move on. In case you haven't noticed it's colder than a cobbler's last in here. Get a bloody move on man."

Prideaux did exactly that. Minutes later he returned carrying an armful of snowy logs. The expression on his face pre-empted any jocosity from Bones. He looked as if he had seen or possibly even touched a ghost in an inappropriate spot.

"What on earth is wrong with you Prideaux? I know how cold is but you are wrapped up like Nanook of the North so it is to be hoped that you are not suffering from frostbite or snow blindness or any of those nasties."

"It's just that, you know how you can see the guest bedrooms from the log store at the front of the pub. I happened to look up as I was picking up these logs which, by the way, I am about to drop on the floor as my fingers are starting to go numb."

He was a good as his word as half a dozen logs dropped to the floor.

"Come on man. Spit it out. Never mind logs. What is it that causes you to look like Banquo's ghost with a nasty touch of norovirus?"

"As I said, I looked up and even I couldn't fail to notice that the window to number ten was wide open. Now I know that Cornelius can be an odd sort but in these conditions anyone trying to sleep in a bedroom with the window open would likely have frozen to death.

"Last night was around nine degrees below. I think that we should go up to the room together. Just grab the pass key and let's go. I have a really bad feeling about this. I just hope he is alright and being purely selfish for a second; can you just imagine what will descend on us if he is not. It is easy to forget because the man is such a twat that he is, or was before being retired, also one of the highest ranking intelligence men within MI7. Those buggers look after their own whether they like them or not. And perish the thought, what if he is not one of their own any longer? What if....? It doesn't bear thinking about what they would do to him. It's not as if he was one of those oafs in MI6. Most of those should be on school crossing duty. The heavy stuff is always delegated to MI7."

Prideaux looked at Bones who by now had armed himself with one of the fire irons from the fireplace in the bar. He was holding it in two hands and playing some stylised cricket strokes. Despite his unease Prideaux could not help smiling at his friend. They began to walk up the stairs towards guest bedroom number ten.

The subject of their attention was startlingly oblivious to the interest created by his absence from the breakfast table. Far from sleeping the sleep of the just he was sleeping the sleep of the newly despatched. The big sleep for the man who had ordered quite a few of his own eliminations in his time. He lay still wearing his floral pyjamas with a base layer for warmth underneath. Nothing on earth could breathe warmth back into this body lying stiff and almost frozen at an odd angle across the king size bed.

Someone had gone to a load of trouble to make Cornelius's last minutes on earth as painful as possible. Whoever it was clearly had a twisted attitude to assassination. It had to be that. Whether one of the AF had got there first or an operative from MI7 it was obviously one with a macabre sense of humour. This was not an execution. It was torture followed by execution. The murderer had been following a well trodden path in making Cornelius's last minutes on earth both painful and terrifying.

His ribs had been severed close to the spine and spread out to resemble the wings of an eagle. Both lungs had been ripped out and placed to either side of the body. Cornelius had been disembowelled and his entrails were arranged neatly around the corpse. His head was barely attached to the body and his throat had been cut slowly with a serrated knife. The sheets were soaked in blood. In fact the man had been so well bled that if not for the gaping wound across his throat and the bizarre marks of torture he could have passed for a shop floor mannequin. Somebody had done a very professional job on a man who had breathed his last in the long reaches of the frozen night. He would have taken a long time to die? Jack the Ripper would have been well impressed.

It all looked a bit too pat though. This was not the work of a murderer in a frenzy. It was the work of a careful killer. This was a staged execution. The purpose was to warn and to terrify. Nothing in the room had been disturbed. Cornelius was a meticulous man. His wallet, phone and keys lay on the bedside table. The book he had been reading, Nicolo Machiavelli's Prince lay beside them, a bookmark resting in between pages fifty six and fifty seven where he had placed it before taking his final sleep in this world. The suit he had been wearing hung in the wardrobe the shirt hung alongside.

"You open the door with the pass key and go in first Piers," breathed a scared looking Bones in a husky whisper. "If there is any problem within, a burglar perhaps, I shall spring into the room as your wing man marginally in your wake, armed with my trusty fire iron making bloodcurdling shouts and threats. Any intruder will be reduced to a panic and gratefully give himself up to arrest by two solid citizens. That will have to serve until we can arrange to get the local plod out."

"Bonesie, in the unlikely event that there is an intruder he is more likely to laugh himself to a hernia than anything else. Your problem is that you watch too much television. What we are likely to find behind this door, when I finally get the bloody thing open, is an irritable and abusive Cornelius. He might need thawing out but if the clown left his window open overnight then serve him bloody well right. Right then in we go. Geronimo Evans."

The key clicked in the lock and with a little pressure yielded to a nervous Prideaux who stepped into the room closely followed by Bones who had now inexplicably taken up a fencing stance holding his fire iron as if it were a rapier. The sight of what was too obviously a corpse on the bed stopped both men in their tracks.

"Bloody hell, Piers. He doesn't look very lively. Good God the bastards have ripped out his teeth." Prideaux couldn't find it in his heart to explain that the teeth were false and in all probability Cornelius had removed them himself before taking his final snooze.

"The poor bastard has obviously left this vale of tears and with head barely attached. I should appreciate the absence of any cod Monty Python dialogue involving parrots and invisible choirs. I know the Python boys are on their last ever tour in an attempt at recreating the old days and making a few quid but some respect in the presence of the dead would not go amiss."

"Cornelius is definitely dead and we my wayward aristo are in deep shit. I suppose you recognise the pose in which the corpse has been tactfully arranged?"

Bones replied with a shrug. He had no idea what Prideaux was rambling about other than someone had taken several hours to cause someone to die in the most grotesque way imaginable.

"I've never seen it in real life, or real death," explained Prideaux. "I'm pretty certain that this is an attempt at recreating the Viking Blood Eagle. That particularly unpleasant bunch used this method of torture and execution to terrify the communities they raided. The Normans occasionally used it too. As you know they were Viking descendants and just as bloody."

"Piers, I hope you are not trying to tell me that there are raiding parties of Vikings marauding around the village."

"Not exactly. But someone is obviously trying to frighten us."

"I've got news for you Piers. It's bloody well working. So much so that I feel a change of trousering coming on."

The sound of the heavy oaken front door splintering allowed Prideaux the opportunity of observing, "I think that shit you mentioned just got a lot deeper, Bonesie. Please tell me that we are not about to be visited by a Viking raiding party. I think that would be too much for the old dicky ticker."

5

DEATH IN THE COUNTRY

There was nothing for either man to do. They had touched nothing so fingerprints would not be an issue. They had not even approached the bed where Cornelius had breathed his last. Bones had swiftly deposited the fire iron behind the wardrobe. They turned in unison to face the door as the sound of footsteps coming up the stairs got louder. In an involuntary reaction to the unknown both men raised their hands in a gesture of surrender. The door that had closed behind them when they entered the room burst open and four large armed men burst in. They were all armed with machine pistols and democratically aimed their weapons two at Prideaux and two at Bones.

"You can lower your hands but for appearances sake I think you should assume the position. You don't look the type to be familiar with such things. Bizarrely the gunman shouting the odds seemed to make the effort to chuck a wink in Bones's direction before continuing with his orders, "If you wouldn't mind lying face down with your arms stretched palm down in front of you that should prevent any unseemly shooting. There's more than enough blood been spilled in this room already." He followed his latest order with what Bones was now convinced was another theatrical wink as though he were making some sort of advance. He whispered as much to Prideaux.

Prideaux's reply was simple and direct. "If I were you I'd keep my bloody mouth shut and my imagination on standby." Their final instruction followed and was as unequivocal as all the rest, "as soon as the boss gets here we'll see what comes next."

Bones and Prideaux knew in their hearts that the best policy was to stay as still as possible and say nothing. If they were any further outside their joint comfort zone they would both be in another country. There was no doubt that the men currently pointing Glock 9mm machine pistols at them were professionals.

The one who had spoken appeared to be British. There was something about his accent that sounded familiar but neither Bones nor Prideaux could identify it. But that was at least something to cling to. As always when one is in an impossible position time seems to slow to a funereal tread. Seconds become minutes and all the rest. It could not have been more than five minutes though it felt more like thirty before the door opened for a third time that morning. Lying face down Bones and Prideaux could not get so much as a glance at whoever it was who had just entered the room. The fact that the tone of the four armed men had become reverential suggested the arrival of the boss. Some subdued chatter followed until the lead voice who had ordered the two men to the floor ordered them to resume their feet.

"OK for you to turn around now," came a voice neither recognised. "You might as well know that I am mightily pissed off to be dragged all the way here on business, but on balance it is quite nice to meet you both. I have heard much about you. Granted none of it is very flattering but I always like to know who or what I am dealing with. OK lads stand down. Send in the cleaners and we'll sort this place out.

"Just keep an eye out as unobtrusively as you can manage. You know the drill anybody other than a busybody appears and shoot their balls off. Now then Dastardly and Muttley please assure me that you have touched nothing in the room."

"Who the hell are you?" said Bones in his most irritated tone. "You do know we had nothing to do with this. I mean I never liked the man but I had no reason to cut his throat, much less almost decapitate the poor bastard. And as for arranging his corpse in the style of the Viking Blood Eagle…well I know the Vikings were a cruel bunch but this is taking things a bit too far. We are not savages in this part of the world you know despite what is written to the contrary by the London press most of whom think that the world is flat and they would fall off the end if they ever ventured outside the M25. Who the hell are you anyway?"

"You won't know who I am Bonesie, though I probably know more about the pair of you than you know about yourselves. Just think of me as your guardian angel. I suppose I'm rather more an archangel really. If it helps you can call me Gabriel, and my current task is to help you two out of an awkward spot.

"I'm afraid that Cornelius was acting under his own steam in coming here. He was entitled to contact you and I had intended to follow him eventually anyway but when I received the black alert message I got here as soon as I could. The thing is chaps it looks very much as if Cornelius has been turned."

The two looked at him blankly. They were aware of rivalry between MI6 and the anti-Spriggan unit in MI7. It was impossible to penetrate such secretive units: if you were on the outside then a lot had to be taken on trust. After all Cornelius had been directly involved in the events that had ultimately led to the deaths of their friends Mark and Ginny Williams. But hearing this from Gabriel unsettled them more than a little.

"Listen Gabriel, as far as I'm concerned you are no angel. You're just another spook or whatever they call your lot. I'd really appreciate some honesty. I realise that is a strange concept to you but perhaps you could make an exception just this once.

"Explain to me how it comes to pass that we have a high ranking government agent in one of our better rooms with his throat cut so deeply that his head hangs by a thread. Not only is the poor bastard dead but it appears that there is every chance that Eric the Red or some similar marauder has decided to show off his mastery of the Viking Blood Eagle pose. It's not fucking right. Now much as I respect our secret services I must point out that I am unhappy at your turning our pub into an episode of CSI Abergavenny. I'm sure that the last time I saw him his full ration of blood was somewhere inside his body rather than soaking through those rather expensive Egyptian cotton sheets of ours."

"Piers, my dear old soul. It is marvellous that you and Bonesie are carving out a lovely career for yourselves lost out here in the backwoods. It almost runs like a Welsh Walden. I am genuinely happy for you. I must tell you that such pleasures are denied to those of us tasked with keeping the country safe in these troubled times. So you enjoy yourself luxuriating in your bosky woods and I shall carry on in the frontline denying nutters their every effort to derail democracy."

"And a right old Horlicks you are making of it. I wouldn't trust your lot to run a sweet shop," Bones never did master the art of keeping his mouth shut.

"I'll let that one go Bones. But for the record do not jump on that high horse of yours too often with me or you'll be accompanying the beast to the local knacker's yard. Look, I assumed he was headed here and knew he hadn't the clearance to come alone. I'm just sorry I didn't get here in time to save him. Now I want you two to tell me the story from the beginning while we give the cleaning squad the opportunity the do their valuable work. You won't recognise the place once they have finished.

"Whoever did this knew he was here. I'm guessing he was local as he knew how to get up here from downstairs which in this ancient warren is not a given. He also made good use of the snow by leaving through the window and dropping into that convenient drift right below. It broke his fall and last night's snow covered his tracks so no point in trying to trace him. Now come on you can sort out some food for me and we can have that chat downstairs."

"Well I must say Gabriel that you are one cheeky bastard. What exactly is it that you would like me to rustle up for you at the drop of a hat. Breakfast is long gone and in any case our chef is snowed in miles away. I might be able to serve you up a steaming plate of bread and spit, it's about all you deserve with your attitude." Like Bones Prideaux was getting more than irate at the turn that events had taken. He was all for the defence of the realm but not at the spectre of these London cowboys charging in like John Wayne on speed.

It took Bones longer to tell Gabriel what little they knew of the reasons behind Cornelius's visit than it took Prideaux to rustle up some acceptable sandwiches, sans spit of course, in the chef free kitchen. There wasn't much to tell and both men hoped that Gabriel would be able to give them some hard information.

"The only thing we got from Cornelius was that he wanted us to go out to Puglia," explained Prideaux. "It sounded as if he thought we might be able to help smoke Slope into the open. I can't help thinking that there was more to it than that though. He would have told us this morning I think, well if someone hadn't taken the trouble to slice through his vocal chords that is. You could let us know what is going on, Gabriel? You obviously know far more than we do."

"That's one of the reasons I'm here. We have had our concerns about dear old Gawain for a while. He was one of our best men for many years but since we sort of retired him he has lost focus. He knows that the rules do not allow a lone wolf approach. He was becoming a bit vague and we are aware that Slope has been dormant for some time that is also not like him. The idea of sending you two to Puglia for a bit of gentle and very amateur sleuthing makes no sense at all, it all sounds pretty amateur. Not like Cornelius at all.

"The murder of Cornelius changes the picture significantly. If he wanted you two out there then there must have been a reason other than the one he gave you. I don't suppose he gave you any documents, codes or perhaps data sticks, did he? Any mention of items of antiquity or Norman history at all?"

A couple of bewildered looks gave Gabriel his answer. Neither had the first idea what he was talking about. "The things I do in defence of the realm," thought Gabriel.

"We have little choice but to send you out there. Whatever Cornelius had planned you two were obviously central to it. I'm sure that you can get this place covered for a week or two. The government will pick up the tab for any losses over and above what the pub would have taken with you two here and in full flow."

"Sarcasm doesn't suit you, Gabriel. As a matter of fact we do have a very loyal following here and before all this happened we were all for a trip to lovely southern Italy. We have excellent staff who would have been more than happy to cover for us. You should know that Bonesie and I are not violent men, and if the Grim Reaper had not been upstairs sharpening his scythe on Cornelius's throat and all parts south last night we would be hurrying off to complete our packing. This changes everything. We could now be going out there to certain death. I don't know the Italian for Grim Reaper but I'll bet they have their own version of the old bastard stalking the badlands of Puglia and Basilicata.

"Now just suppose that Slope is lurking in the undergrowth just outside Ostuni or Locorotondo. Suppose he has decided to take a closer look at trulli land down there in Alberobello. Just how long do you think it would be before someone was digging our mutilated bodies out of a disused olive grove? That is what I fear may be our fate."

"I would no more send you two to Puglia on your own than I'd expect the queen to abdicate in favour of Prince Charles. It would make no sense at all. You are a very unobservant pair aren't you? Did none of the four men that came into room ten in something of a hurry stir any memories for you?

"Well one of them, the one that did all the talking, I should say ordering us about seemed to be giving me the glad eye. And there was something about his accent that I couldn't quite place."

"That should have been enough done because two of them were the twins Bob and Robert Job putting in a shift as members of the poor bloody infantry. I'm sure you remember them. They are not easily forgotten. You should also know that in the current climate wherever I go those two forces of nature are never far behind. Not that anyone in their right mind would ever tangle with them mind but they are my most reliable men. They would be coming with you almost as personal bodyguards. I'll tell you now that you will not avoid weapons training this time as you have done in the past. You will be taken to the range up near Brecon and given official issue Glock machine pistols."

"Just a minute old fruit," blustered Bones. "I have said it before and here it comes again, by the sacred memory of the Tufty Club please remember that we are not active soldiers. I for one have never been an active anything. Trying to turn us into cut price James Bonds simply will not work."

"I'm sorry to offend your sensibilities but the fact is that the twins have been deputed to be your arms instructors. You know them well enough to know that they are never to be trifled with. For some odd reason they seem to like you. Must be the old alma mater I suppose because I'm damned if I can see the attraction. They'll also make sure you have some basic grasp of self defence. Well just enough to stall someone until one of the boys can get to you at least."

"Well Gabriel, it's a fine offer and one that I am actively considering," interjected Prideaux. "Just a tiny questionette or two if that's OK?"

"Fire away old chap and I'll give you my answers as fully and as frankly as you'd expect."

"Well I was wondering where we would be expected to stay. I know that Cornelius has a trullo out there but is it one of those nicely appointed ones or basically a shepherd's hut? Old Bones here is not getting any younger and in all things these days comfort is the determinant. I am the first to answer the call when my country needs me but really I think some consideration is in order. I should also like to know whether said trullo is within spitting distance of civilisation or in the back of beyond where the opportunity for wine, women and song is severely limited."

"Well said Piers, always the eye to the main chance. I think I can put your mind at rest. You will be able to stay in what was Cornelius's trullo. It didn't belong to him but was a sort of grace and favour arrangement. It reverts to the department on his death.

"I'm having it cleaned and swept by the ferrets as we speak. I shall be out there myself to make sure everything is tickety-boo and don't worry I'll ensure that all security is ramped up. You should have guessed that an aesthete like Cornelius would not have been roughing it."

"As you know Bonesie Italian food is one of my favourites," Prideaux winked as he said it. "Just think we could be bimbling around the local trattorias and restaurants sampling the local delicacies. Something not to be sniffed at you know."

"Look you two I haven't seen it myself but apparently it is a beautifully restored example of the traditional trullo able to sleep six. It has thirteen acres of olive grove around it and a swimming pool outside the back door. From the roof you can see the Adriatic in one direction and Ostuni in the other. You will be equidistant from both places which makes the sea and the city walkable or if you prefer very easy to cycle to. Before you start bleating there will be a car on hand too. And should Slope show his miserable head the Job twins will be there the lop it clean off."

"Well, old chap if Piers and I are to put our lives on the line to help out the intelligence services one last time then I'm not averse to a bit of pampering. And if we are going to fulfil the role of tethered goats then I shall expect fine wines and very haute cuisine.

If that is to be the case then perhaps I could reconcile myself to visiting Italy for one more adventure."

"Now, you two I need to go back to base with the twins. All you need to do is finish your packing and be ready to leave first thing in the morning. The twins will be back here to pick you up and bring you along with luggage up to HQ. You won't need your passports because we will fly you in under an agreement we have with the Italians. Now remember that the twins are in charge since I wouldn't leave you two in charge of the school tuck shop. So you do what you are told or you will be back here quick smart."

"Just one more thing Gabriel I hate to mention it really," said Prideaux mentioning it anyway. "The thing is I can see that this will be a good opportunity for a break for us and all that but just what are you expecting us to do while we are there? I mean it's not as if either one of us is fluent in Italian and won't we need some sort of cover story?"

Exasperation flitted across Gabriel's face as he managed to choke back a sarcastic remark. They weren't much but they were all he had. Best to keep them onside for as long as possible anyway. It wasn't as if this was a master plan or anything like it. It was just a response to very limited information that might just have tempted a resurgent Slope into breaking his cover. In that case he could be liquidated and that would go a long way to persuading Zebedee that he, Gabriel was made of the right stuff. There was also the thorny issue of what Cornelius had lifted from the security archives. It could be anywhere but the place to start looking would be the trullo and surrounding olive groves. Recovering that item would give his career a boost of rocket proportions. There was no need for Bones and Prideaux to be aware of this aspect and if the two became collateral damage then that would be no skin off his nose.

If this plan did work then the corpse currently in a body bag being dragged down the stairs and across to the waiting helicopter in the field over the road would not be the end of it. Cornelius could well be the first of many.

"To be honest you are going to be in an exposed position. That is why you have two of our best men with you. There will be others there too. What I want you to do is simple. You are two old friends taking a holiday at the trullo that belonged to a mutual friend who has tragically died in a road accident, speedboat accident or of a surfeit of lampreys. Because of the sudden nature of his passing you are there to finalise his affairs.

"You don't need to tell anyone anything unless they ask and you feel you need to. Since you have not visited Italy for many years you both thought it would be nice to spend a few weeks enjoying the area whilst completing the sad task of tying up Cornelius's affairs. Now apart from the possibility that you could both get killed it should be the best holiday you have ever had. Does that answer your question, Piers?"

"Admirably, thanks. That's all I needed to know and thanks for being so frank. Bones and I will now get our heads together and start packing. We are already looking forward to doing our small arms training and self defence classes."

"Cut the crap Piers. When the twins return to pick you up tomorrow they, like you will be kitted out to look like a couple of Brits on holiday. And don't worry about not speaking Italian they are both fluent in the language and the dialect of the area. They won't let on unless they have to but pretending not to know the language is a hell of a good way to ferret things out. It's amazing how freely people will talk if they think you don't have their language.

"You will do both your small arms training and self defence work at the Brecon range. It's not going to be onerous as you are not being parachuted in behind enemy lines, nothing as gung-ho as that. You two, God help us all, are the best chance I have of determining whether there is a need to put some real heavies into that area.

"Remember that there is an existing death sentence still extant on Slope. It is currently held in abeyance and we would prefer not to activate it. But if he is rearing his extremely ugly head again then we might need to remove the offending article.

"Who knows, do your part well and you might even get a medal. Or perhaps a knighthood, just imagine that! See you in Puglia. Arriverderci."

Gabriel was out of the bar and through the open front door of The Hand of God before either of the two men could move or even say a word. They looked at each other in silence. This wasn't how they expected to be spending late winter and the early days of spring. The element of danger was tempered by the appeal of a comfortable place to live in an area where the food and wine was legendary. Prideaux in particular felt an obligation to do what he could to ensure that the bastard Slope and the bitch Bennett got what they deserved.

The following morning Bones and Prideaux were seated in the vestibule waiting for the arrival of the twins. The snow still lay thick though there was a breath of warmth in the air. It could have been the beginning of thaw or yet another false alarm. It was still officially winter and this part of Wales was well used to spring coming late if it bothered to come at all. There were years when the season jumped straight to summer.

None of this bothered Bones or Prideaux as they were expecting to be in the deep south of Italy within the next few days. Beside them in the pub vestibule were their bags packed and ready to go. Neither man had any real idea of what to expect but it was Brecon not Puglia that dominated their thoughts as they whiled away the time in inconsequential gossip. Try as they might they could not avoid idly speculating on the imminent small arms and self defence training that was waiting them.

Neither man had any real experience of guns or hand to hand fighting. Both were singularly ill equipped for such activities. Prideaux was a dreaming academic and Bones an old unreconstructed aristocrat. If you gave them time and a glass of wine they could probably tell you that the guns the twins carried were 9mm Glocks. They might even recall that Rosie the barmaid down there in darkest Truro was skilled in an ancient art of Chinese street fighting and that she tended to prefer a Ruger pistol. Beyond that their knowledge of aggression tended to tail off. Still if that was the deal then they would have to comply.

Their cosy little chat was interrupted by an eruption of twins as the Job brothers burst into the vestibule from the rear of the pub. Yelling and screaming they scared the living daylights out of the two older men who found themselves on their feet with their hands in the air muttering, "Please don't shoot, we surrender."

"This is not the bloody Alamo," yelled a delighted and near hysterical Robert Job as he lowered his Glock. Bob Job was rolling hysterically on the flagstone floor with a fist jammed in his mouth as he tried to prevent the laughter. For the twins this was just normal behaviour. For Bones and Prideaux it was the portent of exciting if unsettling times just around the corner.

"These silly sods are supposed to be on our side," the two were to mutter to each other in the months that followed, on more than one occasion.

The silly sods, in truth highly trained killing machines, had a quality of presence that strengthened the resolve of both Bones and Prideaux. Their very exuberance allayed some of the natural fears that this whole business had aroused in two men who would prefer to be as far behind the front line as possible. They were soon to realise that their quiet little lives were to be disrupted for a second time.

6

SPRINGTIME IN ITALY

January had turned gradually into February which was reluctantly making its way towards March before the twins with their bodyguards left Brecon for the distinctly warmer climate of southern Italy.

Flying into Brindisi airport had been something of a trial. Neither Bones nor Prideaux were comfortable fliers. For Prideaux it was the boredom coupled with the sheep-like obedience of passengers that saw them move through airports as if all individual intelligence had been put on hold. Not that this affected the two as their flight landed at the perimeter of the airport at a station reserved for private jets and military aircraft.

For Bones the grumble was a steadfast refusal to understand any aspect of aeronautics. It was the simple old fashioned refusal to believe in heavier than air machines. "Makes no sense at all," was his regular reply when the science was explained to him. He had a policy though and of course it involved alcohol. Fortunately for Prideaux his old friend always carried a large hip flask filled with industrial strength whisky. Even on a short flight such as the one to Brindisi he would be nigh on comatose within the first half hour.

The twins were much more comfortable. They were frequent fliers and the experience always left them slightly underwhelmed.

Arriving at Brindisi airport the four men boarded the 'A' bus that took them to the train station. The twins though normally affable were having no truck with Bones's protestations that he was jet lagged and in need of a restorative drink. They seemed impatient with everything and once they had retrieved their luggage they were on the bus and heading for the stazione ferroviaria with Bones still muttering darkly about 'young whippersnappers'. The bus was at the train station in a matter of minutes with Bones still chuntering.

"For God's sake Bonesie," advised Prideaux "get a grip. Look we're at the station now and we'll be in Ostuni in no time. Please cheer up. I should point out that your attitude is beginning to piss off the twins. Sunny as they can be when things are going well I am not keen on the idea of two severely pissed off Job twins on the loose in southern Italy. They were a bloody nightmare in Cornwall. I can't even begin to think of the mayhem they could cause in this part of Italy."

"I'll do it for you, Piers, mind I wouldn't do it for just anybody. I hate travelling. Once I can settle down in a friendly bar I shall be as right as rain. I've just heard Bob tell Robert that there will be a car parked at Ostuni station waiting for us to drive to the late and unlamented Cornelius's trullo. Now that is something to which I am looking forward."

"Me too, a wash and a change of clothes are a must."

"I think, however, a quick pit stop in Ostuni itself would be just the ticket. Il Gatto Verde would be just the very fellow. Just off the piazza in the centre of town and they do great steaks and their mighty fine pizzas are very good too. If I'm not mistaken the local vino rosso is a great restorative and one which I am very much in need of round about now. I know this is not a holiday but neither should it be an opportunity to deny an old trouper the consolation of good Italian food and wine."

"All well and good and if the twins are in agreement then it might be on. But give it some thought. I know those two can be very professional when on a job which is essentially why we are here. They can also be the world's worst nightmare with some local plonk inside them. What we can do without is the terrible twins deciding to test the mettle of the carabinieri or worse still the local mafia or its offshoots. On reflection the twins versus the Mafia would be worth paying money to see. Let's just see how things pan out when we get up the line to Ostuni."

Bones seemed mollified by Prideaux's assurances at least for the present as the four men boarded the Ostuni train. Conversation ceased as they settled down for the short trip. Each man became wrapped up in his own thoughts. There was that impression of melancholy that often settles over rail travellers in any country. In southern Italy that melancholia seemed to be of a deeper strain than in more prosperous parts of Europe. This was the part of Italy that the north had not forgotten about. Southern Italians as a matter of honour made sure that it never would be able to ignore them. The south hung around like a persistent suitor. It would not take no for an answer and would keep posing new questions.

Through a train window some of the features of this landscape took on an added poignancy. Scrubland enlivened by the occasional abandoned half built hotel filled the vista as the train ploughed on. Thousands of acres of olive groves ensured that Italy would never run short of one of its most popular products. Behind all this was the miasma of bent politicians, secret organisations and a culture of corruption. These days the southern part of Italy was a template for what the UK looked destined to become.

Conviction politicians were a thing of the distant past, that is unless the convictions were criminal ones. Ethics and morality had gone the way of all flesh. Bankers were rewarded, especially when their banks collapsed under them. There were no certainties anymore. It felt like the end of days. Such were the depressing thoughts that intruded on Prideaux's unquiet mind as the train made its way from Brindisi towards Ostuni station.

Shaking himself back into acknowledging the task in hand Prideaux was first to step off the train onto the platform. There were not many passengers alighting. Those who did ambled towards the exit in a desultory way. Nobody could do animated like the Italians but nobody looked particularly fresh as the small group moved through the station and out into an Ostuni evening. It was early for Italy. At 7.30pm the cafés and bars would be quiet. Later they would fill with residents and locals looking for food and some of the older generation in search of 'gelato' and perhaps a little light promenading. Customs die hard, if they die at all, in this part of the world.

Gradually, Prideaux's attention was taken by two middle aged men who walked just in front of them. There was something he couldn't quite put his finger on. They were nondescript. Both wore sharply tailored suits and good shoes. Nothing unusual there. Both wore long overcoats, nothing unusual there either. What had attracted Prideaux's notice was the fact that neither man spoke even though they were clearly together. Logic suggested that they were simply travelling companions who had run out of things to say to one another. When had logic ever had any force in Italy? He slackened his step allowing them to put some distance between him and them. Turning to see where his companions were he saw that they were in conversation with the capostazione. Bones was clearly waxing eloquent in the face of some determined arm waving. The twins stood behind him obviously trying to bring order to the proceedings. The two men who had attracted Prideaux's attention had got into an old black Mercedes saloon car. Something was niggling. Another person had got into the car with the two men. From a distance Prideaux thought there was something familiar about the woman. It was that anomaly of someone whose movements did not match her apparent age. It was one of those things with an irritating resonance. Could it be that the old woman had been following him recently? He was aware of something in the way she moved that was not quite right. Putting it to the back of his mind he noted the darkened windows as the car had roared away up the hill towards Ostuni. He was unable to commit the licence plate to memory.

Back on the platform the capostazione was losing patience with Bones. There was what was obviously a 'failure to communicate' in full flow. At last Robert Job had also had his fill of the nonsense. He picked Bones up as if he weighed no more than a child and handed him to his twin.

"Sit on him Bob," was all he said.

This is exactly what Bob did. The still protesting Bones soon calmed down while brother Robert explained, in flawless Italian, that what he wanted was the key that had been arranged for pick up from the capostazione. The upshot was all four leaving the station in possession of the key to the Range Rover parked on the station forecourt.

With a laudable attempt at making himself useful Bones had offered to explain to the capostazione the arrangements concerning the key that they needed to pick up their transport. Sadly his idea of explaining anything to a non-English speaker was to incorporate a few words of their language into a good deal of hand waving. This was not calculated or even nascent racism but a genuine belief that an individual without a command of the English language did not exist. That belief was accompanied by the old money conviction that a non-English speaker could be converted into one by virtue of the combination of some continental hand waving and a significant increase in volume. The twins led the way to the parked Range Rover. They were trained operatives so their approach was careful and basic precautions in examining the vehicle were undertaken. There was no reason to expect any foul play but training ensured that the proper procedures had been followed. Bones and Prideaux would have taken no such precautions but they were innocents abroad.

Robert took the driving seat with his brother riding shotgun. They had agreed that a stop off at Il Gatto Verde would be acceptable not simply as a means of shutting Bones up but also because as healthy and fit men they were about due something to eat. They turned right out of the station to drive the two kilometres along road SP20 up the hill to Ostuni.

The White City sparkled in the late evening sun. Reflected light from the white painted houses made clear the reason the town had its alternative name. The effect of sun on the brightly whitewashed houses gave the place an appearance that was other worldly. It is almost as if the city had been parachuted from above to settle in the middle of the surrounding olive groves. Mediterranean architecture at its best and at every turn the middle ages announcing its continuing presence. The twins knew the city well and parked near the Palazzo de Liberta in the centre of Ostuni. From there to Il Gatto Verde was a short stroll.

Only two of the four men were at ease. The two who might have been holidaymakers were the Job twins. Fluency in the local language is always a confidence boost but when you are one half of the terrible twins then that is an altogether different prospect. Prideaux and Bones had no such confidence.

In Ostuni when evening starts to fall there are many shadows. The varied roof levels, house shapes and mediaeval streets are willing participants in the shadow show. In each darkened corner on the walk from the car to Il Gatto Verde Prideaux was convinced he saw the form of a man wearing a long overcoat. In his mind's eye he saw one or other of the two men he had seen earlier getting off the train from Brindisi with the old lady He was convinced that they were being watched. He had nobody to tell about this fear. The twins would laugh at his timidity, Bones had already gone so long without a drink that he could see a whole herd of pink elephants as he moved towards the always tricky state of near sobriety. Arrival at the door of the café/bar was a godsend.

The place was quiet. Several couples sat at the tables outside underneath an advertising awning for Birra Moretti. Inside the bar was dimly lit. The air conditioning was working and the atmosphere friendly as the four took a table towards the back of the room. Il Gatto Verde was one of a number of bars in the city and immediate area that had once served as a wine cellar. It was hewn out of the rock on which the city stood. The effect was something like one might expect if Fred Flintstone had opened a coffee/wine bar in Bedrock. The bar was newly opened but it already had the atmosphere of one that had been here since the beginning of time. Its clientele was a comforting mix of locals and visitors. The Job twins went to the bar returning to the table with four bottles of birra.

"What the hell is this," grumbled Bones to the amusement of the others.

The twins had brought him bottled beer without a glass, something they knew would annoy him. Bones was determinedly old school. Drinking from the bottle might be de rigueur for modern youth but not for the scion of an old titled family. The impulse for the insult was the natural inclination of the twins to get as far up the old aristocrat's nose as possible. There was more to it than this, however. A William Radleigh de Beaune abroad would automatically assume that he was on holiday and behave accordingly. This was no holiday. It was work and there was every possibility that the work would prove to be dangerous in the extreme. The twins relished the challenge: Bones and Prideaux weren't so sure.

"Cheer up Bonesie, for God's sake. We're only stopping for one and then on to the trullo. It's only a few miles from here and it's even closer in kilometres. I'll bet you there will be a well stocked wine cellar there. And you know, or used to know, old Cornelius so we will be sharing digs with a fine section of wines from all over Puglia. He was not a man to stint himself, as you know. Make the most of a safe and comfortable bar. The chances are that other venues may not be so welcoming."

"Piers, for your sake I shall do my level best to be cheered and cheery. I will not, I absolutely refuse to drink out of a bottle. One of you cheeky bastards, perhaps you Bob can damn well fetch me a glass then I shall sample whatever this bottle contains. I am braced for disappointment."

A quietly giggling Bob Job did has he was bidden watching with interest as Bones decanted the pale liquid with exaggerated care into the glass. There followed a pantomime as Bones tasted the lager as one might a fine wine. He sipped, gargled before swallowing with every evidence of concentration. He allowed a couple of minutes to pass before placing the glass back on the table.

"Do you know that is not half bad. I have tasted much worse in my time and this is jolly refreshing. Iechyd da my handsomes!" and with a flourish he drained the glass before holding it out towards Prideaux with the words, "your round Prideaux old horse. By the lord Harry I could get used to this. I say Piers old thing isn't that Gabriel over there in that alcove talking to that swarthy type?"

"That's not very likely," Prideaux answered having looked towards the alcove indicated by Bones. "He said he would follow us out here. I wouldn't expect to see him for a day or two yet. Looks a bit like him though. What do you think chaps, you know him better than anyone here. Is that the lovely Gabriel or merely a look alike? You'd better think quickly because he is on his way over here. The twins turned in unison. Although Gabriel was their boss there was little warmth towards him.

"Well, well. Now who would have expected to find you lot in a bar? I'd like to introduce you to my local contact." Gabriel indicated the large man standing to his left. He was, as Bones had pointed out, a 'swarthy type' straight out of central casting. He was also Inspector Pino Rabaiotti, head of the Puglian version of Special Branch.

"Let me introduce you to my men, Inspector Rabaiotti such as they are."

There was a level of contempt in Gabriel's voice that did not go unnoticed. He waved his hand in dismissive fashion at the four who almost imperceptibly had begun to straighten their backs and

attempt to compose their features into something approaching
seriousness. The inspector welcomed them to Puglia and assured
them that he and his men would do their best to ensure that their
time would be as *produttivo* as possible. Only Prideaux at the time
thought the use of the adjective odd. He had not realised that he
and the rest were here to be productive. Helpful, perhaps?
Anything more suggested that if the four were not careful they
could end up as mere cannon fodder in whatever local war was
currently in progress between police and villains. His concern was
not alleviated by what the inspector had to say next.

"Domani I shall expect to see all four of you at my office.
Signor Gabriel will show you where they are. I like the irony that
the offices are situated on the Piazza de Liberta. That amuses me
since the organisation I head is the descendant of Mussolini's
Opera Volontari per la Repressione Antifascista. What wonderful
irony that Il Duce's original secret police remains alive and thriving
in the 21st century. You will present yourselves there at 8.30am
prompt and will be brought to my office. Arrivederci."

The inspector turned on his heel and walked out into the
spring sunshine blissfully unaware that his attitude had been
singularly unappreciated by Bones and Prideaux.

"Bloody cheek," blustered Bones. "Who the hell does he
think he is? I'm not used to being spoken to like that."

"You are going to have to get used to it Bonesie. He is my
contact and effectively you will do as I say while you are here. I
have no intention of pulling rank but I do appeal to your sense of
fair play."

Gabriel had not known Bones long but he already knew
which buttons to press. Bones was a sucker for any appeal to his
sense of fair play.

"I'll do it for you Gabriel but I want it minuted that I am
doing it for you and not that jumped up olive puncher."

"Thought you might Bonesie. You are a decent chap at heart
and I'd prefer to have you onside with this one. There is an
elephant in the room, of course. I hate the phrase but it is
appropriate. Nobody has yet mentioned Slope. Our intelligence
tells us that Slope, and probably the harpy Bennett are somewhere
in the area. Now that could mean anything or nothing but in either
case it needs some investigating. The twins are here for that, you

two are here for whatever you can add to proceedings as well as to draw him into the open. I must stress that this is not a jolly."

Bones snorted. "Not a bloody jolly. I should think not. You have already told us that our position is delicate. On what world could that ever be interpreted as a jolly? More like a bloody death sentence. 'Eat drink and be merry for tomorrow we die'. Isaiah 22:13 unless I miss my guess."

"It's time we moved out to Cornelius's trullo so that I can fill you all in with our most recent information. The twins will drive you out there and I'll follow along later. I have a little bit of business in town. Please do not take things easy and get sloppy. Senior members of units within MI6 especially the leader of MI7's Unit S do not get brutally murdered for nothing. Officially we are here to find Slope. I am also keen to establish what involvement Slope has in the area or whether anything remains of his former organisation."

Gabriel was well aware that in this area of Italy there were any number of secret and secretive organisations perfectly capable of mounting an attack on a member of any British anti-terrorist establishment. Most obvious would be the Mafia, though increasingly the Carbonari were becoming a threat as were the Raccoglitori di Oliva, a much newer criminal organisation. Rabaotti had briefed him on criminal activity in the area. He had also identified the Olive Pickers as the driving force behind the theft of olive trees on an industrial level. He promises to keep Gabriel informed of developments. If Slope is as involved as he appears to be then it will be the ideal opportunity to catch him and Bennett in the act and wrap the whole thing up.

Olives were a staple of this area and consequently olive pickers were plentiful. There could be as many as 60 million olive trees in Puglia. This being Italy nobody really knows for certain. But if anyone ever worried about the world running out of olives then a visit to Puglia would soon put them at ease. The trees themselves have an other-worldly appearance. It is impossible not to discern ancient human faces in the gnarled and split branches and trunks. The olive trees some believe to be a thousand years old seem to be repositories of wisdom as if they were the old men of the woods with knowledge that time and humans had forgotten. So loved are these trees that where a branch has become broken down by age and productivity, that branch will be supported by stones beneath, an echo of an ancient relative resorting to a walking cane as age takes its inevitable toll.

The original olive pickers were men and women who were at one with their land and respected it for the living it provided for them. The Raccoglitori di Oliva of the 21st century were an amalgam of criminals, the disaffected and profiteers who were steadily infecting this part of Italy with their twisted approach to life.

The twins with Robert in the driving seat and Bob alongside drove off from Il Gatto Verde down onto the coast road towards Villa Novello. After two kilometres or so they took a right turn onto a dirt track that led past olive grove after olive grove until reaching the short lane that ran down to the Cornelius trullo. It was a magnificent sight. A confection in shimmering white echoing the hill town of Ostuni they had so recently left. The trullo was surrounded by thirteen acres of olive trees and had been completely refurbished.

Gabriel had left the café a few minutes after the four men and completed his business in town in short order. He knew the way to the trullo and, like them, turned off the coast road and started along the dirt track that led to it. He had barely managed forty metres when his Fiat hit a large boulder. The impact bounced the car across the track clipping a fence post before ploughing into an olive grove. The car came to rest at the base of a particularly ancient olive tree. Gabriel's control of the car was such that the ancient tree was undamaged. He too had got off unscathed but considerably shaken. The driver's door that had taken the impact was jammed and at this point training and instinct kicked in simultaneously. Sliding through into the back seat and exiting through the back passenger door Gabriel found himself lying on the fine tilth that characterised olive groves in the area. He lay there quietly assessing options while shaking his head to clear some very scrambled thoughts. There was no sound apart from the distant hum of traffic on the coast road in the distance. Perhaps he had overreacted. There didn't appear to be a reason for the boulder at that spot on the track, but who knows in a rural environment?

Raising his head to see if he could see anything by the light of an obliging moon he stiffened. Something had moved behind him.

"Alzarsi, signor!" He thought he recognised the voice but the traffic noise masked clues to its owner. He did as he was told getting to his feet and turning slowly to face whatever lay behind him. There was no chance of assessing the odds until he could at least look into the eyes of whoever it was that had laid this obviously successful trap. His mouth dry, heart pounding he slowly turned to witness the grinning face of Piers Prideaux.

"You absolute clown Prideaux," he yelled. "What the fuck do you think you are playing at?"

"That's a nice way to speak to a knight in shining armour," he said. "I thought I'd have a look around so I left the boys at the trullo and bimbled through the olive grove. I heard the crash and walked over to see what was happening and to offer any help I could. I didn't really expect to see Whitehall's answer to Harrison Ford leaping from a car and diving for cover. You only hit a rock after all."

The expression on Gabriel's face left Prideaux in no doubt that the time had come to shut the fuck up, something he duly did. Gabriel silently grabbed a bag from the car and indicated that Prideaux should show him the way to the trullo. The car could stay where it was until morning. Recent events left Prideaux in no doubt that he and Bones had acted too hastily in leaving behind the relative safety of The Hand of God. The winter snow suddenly seemed much more appealing than the blistering Puglian sun.

7

SLOPE SURFACES

Pietro's wine was legendary in Puglia and the surrounding districts. Of all the Spinelli brothers he was probably the most successful. His passion fuelled the wine and his wine fuelled his passion. He had worked hard to establish a vineyard that would give as good as it got to some over-smug French chateaux as well as some of the upstart New World wines.

It was Pietro's wine that lubricated conversation, argument and sex in this particularly passionate region of Italy. The brothers were his staunchest supporters, Marco the staunchest of all and when the grape harvest was due they would put whatever else they were doing on hold. The whole family would set to ensuring that the grapes were harvested at the optimum time to produce the finest of wines. Pietro was the coolest of the brothers. A brawny individual tanned to a mahogany shade from long days in the sun he was at ease with himself. He had found his forte and life could not be better for him.

A few kilometres from the cave where Pietro's wine completed the maturing process that produced the finest wine in all Italy stood an old deserted farmhouse. The Domani family had left many years ago when the south was going through one of its regular declines. Families left without a backward glance travelling northwards more in hope than expectation. There must be a better life somewhere in Italia. Sure as hell it would not be in Basilicata or Calabria. There was at least some hope that it might be found by looking northward where at least there was industry with its attendant possibility of putting food on the table. These regular exoduses helped fuel the melancholy cast of mind in this part of the country. Life was chiefly a matter of survival. Anything else was a welcome bonus. There were similar abandoned farmhouses all over the south. This one differed only in the fact that it showed signs of life. An orange glow dimly illuminated the kitchen of the farmhouse. In the centre of that kitchen was a frightened old man. Securely tied to his own kitchen chair with fence wire his lined face contorted with the pain of the wire that dug into his wrists and ankles. Old blood trickled down to form a pool on the flagstones. The two people responsible for the old farmer's current predicament were chatting to one another as if nothing untoward was happening. Slope, not a man given to praise had eulogised Bennett for her part in taking out the sailor who had been attempting to sell his knowledge to Marco. He was even more impressed that she had come within a whisker of stabbing Prideaux. The icing on the cake though was the envelope she had handed to Slope. After the fracas at Garibaldi's Overcoat Bennett had stolen back to the bar while Marco and his friends were visiting the building that was slated to become his latest business venture. No one was around and she was able to access the bar through a rear window. The safe was a basic security measure that held her up for all of three minutes. She recognised the envelope inside as important and had taken it, carefully disguising both her presence and the access she had managed to the safe. Slope was delighted. A cursory glance had assured him that he now had something of importance that could change everything. The old man's groans broke the spell. Slope walked over to him placing his mouth close to his ear.

"The thing I do not understand about you people is that pathetic determination to stick to some vague hope when it should be obvious to a retarded termite that all hope is gone. Now for the last time all I need from you is the tide tables and the location of the principal sea caverns. Not too much to ask, now is it?" The question was, of course, rhetorical. What else could it be emanating from someone of Slope's academic background? The old man was indifferent to the nature of his questioning. He couldn't muster any answer that would satisfy Slope as he didn't have a clue what he was talking about.

He was a farmer, had been anyway. He had never even been out in a boat. He hated the sea and avoided it whenever possible. Why was this foreigner torturing him in search of answers he couldn't give? His drift towards unconsciousness was arrested by a sudden tug pulling his head backwards by the few strands of grey hair that remained on his head. A female voice whispered in his ear. It was not a reassuring female voice.

"Now listen to me you useless old bastard. Let me show you what I am holding in my hand." Elizabeth Bennett leaned forward placing the stiletto directly in front of the old man's eyes. He focused, with difficulty, on the weapon that seemed to wave before his eyes.

"Now I know you know what this is. And I know you know just what sort of pain it can be used to inflict. The way I see it you have used up all your excuses. Ignorance is not an excuse, so if you are as innocent as you suggest then I suppose it is your bad luck to run across two people who get their biggest kicks from killing people. Now, for the last time. Answer the question."

"Vaffanculo!" was the last thing the old man ever said. As he mouthed the insult through gritted teeth the stiletto bit into his brain entering through his right ear canal.

"That's no way to speak to a lady" said Bennett with a smile as she watched the last vestiges of life leave the tired old body. "What can you expect from the peasant class? They are expendable anyway. I could cut his ears off if you like Sebastian."

"That won't be necessary Elizabeth but thanks for the kind offer," smiled Slope. "I really don't think he knew anything in any case, and slicing ears off is so last year. I should remind you that I put the Spriggans to bed. That is how I want it to stay."

The two exchanged a look of arousal both of them had felt by taking part in the murder of a helpless old man. Violence excited them in several ways, none of them tasteful. "Well perhaps your speciality then. Be quick. I can't control this erection for much longer." Bennett moved with her usual feline speed and with the skill developed from many years of practice recreated the Blood Eagle sacrifice of the Vikings.

"That's so this season Elizabeth" laughed Slope. "Every assassin worth a hoot is performing the Blood Eagle."

"Look Sebastian. The corpse is still warm and the blood is pumping." The mere smell of fresh blood sent both of them into a frenzy. The sex that followed was violent and over in no time to the satisfaction of neither party. But then it was never about the relationship merely the power of death over life that both individuals consistently pursued. Both knew that a change in circumstances could place one in mortal danger from the other. For now in their twisted world all was well.

As quickly as it began all was over and the two stood looking through the window of the deserted house. To the uninitiated the two looked like an old married couple admiring the garden of their new home.

"This is a new situation for us and we need to convince those working with us that we are both serious and efficient," said Slope breaking the silence. If these two ever married the reception would surely have been held in hell.

"It's all about the Olive Pickers now and that means we have to manage this olive tree scam to impress our locals and the really hard men we are dealing with in the north."

Bennett returned his look as the lust seeped from her bruised and bleeding face.

"Darling, you are bleeding," he muttered in a voice of faux concern.

"Piss off, Sebastian. " You know bloody well you mean as much to me as I mean to you. Absolutely fuck all."

"Don't flatter yourself, darling," replied Slope in the especially oily voice he adopted when he wanted to wind Bennett up, "you don't even mean that much to me."

"Spare me the love talk you unutterable shit. Just remember if it wasn't for that twat Cornelius we could be lying about on exclusive beaches, sailing about in expensive yachts and perhaps a little bit of light murder among the uber rich set. Instead we are sullying our hands and intellects with mundane murders."

"There is no such thing as a mundane murder. I must say this wasn't particularly exciting but it has rebooted my appetite for the taste of human blood. Not literally you understand. Can't be doing with all this vampire nonsense. Knew one once of course. What a boring bitch she was. Thinking about it, how much more arousing would it be to prey on the rich and powerful. More of an intellectual challenge and all that. I imagine the sex would be awesome."

"That's all well and good but you won't get near any of that set without loads of money. They stick to their own and thanks to Cornelius you're as poor as church mouse's poor aunt."

"I'll get my fortune back. Don't you worry about that. Or are you only interested in me for my money?" He grinned as he said it.

"Have you thought of stand up? If so I suggest you forget it. You couldn't make a cat laugh. Anyway it's not just that. The bastard has the entire AF on your trail. That must worry you if nothing else."

"Not as such Elizabeth dear. The bastard has passed from this mortal realm. If he thinks that putting up all that cash to fund a fatwa on me will work. Bollocks. Members of the AF are not idiots. They won't take any notice of that. They wouldn't dare, I'm on the board for God's sake. In any case I've already turned the tables on him."

"Brilliant, and where are you going to get the money to pay the bounty? You are broke. You don't have a dime. And the AF have a habit of forcibly retiring board members as you well know Sebastian."

"We'll cross that assassin's bridge when we come to it and when we do you can have the ears my pretty one. Now what about a bit of business?"

"God knows we need the money," lamented Bennett.

"We have to impress upon our northern friends that we are more sophisticated than your average southern Italian. Their impression of the average inhabitant of this part of the country is much the same as a sophisticated New Yorker would regard a dirt farmer from Tennessee. We need to deal with the contempt of centuries if we are to be treated seriously."

"I suppose we will need to abandon this place now and find somewhere else."

"All in hand Elizabeth my dear. I have already arranged a new base for us. It is a bit more in keeping with our status. It's also a bit further up in the hills in a small mountain village populated entirely by Olive Pickers and their families. The place is tighter than a miser's purse. Nobody gets in without the village instantly knowing about it. Sure as hell if they are in the wrong place then they never get out again. We will have the main house in the village. It really is rather splendid. Fresh mountain air, the opportunity for planning and even perhaps some light mayhem.

"We need to find the seaward access to those sea caverns. The Olive Pickers have been struggling because they are far too obvious when attempting to transport them by road. We need to use a less obvious method of transportation and that's exactly what we are going to do. Whether they are bright enough to operate my new idea, is of course a moot point."

The pair left the old farmhouse with its rapidly putrefying corpse to make their way to their new base in the mountains. Slope and his lieutenant Bennett felt no remorse for the senseless squandering of a life. They had a project that excited them. Of course there would be collateral damage along the way. But collateral damage generally followed in the wake of whatever Slope was engaged on.

They were far too distracted and exhausted from the effort of their grim sexual coupling to notice the watching figure metres away in the undergrowth. He was observing through a pair of Special Forces' issue binoculars. His wide face split into a grin as he watched them vanish into the distance their car kicking up a cloud of dust on the unmade road. The Canadian had found his prey and it amused him hugely. Had Slope been aware that this highly specialised killer was as close as a hundred metres or so his buoyant mood would have taken a nosedive.

The Canadian was a figure of myth and legend. Everyone knew of his existence, no one could confirm his appearance. He had been an extra in movies for many years always playing a heavy and always heavily disguised. At two metres tall and around 110 kilograms he was quite convincing in both film and life. His move into murder had come early in his film career and had been the prompt that had convinced him that murder might prove more lucrative.

Although Slope didn't know it yet Puglia was becoming a little too crowded for comfort. If the Canadian was on his trail that meant that some other leading lights from the AF would not be far behind. In fact they were queuing up in and around the Ostuni area.

For the first time in history the AF had removed their Prime Target Initiative (PTI). The PTI was important to the continued existence of the AF as it restricted the actions of assassins to one person one murder. This meant that unless two or more members agreed to work together on a target that the first assassin to receive a contract had sole rights to carry out the murder. With such a competitive career this ensured that there were not too many instances of members turning their special skills on each other. The announcement of the removal of the PTI meant that it was every man, woman and psychopath for themselves. It was sure to end in a pretty bloody massacre at some point.

8

FIREFIGHT AT THE TRULLO

In the trullo life was easy for nobody. Gabriel had arrived back tired, pissed off and on full alert. Apart from two seriously well trained men, neither terribly fond of him he also had two loose cannons capable of inviting trouble by accident or design. The obstruction to the track had convinced him that there was a real possibility of problems in waiting.

"Robert and Bob I want you two on six hour revolving shifts outside the trullo. If either of our resident clowns even attempts to walk outside you have my authorisation to shoot them. I need to sleep and as I hold full authority here you will heed my word or feel my wrath. Now, I am off to bed. You two on guard, Bones and Prideaux to your rooms. The trullo has been comprehensively restructured to sleep six and has all the modern conveniences you could possibly wish. In the morning we will pay a visit to Ostuni and see what the inspector has for us. If either of you is sick in the trullo I shall make sure that you clean up the mess with your tongues. Any questions?"

There were none. They would have been superfluous in any case. Gabriel was doing what he had been trained to do. He remained physically fit and mentally alert. Currently, this was his show and he would ensure that nothing would get in the way. The night passed uneventfully.

The adrenaline-fuelled drive to the trullo had served to calm the twins down to status manageable. They had blown off a lot of steam and were prepared to listen. They took their alternating vigil seriously, one at ground level and one on the stone roof of the trullo even as the sun rose illuminating the olive grove. There was the steel blue glint of the Adriatic in the near distance to remind the visitors that although inland they were barely a few kilometres from some striking beaches. Now was not the time to let slip the guard currently operated by two of the unit's finest. Bob came down the external steps of the building to assure his twin that with the dawn light it was clear of any obvious threats from the immediate area.

"Nothing at ground level either," reported Bob. "A long night though and I hope this is not going to be a feature of our time here. If we are going to get involved I'd prefer to identify targets and get a bit boots and saddles about the whole thing. I feel a bit like bait in these circumstances. I've always hated not being able to see the enemy. The trouble here is that we don't even know if there is one much less what they look like."

His twin agreed. These were men who were used to action. Standing guard and waiting for an attack that may or may not come just wasn't what they appreciated. They decided that it was time to secure the perimeter, an excuse for a walk. The trullo was sited in the centre of the olive grove. Around it as a screen had been planted fig trees and lemon trees which gave it some seclusion from the grove itself. It was an ideal situation. The trees did not grow thickly enough to obscure views or to provide cover for anyone attempting an attack on the building. It was not some sort of military complex but simply a well designed adaptation of the traditional trullo that had originally provided basic shelter for local olive pickers. The interior was now luxurious rather than basic.

The exterior had a degree of privacy that had for many years allowed Cornelius to indulge his penchant for debauchery out of sight of hardworking agricultural workers. Young women, young men it was all the same to Cornelius. The younger and the prettier the better. He liked them best of all if they were athletically flexible. What he did away from prying eyes would have earned him a swift death had he been observed by any of the locals. He stayed safe by having the low cunning to bring his victims in from neighbouring areas. They were not known; he was not caught.

The twins were, as usual, disobeying orders. They had been told to keep guard until further orders from Gabriel. In truth they saw no immediate threat and wanted to stretch their legs after the long night time vigil. At the front of their minds the opportunity for a little light violence could not be discounted and woe betide any local who felt these visitors were fair game for some local machismo. Their perimeter stroll took them a fair way from the trullo. They took turns at looking back in case of any danger threatening from the unseen northern side of the grove. All seemed quiet. It did not remain so.

What the twins had overlooked was the preference for the Vespa scooter in this part of the world. The 'wasp' got its name from the irritating buzzing sound that plagued many Italian towns and cities. It could be tuned so that it could achieve the same top speed but without the insect like sound that immediately gave its presence away. It was the perfect vehicle. With the right tyres it could negotiate any sort of ground and could arrive silently and allow equally muted escape.

There were two of them. They approached from the north side of the trullo. Wordless and soundless they approached. One carried a rifle slung over slim shoulders, the other had a pistol stuffed into a waistband. They looked as if they knew their business and were quickly at the door of the trullo, completely undetected either by the guards or the sleepers within.

The twins had completed their cursory tour of the grove and were headed back towards the trullo when Robert caught a glimpse of a figure he didn't recognise. The slim figure had run up the external steps onto the roof of the building and appeared to be aiming a rifle in the general direction of the grove. His twin picked it up at almost the same moment and without a word they broke into a sprint towards the building.

The figure on the roof was clearly a lookout. The combined presence could only herald disaster. The lookout spotted the fast approaching twins levelling what looked like serious weapons in their general direction. The twins hit the ground simultaneously landing either side of a venerable olive tree as they unleashed a storm from their Glock 17C automatic pistols. It was a shit storm of bullets that sent the rooftop figure diving for cover.

"We got the bastard," yelled Robert as the figure lost its footing and came tumbling down the external steps it had so recently climbed. It lay twitching in the dust at the side of the trullo. The twins covered the ground between them and the target in seconds. Both men were surprised to see the prone figure lying face down with no evidence of a single shot having hit its target. Placing his foot on the character's back, Robert wrenched both hands behind tying them with the cable ties the twins habitually carried. Then grabbing the belt with one hand, the hair with another he turned the figure over dumping it flat on its back. "Well I'll be fucked," blurted his brother, "it's a girl."

"So it is," his brother agreed as they both leaned over to stare into the terrified face of a teenage girl. "Now then my pretty one, my brother Bob and I would like to know just what the festering fuck you are doing here especially since you are armed with a rifle. And before you try the sullen and adolescent approach I suggest you understand that if it suits my purposes I shall put a 9mm bullet right between your lovely dark eyes. Capisci?" He smiled to himself as he used the correct Italian word rather than the American slang heard in so many Mafia movies. Even in extremis the twins prided themselves on their linguistic flexibility.

The girl certainly looked Italian. She had the dark complexion and olive skin typical of the area and she was a beauty by any definition of the term. He also knew that softening his approach was not an option given that they had spotted her with a rifle in her hand and there was a fair likelihood that she could be a hired killer. Still it was hard to equate that possibility with the quivering youngster that lay at his feet. He would not be the first to make the mistake of allowing his attention to wander and paying the ultimate price.

It was the intervention of a clearly nettled Gabriel that interrupted his current reverie.

"That's just brilliant, the pair of you look like a couple of bookends absolutely bollocksed at the sight of a young girl. Take those bloody ties off her now, I've told you before to use standard issue cuffs. And for the record neither she nor her boyfriend are any threat to me or to any of us. They are just a couple of local kids. They knew that Cornelius wasn't at the trullo and decided to come up on their Vespas to have some fun and shoot at the trees with their airguns."

The twins looked uncomprehending and not a little sheepish.

"Yes that's right. The sniper's rifle at the foot of the steps is an air rifle. Her boyfriend is inside drinking coffee and getting bored to death by Bonesie. Fortunately for you I was awake when he came in through the front door. I disarmed him, since my guards were nowhere to be seen. The poor kid was frightened to death especially when he heard what sounded like World War Three going on outside. He knew his girlfriend was on the roof and assumed that she had been shot to pieces. Surely a bit over the top even for you two."

"Now come on Gabriel. We couldn't see what she was holding from distance. It could easily have been a sniper rifle. We were trying to do our job in checking the perimeter. I know that you asked us to cover the trullo but be fair we had been up all night and needed to stretch our legs. We thought we could do both things by having a quick check before waking you lot for breakfast."

"Look, you two are supposed to be the best we've got. Now if the best you can do is to completely mess up the intrusion of a teenage girl and her boyfriend then there is no hope for us. You are the first team. The bench comprises those two daft buggers from Cornwall. I really have a good mind to make both of you sit over there on the naughty step to think about what you have done."

The twins looked suitably chastened at this onslaught of finely honed sarcasm. He had a point but they were not used to being spoken to like this by anyone. Gabriel had done well but couldn't maintain the pose any longer and dissolved into laughter.

"You should have seen your faces. You looked like two naughty boys that had been caught comparing the size of their winkies behind the bike sheds. Sorry lads, but you asked for it. Now come on it's coffee and croissants for breakfast, and we'll say no more about it. There is something positive to come out of this though. These two youngsters have been regular visitors here and have quite a bit of interesting information to impart. They could prove a better source of information than our police contact in Ostuni. We have to see him in town a bit later but for now the appeal of a decent breakfast is too strong to resist. Avanti you members of the lumpen proletariat, breakfast awaits."

"Hail to the twins," shouted a rather bleary eyed Bones as the twins entered the main room of the trullo. "Plenty of coffee here for the bold foot soldiers. And it would seem that you have captured a member of the enemy forces. I suspect a medal for bravery in the face of overwhelming odds may well be on the cards."

"Zip it Bones," muttered the disgruntled twins in unison as they sullenly took their seats on one of the Italian designer sofas that made the room look like a set for a fashion shoot. "Simple mistake. OK? Anyone could make it," snarled Robert.

"There you have it. Right to the nub, a simple mistake. Except it was your mistake and it could have led directly to the death of this delightful young lady. How terrible that would have been. Come on chaps, play up and play the game."

Robert was part way out of his seat as Gabriel entered the room. One look was sufficient to quiet an angry heart. He sat back down with a sullen look of resignation clouding his face.

"Right you lot," Gabriel instructed, "follow me through to the kitchen. Breakfast is laid and before we make our way into town I want you all to be fully aware of what Saro has told me. I should introduce you. This is Saro Rosso and the young lady who is being so gracious, despite the fact that you two almost sent her to an early grave, is his girlfriend Lilla Savino. Strictly speaking they should not be here. They know about the place because they are regular deliverers of food from Lilla's family restaurant. Salvino's is, I should say was, one of Cornelius's favourite restaurants. Cornelius held regular parties and soirees here often with guests of dubious provenance. When they were not wishing to promenade through town they would order by phone directly from the restaurant and Saro and Lilla would deliver. Cornelius was a shit but he was kindness itself to these two. He would always tip them handsomely and they were welcome to come here whenever they felt like it."

"That is true," confirmed Saro. Signor Cornelius could be very difficult at times. I think it was when he had taken too much to drink. But he was always kind to us." He looked at Lillo for confirmation.

"I think that Signor Cornelius had trouble with his soul. When we knew him first he was happy all the time. But for a long time now he has been drinking a lot. It is true. When he drinks he gets aggressive. I have seen him beat women badly when he is like that. He always was sorry after but he never touched me."

"These two probably knew Cornelius better than most," continued Gabriel. "On occasions they made extra money by waiting on at some of the events that he hosted. It was something of an issue with Lilla's dad Gennaro who felt she should be working in his restaurant. He also thought that she should not be in the company of Saro, but he wouldn't have been an Italian father if he didn't think that."

The two young lovers looked at one another with expressions of exasperation.

"What is interesting is what Saro was telling us when you two were outside channelling the St Valentine's Day Massacre. More than once at the parties where the two youngsters acted as waiters there were senior members of the Olive Pickers present.

"That is not the union of olive pickers where the average age is probably around eighty but the criminal organisation that has shamelessly taken their name where the average age is around thirty five. Saro and Lilla knew quite a few of them. They were local lads who had never picked an olive in their lives but always seemed to have money, cars and the latest phones and tablet computers. And here is the knock out detail. On several occasions they recognised Inspector Pino Rabaotti. He had a habit of getting horribly drunk and was not a nice drunk. Often he would be out in the grove taking potshots at anything that moved once he had moved to his second bottle of Vigna Flaminio."

Both teenagers shrugged in agreement.

"They also remember having to call someone when they saw him beating up a woman. She had done something to upset him but his response was way over the top. Whatever it was had obviously enraged him and he looked as if he intended to kill her. It took Cornelius and several other guests to calm him down. Someone took the girl away but she looked in pretty bad shape. Once he calmed down it all seemed OK again but he obviously has a vicious temper. The other little problemette we have is that this uniformed thug of whom we speak is my local contact."

"I thought he was a wrong un' as soon as I clapped eyes on the fella," interjected Piers.

"Now either he is in the pay of the local Olive Pickers or he is one of them. I know enough about Italian society in this part of the country to know that lines of demarcation are blurred. In any event this is going to make things very tricky indeed. Any suggestions?"

"Can't we just pretend ignorance and see what he says," offered Bones. "After all we don't really know what's what anyway. I suggest that this is not the time for attempting any form of bluff. We are a long way from home and while you and the twins are well able to look after yourselves Prideaux and I will be no more than lost lambs in the land of the vendetta."

"I'm not expecting anything from either of you two Bonesie. The twins and I are the professionals although after the last little episode I'm using that word for the twins in its loosest possible sense. What I suggest is that you and Prideaux stay here while I take a ride in with the twins to see the jolly inspector.

"Perhaps you could see whether you can manage to resurrect my car? I know you two are useless in a practical sense but both Saro and Lilla here say they are pretty handy with scooters and cars. If there is no joy then ask Saro to give his father a ring. He runs a small garage near Villa Novello and if the car is kaput he will come and tow it away."

Prideaux looked a little concerned at the turn events were taking and was unable to keep quiet about it.

"I appreciate what you are saying but leaving Bonesie and me out here in the sticks is a bit like a spot of goat tethering. For all any of us know the leopard could well be crouching in the undergrowth. Granted we have the added protection of a couple of teenagers but just for a moment suppose that Slope, or some creature like him is waiting in the undergrowth for an opportunity to pounce. We will be like corn before the sickle. No doubt that particular sickle will be wielded by the Grim Reaper himself. Wouldn't it be better if Bonesie and I came into town with you? Then you could meet with your dodgy contact while we go off for a spot of low level sightseeing."

"Hear, hear Piers. Splendid idea," Bones chimed in right on cue. "That's just the badger. Off we'll go and take a look at the odd spot of rubble feeling safe and sound in amongst all those tourists and decent local types going about their honest business. Nothing wrong with that surely?"

"There is everything wrong with that and you bloody well know it Bonesie. You two would spend a nanosecond exploring what you refer to as rubble before sniffing out a café or bar and proceeding to get legless before lunchtime. Not only would you then be at the mercy of anyone who imagined the world a better place without either of you running loose, but more likely locked up in chokey for insulting the Italian flag or something similar.

"I resent that," chorused Bones and Prideaux.

"Resent what you bloody well like, you are not in Wales now and if I had my way I'd ship the pair of you back home at the drop of a hat. For some reason my masters at home think you two will be of some use in catching Slope. I've told them that you're as much use as treacle toffee toothpaste but still they persist. Too many redbrick types these days though I'm sure neither of you feel able to comment."

"Wrong again twathead. I feel fully able to comment and at some length." Bones was clearly winding up to deliver a long lecture before a sharp dig in the ribs shut him up. They were here on sufferance and constantly annoying Gabriel wasn't a smart plan.

"Anyway, that is my decision you stay here, we go off and will be back once we have had speech with the dear old inspector. I have given strict instructions that you two are to remain strangers to the bottle. And if you behave yourself I shall treat the pair of you to a glass or two of the finest wine in all Puglia."

Gabriel swept out of the trullo closely followed by the chastened twins. The Italian teenagers looked from Bones to Prideaux and back again searching their faces for any indication of mood. It was Prideaux who took the lead.

"Right you two we had better get moving and see what we can manage with the car. Now I know you can both speak English so let's make things clear. I'm not particularly handy, Bonesie here is useless but it appears that you have some mechanical skills between you. Follow me and we'll stroll across the olive grove to the car and see what there is to be done. You'd better get whatever tools you have with you and then we'll see what is available in the boot of the Fiat. Clear?"

"OK," nodded Saro. "I am not a mechanic but I have watched Papa and my brother Vincenzo work on cars since I was a little boy. If we can't get the Fiat going I'll ring Papa and he will bring out his breakdown truck."

It took twenty minutes for the four to reach the crashed Fiat. Saro laid down his tools, popped the hood and began applying a torque wrench with abandon. After a time he stood to ease the pain in his back. As he stretched there was a popping sound like a balloon being burst by a pin. The bullet took him in the left shoulder and spun him around. He dropped into the dirt at the front of the crashed car dropping his wrench as he fell. He grabbed at his shoulder dumbly attempting to stop the flow of blood. He squealed with the pain as Lilla rushed to his side. Prideaux pushed her to the ground and the two teenagers lay together hidden from whoever had fired the bullet.

"I bloody knew this would happen," he spat. "Bloody Gabriel just wasn't listening. What the hell are we to do now Piers?"

"I suppose it would be tempting fate to ask whether you have your phone on you? Mightn't be a bad idea to ring somebody, say Gabriel or the twins, just on the off chance you understand. Seems to me young Saro there is about to go into shock and someone with a bit of medical knowledge would be handy."

Lillo was the one to produce a phone. She spoke rapidly some aggressive sounding Italian sentences. Hysteria seemed close. It was the urgency of her voice that demanded a response. As soon as she had relayed her message she translated the minute or so of machine gun Italian into, "I have phoned Saro's papa. He will be here very soon. He has a doctor with him. And he is very angry." She was suddenly calmer than any of the men.

"Ah! The efficiency of youth," Prideaux mused as he and Bones carefully raised their heads to look for any oncoming truck.

9

THE OLIVE PICKERS

It seemed like hours later but was only fifteen minutes when a rusty, dusty old truck screamed to a halt in front of the damaged Fiat. Two men jumped out of the truck and ran towards the four who were doing their best to stay out of any line of fire. The men didn't look the type to take any notice of a sniper of any description. They looked much more like trained soldiers than civilians and their demeanour jerked a cowering Bones and Prideaux into action.

"It looks as if these two mean business," Bonesie. "I think it would be helpful if it looked as if we were trying to do something positive in the circumstances."

He looked around. Bones had already crawled to the front of the car and was attempting to staunch the bleeding from Saro's shoulder with the large yellow spotted handkerchief that he usually sported in his jacket pocket. It was typical of Bones that he should appear to be actively helping rather than cowering but his stance certainly seemed to mollify the two gorillas who threw themselves down in the dust, crawling the last few metres to get to Saro.

"It was a single shot," stuttered Bones as he was unceremoniously pushed out of the way.

The two men dragged Saro further back behind the car for safety. Turning him on his side Luigi, the doctor, discarded the handkerchief and ripped off his T-shirt to access the wound. After a fraught few minutes he looked at Gennaro and nodded. "He will be OK. He is a lucky boy. It is only a flesh wound. I'll just clean it up and bandage him then we can take him to the hospital in Villa Novello. I have already told them what has happened. They will be expecting us."

"You two will need to tell me what happened here. Let me tell you now that if anything bad happens to my Saro then you had better have a damn good explanation. Saro's father spat menacingly into the dust. I suggest you go back to the trullo and lock the door. The carabinieri know that something happened out here and will be here soon."

He picked up his son and walked back to his truck seemingly oblivious to any possibility of any sniper waiting for the luxury of a clear shot.

Bones and Prideaux needed no further bidding. They scampered back through the olive grove as if the hounds of hell were after them. Reaching the main door they gratefully slammed it behind them firstly locking and then bolting it. The heavy oak door had a sense of permanency to it. If the local police were on their way that would keep out any possible intruders for long enough for the cavalry to arrive.

"I think we got off pretty lightly there Bonesie. I can't think that bullet was meant for Saro. Somebody must be out to get us."

"Seems likely, Piers old pal. Why is it that I have this extremely unsettling feeling in my water that Slope or Bennett could well have us in their sights. We need to get hold of Gabriel and the twins, just in case."

Both men were thinking the unthinkable. Unless Saro was involved with some youth gang or something then the bullet in his shoulder had been intended for one of them. If so who would take the trouble to take a single shot then disappear? Whoever it was could have walked up to the car behind which they were hiding and shot all four of them. None of them were armed and there wasn't a fighter among them. It could easily have been a massacre.

"What the hell have we got ourselves into this time?" "You know that I love you like a brother Piers but I'm afraid you've let both of us down this time. You are supposed to be the brains of this duo. I am merely the sage old philosopher who becomes cuter when given a decent claret to gargle. Like you I abhor violence but at the same time it fascinates me. I simply don't want to be a victim of it that's all. Someone, however, is severely pissed off with us. That shot was a warning. I'm not sure whether it was intended for one of us or if it was a shot across the bows so to speak"

Ferreting in his pocket Bones eventually found what he was looking for. He tossed something across to Prideaux who caught it in one hand. It was a stiletto. What Bones knew and Prideaux was about to know was that they were in the land of the stiletto and it was much more than a close quarter weapon used by gang members. Like most weapons it had a long and bloody history.

"Bonesie I can feel that you are about to set sail on a long lecture detailing the development and use of this particularly nasty weapon. For the sake of my sanity please just get to the gist and explain why this rather well crafted piece of steel is a warning."

"It is an assassin's weapon my old fruit," replied Bones slightly needled at his friend's tone. "It goes back to the Middle Ages and has had several uses over the years. It is a stabbing weapon and was once used because its slender nature allows it access to gaps in armour. It can get through chain mail or even through the helmet of a knight. The Italians, always an inventive race, developed it to become the dominant weapon particularly here in the south. Assassins love it because it is so easy to hide up a sleeve or in a pocket and with practice it can be particularly lethal. Take a close look, you'll see what I mean."

Prideaux took the dagger and examined it closely. It made his blood run cold that such artistry could be used to produce such an effective killing machine. Accordingly he listened as Bones expounded .

"Because the knife has such a sharp point and is so thin it can penetrate the body easily. Efficient users can then twist it so that it inflicts a fatal wound with the minimum of blood loss. No spouting claret to disfigure the expensive Italian hand made shoes you might say. Good God some assassins even had them hand made with grooves running the length of the blade so that particularly nasty poisons could be introduced into the wound. It is not a weapon to be trifled with. And in these parts it is often used to convey a warning. Many of them are decorated with elaborate patterns. They are the ones that convey the warning. You will never see the one that kills you. The one you are currently holding bears engraved olive leaves along the blade. That means that it belongs to someone who is a member of the Olive Pickers."

"Just a second Bonesie. Didn't Gabriel say something about Slope being involved with some organisation with connections in the olive business? Something to do with nicking trees, I think. It'd be a hell of a coincidence if this didn't have something to do with him."

"I'd thank you not to interrupt while I am on a roll Piers old horse. In fact the Olive Pickers developed their own version which has always been brilliant for stoning olives. Later they found a more macabre use to put the weapon to and that my dear old friend is what you are holding in your hot little hand. The arma insidiosa my old fruit pie. The favoured weapon of assassins operating on behalf of the Olive Pickers, and in all probability Slope himself.

"And before you ask, I found it sticking out of the olive tree that dear old Gabriel laid his car so carefully up against. I pocketed it when all the fuss was going on after Saro had been hit. I knew what it was and now you do too. Question is what do we do now? I'm up for running swiftly back to dear old Blighty and I really hope you are not going to get all brave on me. We are out of our depth here; let us leave it to the experts."

Bones took one look at Prideaux and realised that cutting and running was not going to be an option. He might have known. His blood was up now. A young man could have died and he was being warned that sudden death could be waiting for him here in the olive groves or in the twisting mediaeval streets of Ostuni. A sane man would have already been booking a flight. Amongst his friends Prideaux was rarely referred to as a sane man. Here we go again thought Bones.

"I yield to your superior knowledge concerning the origins and uses of the stiletto Bonesie but I have to ask, how do you know that this one doesn't belong to a peasant who was using it for its original purpose. Why does there have to be all this drama and intrigue? And if you think about it why couldn't the shot that injured young Saro have been a wild effort from a hunter of sparrows or any tiny birds that Italians like to blast out of the skies at any opportunity?"

"If you had listened you would know that I told you this particular stiletto was engraved and is therefore a warning and not a mislaid olive stoner. The more intricate the engraving the more serious the warning. I'd say that we are in red card territory with this one my old darling. And if you really think that a single shot equates to some Italian peasant getting all John McClane on the local bird life then you are more naïve than even I thought you were. We are most royally in the shit and something must be done."

"There is nothing we can do until those three get back from their jaunt into town. Given what the kid told us I don't hold out much in the way of hope for any support coming from the laughing policeman, that bastard Rabaiotti in Ostuni. I'll bet he's is up to his neck in cahoots with the local Olive Pickers. Nothing for it but to hope that door holds against any marauding Mafiosi of whatever persuasion. In the meantime perhaps we should arm ourselves with those pistols that the twins trained us up on before we flew out here. I was getting quite good on the range."

"Listen Piers, shooting at paper targets in the sure and certain knowledge that they are most unlikely to shoot back is one thing. It is a horse of a very different colour when some hairy gangster bursts in with a sawn off shotgun in one hand and a machine pistol in the other. You have never killed a man, neither have I. Given time I am confident that I could bore one to death but that is not a likely scenario to consider.

"There is one other tricky bit. As far as I am aware those pistols are looked away in that bloody great trunk that the twins turned up with. There is a combination lock on it and I have no idea what the combination is. I am also fairly certain that the bullets are locked away in a separate trunk in line with company policy. Probably some daft health and safety ruling or something. Either way while Gabriel and his ever reluctant companions are armed to the teeth, we, my friend, are as helpless as babes in arms and…"

A ferocious knocking on the front door broke into the typically rambling conversation that proved the default mode for Prideaux and Bones whenever they were threatened with danger. It never got them anywhere but was merely displacement activity until something turned up. They would have been just as well advised to adopt the alleged strategy of the ostrich and simply bury their heads in the sand.

"Open this bloody door before I kick it down. What are you two clowns doing skulking in there with the door locked? Get it open now or I'll shoot the damned thing open."

Never had the two friends been so pleased to hear the dulcet and clipped tones of Gabriel. They were not under threat of torture and a slow death after all. However, although the threat level had moved from red to amber they were most definitely under threat from a nasty blistering from the tongue of one heartily pissed off senior intelligence officer.

Prideaux moved with alacrity to start throwing back the bolts and removing the bar that was all that separated them from a bollocking of nuclear proportions. Sometimes the day just doesn't go the way one would like it to.

The prediction of a severe blistering was to be an accurate one. Gabriel raged through the trullo calling down fire and brimstone on every creature that walked or crawled. The twins simply stood to one side. They resembled two giant schoolboys who had been caught out doing something unspeakable in the headmistress's hat. He was not to be placated. All four men knew that his anger most resembled the tornado in its pattern. It was unstoppable and therefore honeyed words, common sense or any attempt at opposition was a pointless exercise. In time he would, like the tornado, blow himself out. Until that time it was best to stay out of the way: if at all possible.

"That bloody man. Arrogant, patronising sod. No bloody use to man nor beast. If that is the best the local plod can offer as a contact we might as well go home now. He is either one of them or too bloody scared to stand up to them. If we are going to get anywhere at all we will have to do it all ourselves. I'll have the slimy bastard busted back down to traffic cop. I wouldn't trust him to do that even."

"I take it things didn't go that well then," interjected Bones. Gabriel switched his full attention to Bones and Prideaux who had been desperately trying to shut Bones up. It hadn't worked. Bones interjection had immediately diverted the Gabriel hairdryer from the twins directly onto him and Prideaux.

"You two were worse than useless." He completed his tirade turning on his heel to face Bones and Prideaux.

They knew their turn had to come but hoped that some of the energy might have dissipated by then. They were wrong.

"Look I know that you two are civilians. I also know that you have both regarded this trip as a jolly. It never was and as of now I'm deputising you both as field agents until the unit can get some more reliable muscle out here. And before you start waffling Piers, remember that we are in a very exposed position. Forget any ideas you had for sun, sea and too much Montepulciano d'Abruzzo I intend to arm you both and since there is nobody else you will do your best to give a passable imitation of field agents attached to Unit S."

There were vague signs that this particular tornado was at last beginning to blow itself out. The signs were sufficiently auspicious to persuade Prideaux to at least seek some clarity. Why would Gabriel be invoking the anti-Spriggan unit here in Italy at this time when there was no hard evidence that they had a presence? Taking a deep breath he decided to at least ask the question.

"I was wondering whether something had happened to persuade you that the unit actually had a target down here in Puglia. Now I know that Bones and I were invited along for the knowledge we have of Slope and hopefully to draw him into the open. We are also aware that when Slope escaped from the secure facility there was an idea that he might be headed in this direction. I accept all that along with the fact that we are here because we know more about him than most. If I'm honest I'd also like to see him with a bullet between his eyes, but to date all I've heard is vague rumours of an organisation called the Olive Pickers.

"And while you were away somebody took a pot shot and hit young Saro. He was lucky. Ended up as a flesh wound. Nasty though. And I don't think that he was the target. It also appears that we have received an official warning from the Olive Pickers through the medium of stiletto. So something is going on and why do I get the impression that you know all about it? You might like to elaborate Gabriel."

"That's one of the reasons I am so bloody mad Piers. From the brief conversation I was able to have with the laughing policeman in Ostuni it is clear that the Olive Pickers have overnight become much more active and violent. He admitted that there have been at least four murders in the area bearing the hallmark of that particular organisation. Eventually, he deigned to admit that the upsurge in violence coincided with the arrival in Villa Novello of an Englishman. As far as I could tell he looks nothing like our old friend Sebastian Slope but as you know that bastard is adept at changing his appearance at the drop of a hat. He is even better at doing that at the adoption of a hat."

The remark was not funny but certainly indicated that the angry winds were not blowing as strongly as previously.

"Well if that's the case it should be fairly straightforward to toddle off down to the lovely harbour in Villa Novello and establish whether the mysterious Englishman is our escaped murderer or not. Slope needn't hold any power here. The Spriggans are more or less over and I can't see an organisation rooted in Britain taking hold in Italian soil. We could at least take a look and report back," said Piers.

"If you could restrain your natural propensity to babble you would realise that I have not yet finished." Prideaux had no intention of fanning a wind that had dimmed to a dull roar. He kept his counsel.

"About a month ago," Gabriel continued, "a woman turned up in one of the sea front bars down in Villa Novello. She was alone and made it clear that she was not interested in meeting new people. She stood out because she was not local and did not appear to be a holidaymaker.

"Because she didn't seem to have any reason to be there the local plod decided to check her out. One of their men began following her. She spent time in bars but was never approached by anyone and simply kept herself to herself. One morning around 5am when the garbage truck was doing its rounds they found a body in one of those massive bins where the cafes and restaurants put their waste. It was the man who had been trailing her. His neck was broken and he had been dead for some hours.

"I didn't get that information from our so called contact. Inspector bloody Rabaiotti conveniently neglected to tell me. I dropped in to the newspaper office and found the report of the murder which the local police are attributing to person or persons unknown. It could well be that the woman in question is Bennett."

"I see," responded Bones stroking his chin in what he believed to be an impression of an intellectual detective pondering the meaning of a vital piece of evidence. "Well if that's the case we had better take a trip to the seaside. There is a fantastic restaurant I just happen to know down there in Villa Novello and the pizza there eclipses the best that Naples can offer. Could be fun. One thing though. I know that the twins brought the pistols we were trained on in Brecon with them. I should sleep a lot happier if we could be trusted to be issued with them and perhaps a few of those bullets that go with the ensemble that will turn Bonesie and me into the least convincing special agents in the history of the known world."

This last brought a thin smile to the face of Gabriel and big wide grins to the faces of the twins. If this whole situation was opera then at least the elements were in place to make it a comic opera.

"Villa Novello it is then. We are here for a purpose and if a small slice of danger means we end up doing what we came here to do then so much the better. Having said that I do not want any heroes. And that remark as I suspect you know is directed at the twins rather than you two. The twins will go with me to Ostuni. I'm sure they would prefer to accompany you two down to Villa Novello but I need to get a handle on just what is going on in this area. Just try not to get into any trouble."

Bones and Prideaux bowed their heads in mock recognition of the warning. They smiled as they did so recognising that Gabriel genuinely wanted to keep them out of the line of fire if at all possible.

Two hours later and Bones and Prideaux are seated in a pizza restaurant overlooking the harbour. Gabriel and the twins are ensconced in a villa around a mile away inland. The town is reminiscent of those abandoned towns that crop up in spaghetti westerns. There are shops. There are bars. There are restaurants. Somewhere there are people but they are not in evidence.

Right next door to the restaurant are the bones of an hotel. Building was started, it was never finished. The skeletal remains mock the optimism that flared briefly before the money ran out. Stray dogs lounge in the sun or lope hopelessly through dusty back streets. Lizards sunbathe on warm rocks and concrete. The air is clearest on the front where the fishing boats bob in a crowded harbour. This is the picturesque part of town. There are no visitors visible. This is not tourist Italy. This is the real place.

Prideaux is fascinated by the small lizards that seek the sun on the sea wall. The pizzas are being made to order by the chef and will take as long as the chef decrees. This is no fast food restaurant. The chef is an artist in dough and he knows it. It is incumbent on customers to treat his creations with real respect. You can order what you like; you get what you are given. He is too big to argue with and he makes great pizza. The owner of the restaurant is tapping on the restaurant window to call them back in to collect up their order.

On returning to the restaurant the two received their order from the hands of the giant chef. They also received their instructions in how the food was to be conveyed. They were left in no doubt that these works of art were to be carried horizontale or the chef's revenge would be swift and far reaching. "Excitable chaps these chefs," muttered Bones as they left the restaurant carrying the food exactly as directed.

The two men sat near the breakwater just beyond the Customs House. They ate some of the very best pizza they had ever tasted as they watched the young men and girls of the area impressing one another with daredevil dives from the highest part of the harbour wall. Perfectly tanned they cut through the water like so many golden fish. Excitedly they shouted to each other as the day wore on. It was all a pleasant diversion for Bones and Prideaux as they slipped towards the level of relaxation that epitomised an Italian holiday in the sun. Always the gannet Bones finished before Prideaux was halfway through his.

"Just shout out if the dish is too much for you old chap," he shouted making a grab for a piece of the Prideaux pizza.

"You are a greedy bastard Bones. I thought you bloody aristos learned table manners at the knee of some nanny or other."

"It may have escaped your notice but we are not at table. We are sitting on an outcrop of rock eating dough, tomato puree and several sorts of cheese with our fingers. Delicious as it all is normal protocol does not apply. Besides which you are beginning to look like a three year old who has been deprived of the customary bib and has decided to decorate himself with his lunch. If a critic asked I'd say somewhat in the style of Jackson Pollock."

"Bonesie old chap. Just to refocus your mind for a moment do me a favour and as casually as you can look over my right shoulder. There is a woman walking along the harbour wall towards the village. There's something about that walk that seems familiar. What do you think?"

"A bit far away for these fading peepers I'm afraid but I think I see what you mean. Walks a bit like a man. Bit of a swagger that sort of thing. Is that what you mean?"

"More or less. You don't think it could be the loathsome Bennett do you?"

"I bloody well hope not. We've already had more than enough nonsense to deal with without that devil's spawn putting in an unwelcome appearance. Plenty of women walk like that. I'd need a better look. It might be worth following her. She's almost out of sight but if she turns left when she gets back to the track, that only leads to Marco's bar. He wants to see us anyway. He's not sure but thinks he might have some news on the Englishman involved with those blasted Olive Pickers. You know what he's like. Half Cornish is Cornish enough. He'll talk to us but he won't trust Gabriel. Tighter than a chough's chuff we Cornish. We could take a chance and follow her. The alternative is to wait for her to come back. There's nothing else down there as far as I know. It'd be worth popping in to see Marco again anyway. He's a real character and I haven't had a drink for ages. We can pick up that letter that Cornelius left as well."

"One rule Bonesie. A drink. That is all. Let's stay in the singular for once. I don't fancy another bollocking from Gabriel. Neither do I wish to suddenly find a stiletto nestling between my ribs. If you promise we'll take care then that's OK, if not then we'll be out of there sharpish."

"Lead on Macduff, and sober be he who first cries hold enough."

Bonesie and Prideaux left the harbour heading towards the track blissfully unaware of the large man in the small boat who was following their every move through powerful binoculars.

10

PIETRO'S VINEYARD

With the noonday sun glinting off the white stones surrounding hillside vines on the outskirts of Villa Novello di Ostuni it was time to find some shade for those who wished to avoid the cooked lobster look. Brits abroad had long pioneered this particular look for no other reason than ignorance. Bonesie and Prideaux had learned to their cost that there are times when gloom far outweighs bright sunshine.

They had temporarily retired to the cave where Pietro's finest wines were slumbering. In this part of the world food and drink are taken equally seriously. Wine production is less about profit than the pride in producing something beautiful. To Pietro his wine was special. It was a living thing and needed cosseting to prosper. Gabriel was content to hold a watching brief as he listened initially to Pietro outline the quality of his wines. Though he had heard this degree of certainty from winemakers in the past Pietro's fierce determination was impressive. It was a good opportunity to keep an eye on his charges in the hope that they would not attract too much attention to themselves or the vineyard. Bones and Prideaux were able to outline the fracas in Garibaldi's Overcoat to Gabriel. They suspected that the woman who murdered the sailor offering to sell information to Marco was Bennett. He had listened fitfully but seemed more interested in the stolen envelope and its contents than in the whereabouts of Bennett or Slope.

In the cave it was cool by comparison with soaring outside temperatures. Semi darkness made it easy to understand the concept of wine as a living thing. The age-old casks creaked like old bones settling in for a long rest. Pietro stood behind a stained old oak table, a range of wine bottles assembled on the table. There were no spittoons. This was the best of Italian peasant wine. Nothing wasted here. Pietro was fervent about his wines. He did not make bad wine. It was simply a case of good, very good and the nectar of the gods. At Pietro's vineyard you started with the good stuff and kept on going. A tasting here was self regulating. Drinkers knew what awaited them at their destination and overindulgence on the journey was not an option. It would have been an insult to Pietro, his entire family and this part of southern Italy to treat his wine with anything less than reverence.

Apart from brother Marco there were assembled some of the finest drinkers in all of Europe. However, that is not why they were here. The happenings in Marco's bar had led to a lot of local soul searching. The brothers had been doing some sleuthing. The recent murders in the locality had changed the easy going approach of local families. This wasn't a particularly lawless area. Where there were problems they tended to be solved by those involved. It wasn't usual to trouble the local police in any case. That was partly because yet another of the cousins was the local police chief but mainly because they preferred a quiet life. Investigation of major crimes such as murder was important but deflected from more important issues such as good wine, good food and fishing. Besides this it was obvious that the late spate of wrongdoing had an outside influence. This was not based on feuds that had festered for centuries. All such feuds were perfectly well understood by Italians. It was the natural order of things. Outsiders interfering in little local difficulties were as welcome as fish pox.

"Welcome to my vineyard," Pietro announced when the group had settled themselves in some comfortable armchairs in the tasting area. "I know that you have things to discuss with my brother Marco but little is ever achieved here in Puglia without the benefit of fine wine. So I present to you the three stages of enjoyment. And remember this is a drinking not a tasting. Tastings are reserved for buyers. You are guests so enjoy the wine. Just drink from the bottle on the left and move to the right. By the time you have sampled all three wines your minds will be as sharp as an assassin's stiletto. I'll leave you to it." With a wave of the hand Pietro left the group to their enjoyment of some of the best wine made in Puglia.

Embarrassing silences are always the worst kind. It was an unusual situation for Bonesie and Prideaux. The silence weighed heavy since the next step was not an obvious one. If not for Pietro's obvious sincerity four of those present would have fallen on the bottles arrayed in the cave like wolves on the fold only without that level of restraint. It was all like the worst sort of dream. For wine lovers to be let loose in a cave full of the stuff. No restraints. No regrets. Nothing to hold them back. Too good to be true surely. Marco broke the spell. Initially it looked as if he was of the Billy Bones school of wine drinking as he walked casually to the table and poured four generous glasses of wine from the first bottle. He handed the glasses round then settled himself on the wooden pew to the side of the wine table.

"This is one of Pietro's beginner's wines," he began. "Savour it, then I have something I need to tell you." The four dutifully did as they were advised. Consumption was followed by much smacking of lips and pantomime expressions of enjoyment. It was all the result of nervous tension. Marco was alive to the atmosphere and moved to defuse it.

"Right then," he said in a voice that had deepened with authority. "We'll talk about the wine later. You can eulogise it to your heart's content then but let me put your minds at rest. I am not a member of any of the myriad criminal groups that prosper in this area. I am, however, a member of the Spinelli family. You've met my brothers. I have many more cousins and we are as one in rejecting the apparent necessity of southern Italians to belong to some form of mafia type organisation. We can do this because of family strength and loyalty. We have done it for years. We don't bother them so they leave us alone. That is they did until quite recently. The incident in my bar that you witnessed wasn't the first thing to change the balance of power around here. The atmosphere is different. I can tell when I walk around the port. I know that some of my regulars no longer come to the bar. I no longer feel comfortable when I go up to Ostuni. Nothing I can put my finger on but enough to cause me to question things. This has confirmed things for me." Getting to his feet he opened a canvas bag that had been lying on the wine table. Opening it he held up a piece of parchment wrapped around a slim dagger.

"This is an assassin's dagger and as you can see it is the trade mark weapon of a group called the Olive Pickers. The woman who killed that sailor in my bar used an identical weapon. On the parchment is written:

Nessun altro ramo d'ulivo. All that means in English is simply no other olive branch. What it means in reality is that the Olive Pickers are calling off the truce that was agreed years ago between our family and their organisation. Effectively it means that all bets are off. This is something that has existed for generations and with the odd little bit of local difficulty it had never been threatened. These things work if they benefit both sides. Clearly they think that is no longer the case. Now I know these people. I went to school with them. I've played football with them. I've fished with them and drunk with them. Suddenly the old rules no longer apply. What worries me most is that I don't recognise the name on the parchment. On such warnings there is always given the name of the current leader. On this parchment the name is not even Italian. It appears that the leader of the group is someone called Sebastian Slope."

Marco stopped to take a breath. His last few sentences had been gabbled rather than clearly stated as his agitation with the situation had grown. He looked at his audience for a response. Typically it was Bones the fading aristocrat who provided one.

"Fuck me with a bent baguette, so this is where the bastard is hiding. Well, well. So the old sod is up to his old tricks again. I'll bet that bitch in the bar was Elizabeth Bennett. Must have been her."

"Full marks for detection, Bonesie old horse," broke in Prideaux. "It may have escaped your mind but that's really why we are here. I must say I'm surprised to see him break cover so soon. I'm also bloody worried that he seems to be the boss of an organisation that has some sort of structure. Worst of all they seem to have a penchant for puncturing persons with wickedly sharp daggers. This cannot come to good."

"Let's cut things short Piers," Marco intervened. "You tell me what you know about this Slope character and I'll fill you in on the

Olive Pickers. Deal? I've heard from Bones about problems in the past in general terms but what I need to know is what level of alert do I need to put my family on?

"Sounds like a good solution to me. The only thing is that it'll take quite a time to tell the Slope and Bennett story. It seems to me that the best thing would be to open that second bottle of wine tout de suite. That should sharpen up the old mental powers. What say you Marco?"

Marco was aware of his companions and their story telling powers with preference for long drawn out explanations so his agreement depended on Prideaux giving him the abridged version. The deal was sealed with the reverential opening and pouring of the second bottle provided so generously by Pietro. True to his word Prideaux rushed through the events that had transformed his life and the lives of others to bring Marco up to speed.

It was no easy task for Prideaux to rein in his usually convoluted style. The effort showed on his face as he struggled to be brief.

"Slope and I had a major falling out some years ago," he began. "When I became involved I didn't think too much about it. At that time I didn't realise I was dealing with a psychopath."

"I don't think psychopath fits the bill, old chap," interjected Bones. "That bastard should have been locked away in the Laughing College years ago. He was barking mad and, in case you have forgotten, spent a good chunk of his miserable existence trying to put an end to our short stay in this vale of tears. Don't bloody dress it up man. Bloody nutter, and no mistake."

"Did I introduce you to our Cornish Ambassador for political correctness Marco?" Marco smiled as Prideaux continued to explain.

"Bonesie has a point which is essentially that Slope is an unforgiving enemy. He has such a strong view of his own worth that nothing will stop him getting his revenge on anyone who has crossed him. He has already made various attempts at murdering us and we have managed to survive. However, he has already murdered two of our closest friends, an old college acquaintance, and the only woman that Cornelius ever loved. That's for starters and the bastard is not sated yet."

"Told you," shouted Bones. "Card-carrying nutter. Bullet in the back of the neck would be the kindest thing." Prideaux managed to rein in Bones before he managed to attain warp speed and continued with his explanation.

"Bonesie and I are here in our roles as sacrificial goats. The hope is that his hatred for both of us will force him into the open. The unit that Cornelius used to work for knows that the bastard is somewhere in this part of the world and mixed up in some olive tree scam. Cornelius was section head at MI7 and he was the one who bankrupted the bastard Slope obviously setting the cat amongst the pigeons in the process. That would explain his name on the parchment. He has obviously wheedled his way into the Olive Pickers, probably needs the money, hasn't got a farthing to his name."

Now that he was aware of the background the appearance of the dagger and parchment made more sense to Marco. It also suggested that Slope had the confidence to move out of the shadows. It was an unusual development for an outsider. Italian groupings of any kind were not given to inviting outsiders to join them. It must mean that Slope had something to offer the Olive Pickers.

"I understand what you are saying Piers. This is a dangerous man we are dealing with. If he has been accepted into this group then he has some very determined people around him. The Olive Pickers have been bleeding this part of Italy dry for years. They are not just thugs but have some very clever people calling the shots."

"What exactly is their scam then Marco?"

"It is absolutely foolproof. That's the problem. They frighten the peasants into silence by stealing their olive trees. They have buyers already lined up living in the north who will pay a fortune for a mature olive tree. They even have agricultural advisers on board to ensure the trees survive the trip north. Once the deal is done through the kind auspices of the northern Mafia the peasants put in a claim for compensation from the EU."

"Hold your horses old fruit," slurred Bones who was clearly taking every advantage of the quality of the wine that surrounded him. "I thought the educational system down here was such that these peasants couldn't even sign their own names. Back of beyond after all, don't you know."

"Tactfully put Bonesie you old reprobate. They have people here who could fill in the densest form designed by man. The compensation is huge. Once it is paid to the peasants they are forced to hand over the bulk of the money leaving them just enough to live on."

"Surely they send somebody down from Rome or wherever to check on claims?"

"You'd think so, wouldn't you Piers? But no. This is the EU and their agricultural policy is so Byzantine that nobody understands it anyway. It might make sense in Wonderland but not here. When they do send someone down to check all they see is a hole where a tree used to be and a grieving peasant. The grief is genuine, the claims aren't. Some people here have nursed the really old trees for generations. And what do you think happens to the inspector if they feel the need to investigate further. The roads around here can be very dangerous, especially at night. Perfect scam really."

"Whoo hoo!" hooted a clearly inebriated Bones. "Capitalism red in tooth and claw. That's the way to do it."

"Ignore the right wing Marco. He's still getting over the loss of empire and the fact that he's struggling to pay the taxes he owes the revenue on his ancestral pile. Be just like him to adapt the scheme to nicking apple trees when he gets back home. I despair of him sometimes."

"Now, now that's enough of that conchie talk Piers. Nothing wrong with empire. Kept you bolshie lot in your place for years when we superior types were in charge."

Gabriel was growing tired of the way between them Bones and Prideaux were masters of obfuscation. Whether intentional or not they almost always subverted serious discussion and reduced it to mere insult and counter insult. He had enough, and showed it.

"You two can kindly shut the fuck up or find somewhere else to be. This is important. I know these two are friends of yours Marco but I genuinely need your help on the ground here. We have a situation. I know you know this area well. I'm also aware that you grew up in Britain and retain some of the values you absorbed when you lived there. I really need you to be on side. Of course you have a choice. It's Hobson's choice but I don't think you want to see the Olive Pickers becoming prominent in this area any more than we do. Now I don't know how much Bones and Prideaux have told you but if you have any sense at all of what we could be dealing with here then I'm confident you will come on board. I hope that you can persuade your brothers to join us too. We will need every soul we can possibly get and from what I understand your brothers are a formidable bunch."

"Let's not forget that this is my patch," Marco replied to Gabriel's appeal. "But you are right about one thing, I retain my affection for the old country and I have no intention of allowing a psychopath to establish control in this part of Italy. Bonesie and Prideaux told me most of it before they succumbed to the wine and nostalgia that seems to infect anyone with Celtic blood. I realise that you are trying to take out a soulless bastard and since you asked nicely then I think you can take it that I am with you in this instance. I'll get the rest of the family on board. One thing though, they will answer to me not you. The second you start throwing your weight around we'll walk. If that's acceptable to you then I think we have a deal."

Gabriel had kept his counsel. Developments, however, had given him no choice. He needed to be seen to be in charge if this whole thing was not to run out of control. He hesitated for a moment before extending his hand to Marco. It wasn't his usual way but as always he had done his homework. He knew that he would need people who knew the area. He was also aware that the brothers had a lot of respect locally. That would be invaluable when it came to taking out Olive Pickers. This was a close knit area and a wrong move could prove problematic. Nobody was about to welcome a foreigner riding in like the man with no name and taking out half the male population. It could well lead to questions. Marco and his brothers could well prove invaluable in stopping Slope in his tracks.

"Now that we have an agreement Marco perhaps I can ask you to fill me in on the caverns around the coast," said Gabriel. I understand that Slope and his followers have to stay off main roads if they are to profit from their cunning new business opportunity." Marco was more than keen to fill Gabriel in on the impact Slope had made on the villains in Puglia.

"What people frequently do is underestimate Slope," answered Piers. "Many aren't even aware that he was a successful businessman before he ever became master at St Jude's. He knows how to organise and he is ruthless. What else do you need to be a successful businessman?"

"Fair enough Piers. Marco, what I need to know is how is this scam to benefit from the sea caverns?" questioned Gabriel.

"That's simple," Marco replied. "Slope has realised that the scam can't work using road transport. There are thousands of sea caverns that could hide quite large boats. They are hard to find but Slope is likely to find them, eventually. Bones tells me that his main methods of persuasion, in business or not, is torture and murder. If he carries on with the scheme then the olive trees will be far easier to transport by water. The local farmers will be bullied into submission and the EU will be stung for compensation for trees that will have mysteriously disappeared like snow in summer. Classic con really."

"The only drawback might be how long it can retain Slope's interest," said Piers. "He's easily bored and there is a lot of tedious organisation needed to make the whole thing work. He's just as likely to put someone in charge of the con and move on to something else."

As Gabriel received the information from Marco he looked thoughtful. He had good reason to remain thoughtful. "Obviously if they are to use the seaways then they will need a place to hole up and to load the boats, ships or whatever the hell they are," he mused. "Not really my field the sea but I'm sure you will be able to fill in the gaps. I need the knowledge so that I can deploy my men. You clearly need rid of one evil bastard and whatever henchmen and henchwomen he has recruited."

Marco poured two glasses of fine wine passing one to Gabriel with the words: Libiamo, libiamo ne'lieti calici.

"You Italian chaps certainly like your wine," responded Gabriel, "and what exactly am I responding to?" he continued.

"As if anyone needed an excuse to drink the blood red wine of Puglia. You are toasting the wine that tastes of the blood, sweat and soil of my country."

"I think I've had wine like that before. My local doesn't exactly have an extensive wine list. Runs more to real ale though I don't expect you chaps to have much of a taste for that sort of trade."

Gabriel had much on his mind. Marco was generous with his brother's wine and Bones and Prideaux were taking full advantage of the fact. Gabriel was opting out as he was conscious that there was a real possibility that Slope was active in the area. It wouldn't do to be under the influence if positive action should be required without warning. There wasn't much he could do about Bones and

Prideaux who were behaving much as he'd come to expect. Far better to ignore them and concentrate on more pressing matters. The arrival of the Job twins convinced him that this was the case. They had taken time out to visit Salvo in hospital where they had run into his father. Salvo's father was a mine of information for the twins. He was happy to pass this information on as Salvo was clearly on the mend and like many in the area he was no friend of the Olive Pickers. It transpired that the Olive Pickers led by the man who might or might not be Slope had been forced into action. They had various organisations on their trail and such pressure was forcing them to attempt to smuggle their latest batch of olive trees out of the area. Their move was urgent. It had to be now and they believed they had found a grotto that would fit the bill. All that was known was it was close to the caves where Pietro stored his wines.

Marco smiled as he absorbed the information. He had a good idea of exactly where the grotto in question would be. "Follow me," he shouted to Gabriel and the twins. "I know how to access that grotto and it sounds as if we need to move swiftly."

The twins were as twitchy as fitchews who had not killed for an age. Wound up tight the two were like sprung steel just looking for an outlet for their pure and powerful natural aggression. Gabriel on the other hand seemed to be prevaricating.

"Now hold on a minute. We have no idea how many men may be involved. We will need backup as well as clearance. I'll contact Inspector Rabaotti for clearance and as many of his men as he can spare. I'll also need to mobilise the coastguard. We can't go off half cocked on something this big."

"That's the whole point Gabriel," yelled Robert Job. "Salvo's father is certain that Rabaotti and the local coastguard are up to their necks in all this. We have no time we need to move now. Come on Marco show us how we get to the grotto."

Marco ran to catch up with the twins and reluctantly Gabriel followed like the unwilling schoolboy dragging his feet on the way to school. He paused briefly to shout back at the giggling figures of Bones and Prideaux, "I suggest you useless bastards stay where you are. Not that you look capable of movement. Try sobering yourselves up by the time I return or I'll have you eviscerated and your entrails fed to the fishes."

He increased his pace to try and catch up with Marco and the twins. All the while he muttered angrily to himself: "One chance, that's all I need and I'll make those wasters suffer."

The wasters in question were suffering enough at the moment as the powerful Puglian wine began to gain the upper hand over two of Oxford's finest.

11

IN THE GROTTO

The sound of the sea became more apparent as Marco, Gabriel and the Job twins neared the rear of the cave. The odour of salt was almost overwhelming. It stung the eyes and the face. The four men reached what looked like a blank wall. In this part of the world things were seldom what they seemed. Off to one side of the wall Marco reached up at what appeared to be an outcrop of rock. With a sudden movement he pulled himself up on the outcrop grabbing it with both hands and allowing full weight to dangle against the wall. There was a creaking noise and a small door in the wall jerked open. The noise and smell from the cavern intensified as Marco nimbly dropped to the floor and led the way through the door into a large space. It was clear that this had been quarried to extend the reach of the wine cellar probably some time after the cave had been adapted to its role as a wine cellar.

"As I'm sure you will have guessed by now this extension was quarried by my family initially to give us more room for storage of maturing wine. It was coincidence that it also gave us a place to hide both ourselves and any goods we might prefer to stay hidden. And as a final bonus it gave us access to the grotta below giving us direct access to the Adriatic. It has proved useful in the past. I warn you that to get down to sea level is a precarious business."

"Fuck me," Robert said in a stage whisper you could have heard back in Penwithick. "He's not bloody kidding Janner. Look at that lot."

The twins were staring down through a large hole in the floor of the cave. A series of ladders led down to sea level. There was no lighting but it was clear that there were at least four long ladders roped together. There were in fact a total of ten ladders leading down to the floor of the grotta which was sea washed by the Adriatic. There was no artificial light to aid the descent and that descent would only be for the brave or the foolish.

"Heights don't bother me, Janner," said a confident Bob, one leg already over the side of the opening. "Born and raised in Cornwall my handsomes. You know that at the bottom of every hole in any part of the world you'll find a Cornishman. You know the song Cousin Jack?"

Bob began to sing it and it echoed down through the opening and bounced around the grotta walls.

"Very nice indeed," interrupted Gabriel. "Bang goes any chance of a surprise. That racket could have carried on the wind as far as Brindisi so I'm assuming that if there was anyone down there who shouldn't be they'd have buggered off by now. And just to make myself as clear as I can, I am not even going near that hole unless there is some light and some safety kit available. I do a lot for Queen and Country but even I have my limits. Good God man, even James Bond wouldn't go down there without a harness or a helmet."

"That's because, fictional character or not, he was a wimp. All those gadgets, all that equipment. Anybody could be successful with all that back up," said Marco. "I can do you a head torch each and that's it. Oh and just to put your minds at rest the ladders are firmly fixed and I use them regularly when I fancy a spot of fishing in peace. I've never seen the point of a helmet in these situations. The only thing likely to fall on your head is you. And I wouldn't worry about falling off; you'll be dead before you hit the ground or the sea." True to his word Marco pulled four head torches from a rusting old steel cabinet.

"There you go. Wrap one of these around each of your heads. Test the batteries and I'll lead the way. Now one thing I'd advise.

Don't look down. You can't see anything anyway. Hold the side of the ladders not the rungs and take your time. You are about to descend into a grotta that Slope or any of the blasted Olive Pickers would give their eye teeth to find. Follow me."

"Just one more thing before I commit to this ridiculous charade," said Gabriel.

"What is it now," responded an impatient Marco.

"I'm trying not to make a fuss but what if there are Olive Pickers just waiting for us down there in the darkness. I for one am not armed, mainly as I was not expecting to go potholing with a bunch of lunatics. And I'll bet that the twins are also unarmed. We'll be sitting ducks. Personally I'd prefer to make a fight of it if the occasion arises."

The twins looked at Gabriel as if he had run mad. "It is clear that you don't know us that well. If I cared to I could probably quote you chapter and verse of MI7 regulations on the carrying of sidearms. Suffice it to say that neither Bob nor I are ever unarmed. Good God man, we even sleep with our Glocks."

"That's all well and good but what about me. Haven't you got a spare pistol I could use Marco?"

Marco's impatience was beginning to show. He walked swiftly to a cabinet fixed to the side wall of the cave. It was clearly a gun cupboard and opening it revealed an impressive array of machine pistols, automatic rifles and a charming blunderbuss dating to at least the 18th century. "That was going to be Bones's weapon if he hadn't been too pissed to stand," he laughed. Here Gabriel, have this Glock; it's fully loaded. That should give you a fighting chance always assuming you know how to use a gun. Now let's do this."

Marco threw the Glock to Gabriel and locked up the gun cupboard.

In a flash he was over the side and descending rather swiftly into the darkness followed closely by the Job twins who chattered to one another as if neither had a care in the world. A more reluctant Gabriel brought up the rear. One of the things he hadn't told the rest was that he had no head for heights. Strangely though, the darkness helped as he was so intent on clinging to the ladder sides that there was little else on his mind. Marco had been quite right about the dark. It wasn't possible to see how deep they were going so he didn't have that awful stomach churning that afflicts those with a fear of heights.

The going was slow. It took almost forty minutes for Gabriel to step off the final rung on the last ladder. His relief was palpable as he joined the others who stood waiting on a jetty. As he did so Marco threw a switch that illuminated the cavern. The light almost blinded Gabriel as unlike the others his eyes had not acclimatised to the natural light coming into the cavern never mind the powerful lights that Marco had activated. He slipped and almost fell from the jetty. Bob was just swift enough to grab his arm and steady him but the incident shook the usually unflappable Gabriel.

The overall effect of the lighting gave the group a ghostly look. The cavern was vast and brought to mind a cathedral created by the sea. It was a striking and sobering space. Entirely created by the forces of the sea it had been hollowed out over generations to form the edifice it now was. Having regained his equilibrium even the cynical Gabriel was impressed. He would have been more so if Marco had instructed his electricians to have illuminated the place from the outset. It might have been a little less like a version of a descent into hell then. Gabriel wondered to which circle of hell he would despatch electricians who only did half a job. This reverie was interrupted by Marco.

"I suspect this is what Slope is looking for. The jetty allows large boats to sail all the way in to the grotta. There is plenty of clearance and no problem with height. It is the perfect base for anyone hoping to outwit the carabinieri. I'm happy to admit that the family have made use of it in the past in a minor way but it is important that it remains a secret from any of the local crooks or gangsters.

"I would ask that you three," he looked carefully at the Job twins and Gabriel, "tell nobody about this." All three nodded their acquiescence.

"Glad we got that little difficulty out of the way," said Gabriel with little attempt at masking his sarcasm. "Now perhaps I can stress what I see as important. We need enough boots on the ground to ensure that we stop this latest fund raiser from becoming too lucrative. The bastards that Slope is now involved with will take on anything if they think there is profit in it. Inspector Rabaiotti informs me that the Olive Pickers have run through drugs, people trafficking, prostitution, murder to order and this latest scam will just add to their repertoire if they can get the logistics right."

"Gabriel," said Marco "the reason I wanted you to see this place is that it is perfect for the Olive Pickers and their latest scheme. If they could establish regular sailings from here out to sea then there is a chance that their stolen trees will make it to those with the money in the north. If what the twins have just told us is true then there is nothing else suitable in the immediate area."

The Job twins were ignoring the conversation as they whispered to one another. They were both used to moving large loads around the farm back in Cornwall. Like all Cornishmen they were also at home with the sea and knew the art of moving tricky loads by water. Gabriel was irritated by their whispering that was rendered more intrusive by the peculiar acoustics the grotta created.

"Perhaps you would be good enough to share your very important whisperings with us," he said in a deliberately clipped manner. "I realise that I am only the man in charge of this whole operation but far be it from me to intrude on your family musings."

It was never a good idea to use sarcasm as a weapon against the twins. The term force of nature came nowhere near what could be generated if, even for a second, the twins thought themselves patronised. That had been a matter of honour when the two were undergraduates at their Oxford college.

They had made a pact as students never to change their accents in order to accommodate some of the narrow minded garbage that tainted some of the more privileged of the Oxford set. They were quickly aware that complete balderdash voiced in a cut glass accent could carry far more meaning than it deserved. And one thing that tended more than any other to stiffen the Job resolve was any hint they were being patronised. Since neither twin was a respecter of rank or position it was always the best course to have the boys pissing out rather than in. Gabriel was about to discover this at first hand.

"Now then Gabriel, let's get a few things straight." Robert had appointed himself spokesman. "I am fully aware that you are in charge of this operation but if you use that tone to me or brother Bob there then I shall ensure you can admire the beauty of this part of the Adriatic from the sea bed. Now that's no idle threat. We are not challenging your right of command but we are questioning your lack of practical knowledge."

Robert Job was about to launch into a diatribe when he was interrupted by the unmistakable sound of a large boat manoeuvering its way into and through the entrance to the grotto. "Get down," he shouted at the rest of the group.

Marco knew the cave better than the others so he was forced to take charge. "Follow me," he shouted "and for God's sake keep your heads down. There's a tunnel running off the main cave just to the right. Watch your heads as you get through. Now move it."

The small group ran stumbling until reaching the comparative safety of the tunnel gave them a chance to regroup.

"All of you check your weapons. Make sure that you are ready because we are going to have to shoot our way out of this. If it's OK with you Gabriel I'll take charge down here since I know this cave better than anyone."

Gabriel nodded his assent.

"Sorry Gabriel, maybe you were right and we should have waited for back up. I didn't really think the Olive Pickers would have moved this fast. They must have managed to get an experienced captain and a reliable crew."

"Apology accepted," said a curiously subdued Gabriel. "Come on then Marco how the hell are you going to get us out of this tight spot?"

"Maybe it's best to stay hid and see what happens? Marco shrugged.

"We are going to solve nothing hiding back here watching the tide roll in. I suggest we get back to the cave. I have a vague hope that by now Bones and Prideaux might have sobered up. Not that they are ever much use whatever state they are in."

Such blasphemy did not endear him to the Job twins. They had been through hell with the two men Gabriel was dismissing out of hand. His obvious contempt merely widened the existing rift between him and the veterans of the siege at The Hand of God.

"Not trying to influence anyone but there is a fairly high tide on its way and there is no way out other than up once it floods through." Marco was the man who knew the tides and the grotta so his word was sufficient to galvanise the others. "But we have an advantage even so. We could wait until the boat reaches the jetty and take them by surprise?"

"What good will that do?" It was Gabriel who was

appearing increasingly disturbed as the men waited for the inevitable.

Gradually the boat made its way alongside the jetty where it moored. It had an exceptionally powerful engine that allowed it to enter the grotta in reverse. It was obvious from the waterline that the boat was heavily loaded with cargo and men. Through the gloom it was possible to work out that it also carried a significant number of crew. There were several venerable old olive trees strapped to the deck of the vessel. It looked for all the world like a dummy run to see what was possible. Nobody was expecting observers. The level of relaxation was evident from the level of banter flying back and forth. They had proven the ability of the vessel to manage the seas sufficiently well to access the grotto with minimum fuss.

Gabriel reluctantly took charge. "We are clearly outnumbered and if it were not for the incoming tide I should recommend that we stay hidden here until they have left. However, in the circumstances this could be a rare opportunity to nip this particular activity in the bud. I'll call to them in Italian to throw down their weapons. Before I finish my first sentence I want you," he fixed his gaze on the twins, "to open fire. Follow that up immediately by charging the vessel. We will provide cover so that you can get close enough."

"Here we go. Poor bloody infantry as usual," mouthed Robert.

"Nothing of the sort actually," responded Gabriel. "It's just that I know your reputation and what you are capable of. The sight of you two mad bastards emerging from the dark as if the end of days has arrived will frighten most of them shitless. I'd appreciate it if you left a few of them alive. This could be a coup for MI7. It will royally piss off those layabouts in MI6. What could be better?"

The boat was alongside the jetty and two men jumped down to moor it. "I think the time for discussion may well be over," muttered Gabriel. "Hit that boat with everything we have."

The twins were already outside the tunnel and heading towards the target. The two men on the jetty died instantly as the twins opened fire. Those on board were completely disorientated not knowing what to do. The twins continued their frontal assault on the boat shooting at everything that moved. With their battle cry of Kernow bys Vyken! echoing through the cavern they established their supremacy within minutes. By the time fire was returned from those on board chaos was established. They were firing wildly at shadows whilst taking heavy casualties themselves. Suddenly the engine kicked into life as someone decided that discretion was the better part of valour. That someone was Sebastian Slope. His outline could be clearly seen at the wheel.

It was Marco who shouted. "Down twins," they dropped automatically as Marco continued, "I've got him lined up." Marco had his hunting rifle trained on Slope and was gently caressing the trigger. As he was on the point of making the kill a pistol shot rang out from somewhere behind him. The bullet hit Marco's right arm forcing him into dropping the rifle. It gave Slope enough time to put the boat in gear and head for the exit. It did so with the twins in full pursuit firing their machine pistols as though their lives depended on it. The boat cleared the cave entrance and hit the open sea with a hail of bullets splintering bits of the boat and some of the valuable trees on board. Once the boat was out of range the twins began to walk back towards Marco's position. They chatted as if they had just been out on a pheasant shoot.

"Did you get many, Janner?" asked Bob.

"Half a dozen, I think," Robert answered. "I got that bastard Rabaiotti, he's obviously in it with them. You?"

"About the same," answered Bob. "I know I got that Head of Customs and a few foot soldiers to boot. I'm sure that I saw Slope, you know. Pity we couldn't have boarded. We could have taken the lot."

The twins continued their casual stroll until they saw Marco. He had ripped strips off his shirt to bandage his right arm though the blood continued to seep through. "What happened Marco?"

"It's just a flesh wound, but I had that bastard Slope in my sights. I was about to pull the trigger when I got hit."

"Where the hell did that come from? We were in front of you. Must have been a stray from the boat. They were firing at random once they realised what was happening."

"It came from behind boys. It was Gabriel and I'm bloody sure it was deliberate. I know it was because if you look upwards you'll notice that the bloke suffering from vertigo is whipping up the ladders back to the cave like a monkey on a promise."

The twins did as Marco suggested. Gabriel was already near the top of the structure. He was moving quickly for a vertigo sufferer. Something wasn't right. Marco remembered the fuss he had made during the descent. Now he was on his way back to the wine cave he was moving like a steeplejack. Indicating to the twins that they should follow him he moved quickly to the lead ladder and started to climb at pace.

The twins were always alive to any form of danger and followed closely. More than one man on any of the ladder sections would make that ladder swing alarmingly. This knowledge slowed Marco's ascent considerably. However quickly he climbed he was not closing the gap and Gabriel was almost in touching distance of the bar above the rung of the top ladder. Once there he could haul himself off the ladder and onto the floor of the cave. This was looking bleak.

It suddenly became a whole lot bleaker as Gabriel grabbed the bar and pulled himself up and into the wine cave. There was nothing Marco could do. His heart sank as he heard the grating that covered the grotta entrance from above being dragged across to cover the hole. As Gabriel was forcing the bolts into place that would secure the heavy iron grating he leaned down into the hole shouting, "Arrivederci chaps. If you can hold on to your ladders until the tide turns you might be able to climb down and swim out on the reverse tide. If not you will simply drop off like rotten fruit."

Gabriel emptied his gun into the inky blackness for good measure causing Marco and the twins to pause in their ascent. The bullets harmlessly ricocheted around them and thankfully disappeared into the grotto below. He forced the final bolt of the grating into position leaving the twins and Marco hanging.

"Any thoughts Marco?" the question floated up from some fifteen metres below.

"Nothing springs to mind immediately," came the reply. "The bastard has shot the bolts so it would be pointless trying to force the grating. There's no way three of us could get into a position to try anyway. It looks as if we can dangle here and hope we can hold on for a retreating tide. We could, I suppose, shout for help but I doubt that Gabriel will have left Bonesie and Piers alive even if they are sober enough to work out where we are. I'd say we are in a very sticky spot. Best plan is to move down as close as possible to the rising tide rather than hang about up here until we drop like ripe fruit."

As Marco began to descend he heard the grinding sound of the grating bolts being pulled back. "Hold on he shouted. Someone appears to be opening the grating. I'll get as close as I can and make a jump for it as soon as it looks like there might be enough space for me to get through."

"Be careful," shouted the twins in unison again.

Gradually the heavy grill was withdrawn and light from the wine cave began to penetrate. Marco was tensed ready to make the jump. He had calculated the odds and reckoned that if he could muster enough velocity he could force back whoever was currently opening the grating. What happened next was a pleasant surprise.

"Come on you lot. Stop swinging the lead and get your arses up here a bit sharpish. I don't know. One really can't get the staff these days." The booze raddled face of William Radleigh de Beaune had never made a more welcome appearance.

"Bonesie you boozy old bastard. I thought he would have killed you. Is Piers OK too?"

"You'd better climb up and ask him yourself," Bones grinned. "Oh and I have someone here I'm sure you'd like to meet."

Bones and Prideaux stepped away from the grating allowing room for Marco to regain the safety of the wine cave floor. He was swiftly followed by the Job twins who had certainly had their fill of snakes and ladders. The three men sat with their backs against the cave wall as they became acclimatised to the cave. Bones and Prideaux stood together and looked down on them both with enigmatic smiles playing on their lips. Robert was first to gain his equilibrium.

"I suppose we should thank you for saving our lives but I fail to see anything funny about this situation. What the fuck is Gabriel playing at? We could have been killed."

"You could; he was," answered Prideaux trying to stifle a laugh.

"Not really in the mood Piers," advised Bob. "Just tell us what the fuck is going on. And who is this person that you want us to meet. It had better be worth it because I'm in the mood to do a bit of damage. That means that Bob will be too and I don't imagine Marco feels like a spot of twerking either."

The twins had regained their feet and were vaguely aware of a figure in the shadows. As he moved towards the three Bones and Prideaux stepped to one side.

Realisation dawned slowly as the men looked from one to another. Each face betrayed a look of total incredulity.

"What the fuck is this? You are supposed to be dead, said Robert.

"He is, was," replied Bob. "I saw the body," added Bob for good measure.

"You saw a body, countered Cornelius. "My body stands here in front of you and apart from a touch of arthritis I am fully fit. Now if you Celtic clowns could manage to close your mouths I'll be happy to explain. But before I do I'd appreciate it if you would take the trouble to throw the garbage down the chute."

Turning, he indicated the lifeless body of Gabriel. He had been stabbed through the heart with a stiletto. "Died without a sound. I must say they are jolly handy knives to have. I used an Olive Pickers stiletto in the hope of spreading some alarm and despondency among those bastards. I'm hoping that it will stay in the body for when Gabriel eventually washes up somewhere. Slope is going to know eventually that I'm still alive. But hopefully my ruse will continue to keep the bleeder guessing a good while yet. When you've put the trash out make sure you bolt the grating in place then join me in the tasting area. Wipe that grin off your face Bones. If I see you with so much as a mouthful of wine you'll be joining dear old Gabriel in his watery grave." Cornelius turned on his heel and walked back to the front of the wine cave.

The explanation did not take long. Once Gabriel had been disposed of Cornelius held the floor. As always when Cornelius spoke everyone else listened.

"Just in case anyone thinks that I am some sort of zombie or a ghost I should explain that the body in the bed back in The Hand of God was not me. It was one of my body doubles. Decent chap too. He must have dropped his guard. High price to pay but there is never a shortage of volunteers for the job. Anyone in a high profile position is likely to have a double. The idea is quite an ancient one. Most modern leaders have at least one."

"Most megalomaniacs at least," retorted Bones. With a look that could have curdled concrete the recently resurrected Cornelius resumed.

"If you really have enemies you are likely to have multiple doubles. Osama bin Laden, Castro, Montgomery, Churchill all had doubles. Some of them had multiple doubles. They hold regular doppelgänger conventions in places like Brazil and Ecuador every year. A basic resemblance can be helped enormously with a little time taken to perfect a walk or certain mannerisms. Make up these days is an art so it is relatively easy to come up with a convincing doppelgänger although I should point out that it is not general government policy in Britain. They have standby arrangements as do the Royal Family. They make extensive use of doubles. In my case it was a one off so that we could flush Gabriel out. We knew he was dodgy or I should say that Zebedee suspected he might have been working for Slope, which is why he is now bobbing about on the beautiful briny. At least we have reduced the opposition by one."

"Bloody good show Cornelius old chap. While it is nice to see you walking the earth instead of pushing up daisies don't you think it would have been thoughtful to have tipped us the wink?" Bob looked the angrier of the twins fixing Cornelius with one of those Cornish looks as he spoke.

"Not at all. I knew you two mad bastards could look after yourselves and Marco is no slouch. I was confident you'd be alright. Quick update for you since you've finished having fun in the grotto. I have been in contact with HQ and Slope now has his very own satellite following is every move. We are going to know where he is at all times. I've also got two of our agents shadowing him in case he manages to evade our satellite. Boots on the ground, don't you know. There is something else though." He turned to Bones and Prideaux.

"There was an envelope left at Marco's for safekeeping and I wondered whether it is still there or has one of you collected it? It is a bulky piece of kit and the documents inside are pretty important." Cornelius was attempting to play the situation down. Bones clearly rattled Cornelius by informing him that he believed that somehow Bennett had managed to snaffle the envelope and almost certainly had now handed on to Slope.

"Hmm, pity that. There's some valuable stuff inside. I really wouldn't want it falling into the wrong hands. King's ransom, untold wealth and that sort of thing." Bones and Prideaux could tell that Cornelius was trying to underplay the situation. His face was ashen and the envelope's disappearance had unsettled him. Obviously if it contained what he was hinting at then the items were already in the wrong hands. Recovering himself Cornelius revealed that all was not lost and that he had a plan that would lead to the eventual ensnarement of Slope and Bennett."

"What Slope has is merely a taster. If he can determine exactly what he holds in his sweaty palms then his greed will not allow him to ignore riches that go beyond the dreams of avarice. My job is to stay close enough to ensure that if, and that's not a certainty, he is able to work out what he is searching for and where it is I am right there on the spot to ensure that he is taken out of the equation once and for all."

Neither Bones nor Prideaux were impressed with such a vague plan to deal with such an accomplished schemer as Slope.

He turned and walked away relishing the knowledge that his response would have wound the twins up very, very tightly. They worked better that way he reasoned. Bones and Prideaux on the other hand would be delighted to return to their little gold mine in the Welsh countryside. Accordingly he thanked them for their help in flushing Slope out into the open and informed them that as of now they would be stood down and shortly heading for home.

DAI BLATCHFORD

12

THE VILLAGE

The village was around eight kilometres from the port. An unmade road led from sea level high into the mountains beyond, olive groves lined the slopes. After several kilometres the road narrowed to a single track. The groves eventually gave way to uncultivated scrub as the track continued on its vertiginous way. Its twists and turns made it a nightmare to navigate in any conditions. When the rain came it was virtually impassable. Currently, it was passable with care while retaining its intimidating quality. If you travelled the road to the village without a name you really needed to go there. Locals referred to it as inferno di montagne or more usually didn't refer to it all. If a tourist or non-local had mislaid the way and found themselves on the road to hell any question would be batted away with a firm non capisco.

Comfortably ensconced in their villa Slope and Bennett were putting the finishing touches to their plan. Although they were reluctant to admit it the intelligence services were clearly on the trail. The shoot-out in the Grotto had proved a near thing. The bullet had passed though Slope's jacket and they were lucky that the captain had managed to get the boat out of the grotto at such speed. They had spent some time examining the contents of the envelope. Slope was convinced that if he could interpret the documents and the maps he had in his hands then he could track down the whereabouts of a fabulous treasure. In addition he became aware that there were indications that he might just be able to find out what exactly Cornelius had done to his own considerable fortune. His one hesitation was that perhaps the whole thing was an elaborate trap with the erstwhile leader of the Spriggans the target. He was in no doubt that to get to his goal he would have to return to the UK. As always on occasions such as these the lone wolf in Slope surfaced. He would not take Bennett with him. She could only slow him down. The planning at least he must do alone. For now though they were both safe in the knowledge that nobody would enter the village unless they were welcome. One who was welcome and had been escorted to the villa by two of Slope's trusted henchmen was about to make his way to the safe house. Even a careless observer would have noticed that there was something familiar about the man. The escorts who delivered the man to Slope's front gate noticed but knew better than to comment. They led him to the electronic gate, buzzed the intercom and motioned him inside as the gates swung open. The man limped inside just quickly enough to avoid the gates as they slammed to a close. Two heavily armed bodyguards greeted the man in English and indicated the direction in which he should walk. Flanking him they approached the front door which was opened by Bennett. She dismissed the bodyguards and grabbing the man by the crotch pulled him inside slamming the door shut.

"Not bad I suppose," she mused fondling his genitals in the style of a butcher disembowelling a chicken. "You'll pass in a bad light but you need to be able to do the business if you are to be convincing in action. If you like I can give you a trial. Sebastian isn't here at the moment but I'm sure it would please him if I was able to tell him that I'd given you a run-out on the crash mat. Are you up for it?"

Not the brightest of men he suddenly realised that his latest career change might have some drawbacks he hadn't considered. It had seemed like a good idea when failed entrepreneur, wine importer, and newly minted double for hire had been offered a contract that involved spending some time in this lovely region of Italy. Not much to do other than to make himself obvious in his new role as Sebastian Slope.

He wasn't quite prepared for the violent approach of Elizabeth Bennett. Her favoured approach to sex tended towards the dark side. That was immediately clear to him. What he was unsure about was how Slope might react. He needn't have worried on that score. Slope was in the film room. He would monitor every part of the congress between Bennett and Charles Nerval. He would do it for two reasons. Firstly because he enjoyed watching pornography, secondly because he needed to convince himself that this lookalike he had invited to the village could hack it in his absence.

An hour later when Bennett and Nerval were washing off the detritus of sex in the shower Slope had his answer. Now should he be tempted by any of the willing women in the hills he could be convincing enough to avoid any suspicions that he was a mere stand in. Men rarely looked too closely at Slope anyway, to do so could prove fatal. Nerval had enough of Slope about him to pass muster. He had the walk, the general height and weight and facially he was very convincing. Slope had offered him huge rewards for a couple of months work. There would be no payoff, of course, since his corpse would eventually surface in a place and at a time to suit Slope's purpose. Nerval was unaware of any of this. He had enjoyed some of the less violent aspects of Bennett's approach to sex. He was sure that the cuts and incisions would soon heal and that his battered genitals would eventually recover.

The three ate dinner together later that day when Slope deigned to join them. They dined on orechiette with meat sauce and turnip tops accompanied by several bottles of Graticciaia Vallone. A powerful 14.5 % wine made from fine clusters of negroamaro grapes part air-dried on bamboo slats. A wine that tasted of the soil of Puglia but in a good way. It added the real taste of Puglia to the food. There was little conversation over dinner.

Nerval left the table for his quarters in the garden room carrying a dossier of information and a laptop. His only instruction was to absorb all the information both digital and written and to ensure that he was word and touch perfect in the impersonation. He could be expected to be tested to near destruction over the coming few days.

He walked unsteadily towards his new accommodation with the appearance of a fresher retiring to his room having just met his lecturers who were way cooler than he could ever be, and a hell of a lot scarier. He had heard rumours about the couple but rumours are generally exaggerated versions of fact aren't they? Charles Nerval was in the perfect place to find out. For now he had a huge amount to get through and the quantity of wine wonderful though it was did not provide the best preparation for some heavy duty study. His resolution weakened as he reached his room and dropped his bag on a chair near the bed. His mistake was to sit on the bed. He fought sleep for as long as possible but soon and without undressing he lay back across the single bed and was lost to the world.

Nerval woke with a head like a furry bucket. His first thought was he needed black coffee and to soak his head in the coldest water he could stand. This was a habit he had picked up when as a young man he had read that Paul Newman made a habit of sluicing his face in ice cold water to keep his skin looking young. If it worked for the actor he reasoned then it could work for him. He was less worried about the state of his skin than the state of his head on this occasion yet it seemed to have the desired effect. The reluctant double sat at the rickety old table and began to learn all he needed to know to make his impersonation convincing.

Slope was the type of man who always insisted on an alternative plan. He was disappointed in his experiences in Puglia. The Olive Pickers had not met his high expectations. This was not good enough. The rewards he had hoped for through his collaboration with the Olive Pickers had been as nothing when compared to the wealth that Cornelius had appropriated from him. He had to get that fortune back. If nothing else it was a direct affront to his dignity. Added to all this the latest irritation was the failure of Gabriel to respond to his prearranged check in time. It wasn't like him.

Slope couldn't know that the remains of Gabriel were currently being buffeted by the waves and nibbled by fishes of various sizes. His absence was enough to irritate Slope and an irritable Slope was most certainly not a thing of joy forever. The decision to activate Plan B was inevitable. It would involve a return to Britain and some careful planning but it could be done. This would allow him time to unravel the web of mystery and intrigue that lay at the heart of what he now had in his possession. He was pretty sure that he had the means to crack the secret. He had the book, he had the original drawings for the Black Castle and best of all he had all three parts of the medallion that was typically Norman and was the final piece in the mystery. The first phase was in place. Slope's double would ensure that his absence would not be noticed. The Olive Pickers could easily be left to their own devices, what was left of them after the firefight in the grotto that is. After all they had centuries experience even if their current malevolent manifestation accorded with the arrival of the malignant Slope on the scene.

Slope's managed return to Britain was his current obsession. Puglia was enjoyable enough. Plenty of sun, good food, good wine and the opportunity for some low level crime with the odd foray into murder had kept him occupied. As always he wanted more. His real obsession with Prideaux and his ever present companion Bones was never far beneath the surface. He was now aware that Bones and Prideaux were in Puglia and that was troubling him. This knowledge had driven him to his favourite restaurant on the outskirts of Ostuni.

Slope ordered freshly caught local fish with some orecchiette, asparagus, peas and lemon ricotta. It was a local delicacy and one that he ordered regularly when visiting Angelo's. Like all psychopaths Slope could not stomach the slightest lack of control. His mood became dark as he tried to control himself. Regular diners at the restaurant were wary of his occasional explosions of anger. Angelo tolerated them since he was one of his best customers. Occasional outbursts were forgivable but of late these were becoming a little too frequent. Other valued customers had begun checking whether he had booked a table before confirming their own bookings. This could not be allowed to continue. Easy to say but a real problem to do with a creature as volatile as Sebastian Slope.

The man himself was aware of this and realised that drawing attention to himself would not be a clever move given his recently laid plans. It took a massive effort but he was able to control himself long enough to finish his meal and leave Angelo's with little outward evidence of the darkness of his mood. That would come later. For now his energies had to be channelled into the task of getting himself back to the UK. It was not going to be easy but travelling light would make it a damn sight easier. He resolved to persuade Bennett that it would be better if she stayed in Puglia. His double could keep her occupied. The poor bastard only had a vague idea of what he was taking on but he travels fastest who travels alone was the sort of mindless aphorism he would usually dismiss with a snort. On this occasion it made perfect sense. Bennett would do as she was bloody well told. The decision helped the rage to subside as he backed his car out of Angelo's car park straight into a goat. Slope drove off laughing as the goat bleated its last in the dust of the unmade road. Strange are the things that will make madmen happy.

Several miles away two other madmen were making their preparations to return to Britain. Bones and Prideaux were happily packing their cases in the trullo near Ostuni.

"Happy to be going home, old fruit?" Bones was shouting to Prideaux from the kitchen.

Prideaux was wearing his latest acquisition, noise-cancelling ear phones. The perfect way to hide from Bones's burbling. Bones was an inveterate burbler. When excited this became extremely distracting, the reason Prideaux had paid quite a few euros for his new ear phones. With albums like Field Commander Cohen to listen to there really was no contest. By the time the strains of So Long Marianne had died away Prideaux was packed and ready to go. He unpacked his ears and made his way along the corridor to Bones's room. Bones too was lost in sound but in his case it was Rachmaninov's Piano Concerto No. 3 in D minor, Op. 30 wheezing its way out of an ancient wind up gramophone.

"Why on earth don't you get yourself a decent sound system Bonesie old trout?"

"Because my cloth-eared little pal there are still a few of us left who prefer things to be the way they were. So you go your way and I'll go mine. I believe that's a line from one of your favourite raspers, Bob Dylan isn't it?"

"Bonesie we need to talk. I'm getting a bit pissed off with all this subterfuge, secrets and lies the whole time. Cornelius can sort out the whole bloody mess as far as I'm concerned. Now that the daft bugger has gone and done a Lazarus he can damn well carry on and finish the job. We'll leave it to the professionals and get back to what we do best. Why not as the great Satchmo used to say when he advertised laxatives, 'leave it all behind ya'."

"All well and good old horse but I've been doing a bit of thinking. Slope will have made a good deal of money already from the olive tree scam. He will have placated his friends in the north and has a ready prepared bolthole here for when he needs it. Here's a 'what if...'. What if Slope has been playing the long game? What if all this olive business is a ruse to take our minds off what is going on back home? Let's be honest, you never expected half of the stuff going on in Britain never mind the wider world to ever happen."

The two men looked at each other and began to laugh. They were of an age when they thought that they had seen just about everything there was to see in the modern world. Too young for the last world war they had watched the Berlin wall torn down with pleasure mingled with amazement. Who the hell would have predicted that? Now, in the wake of Scotland voting for independence Wales had swiftly followed suit. That very act had set the larger northern English counties howling with rage until a promise was made that they too could have a referendum over an assembly. Some comedian suggested that perhaps Lancashire and Yorkshire might like to discuss a joint bid for a sort of combined northern parliament. It was a dangerous thing to suggest and sent the activists from both counties running for the barricades. For two men of the world the only correct response was laughter. After hundreds of years of cooperation old sores had been picked again, long dead grudges had resurfaced and nationalism in all its forms was stalking the green and pleasant land. You really could not make it up.

It was Bones who stopped laughing first. "I'm serious about what his intentions are. He needs to accumulate a lot of bucks to replenish the coffers to anything like their original level. He's made a good start but he's an impatient bastard and he will want a big hit sooner rather than later. I have a shrewd idea of what his overall plan might be."

"OK Bonesie, I am all ears."

"Promise you won't take the piss and I'll tell you."

"I promise," replied Prideaux his fingers firmly crossed behind his back.

"Suppose you happened to know roughly where a lost fortune was hidden. I'm not talking fairy stories but a king's ransom, almost literally. If you could get your hands on that then you would have the wherewithal to fund any twisted scheme that took your fancy. What a tempter that would be for someone like Slope."

"Fine so far. I can concede that much. But it would be too much of a coincidence for such a fortune to suddenly appear. Are you sure it's not fairy gold."

Bones answered with a wicked grin creasing his face, "Well I suppose that in a way it is exactly that. At least because it was some of the accumulated wealth of Edward II a king well known for his penchant for his own gender. It just happens that his gold, the crown of England, and a whole lot besides is believed to be hidden somewhere in a massive Norman castle that lowers over a small fishing village in Wales. I got old Cornelius sizzled that last night in The Hand of God and he let slip that the envelope he left for me at Marco's was testament to that fact."

"Nice try, Bonesie. I'll bet there are a thousand stories like that in Wales," Piers laughed. "Cornelius is pulling on your leg old pal. Besides that envelope was never found, completely disappeared into the ether."

"That's as may be Piers but I'll bet not more than one in a hundred have the documentation to give proper credence to the story. This is not some pie in the sky nonsense but genuine mediaeval history. If you have any sense at all you will listen."

"Just for you then Bonesie. Just for you."

13

THE LAND OF THE BLACK SWAN

Slope was arranging to make his return to Britain under the radar. He was not alone. He had, however, persuaded Bennett to stay in Puglia for the immediate future. She seemed unusually amenable in that she had made no attempt to stab Slope when he had issued his orders. In truth she had taken something of a shine to Slope's double as a man with prospects for psychopath and someone a lot more athletic than an ageing Slope.

Two of the country's laziest agents were mistaken in thinking they had landed an easy assignment. Wapping and Thrust two burly men were too young for retirement. There were lots of agents who approached retirement. Few would ever reach that halcyon state. Sitting in an anonymous Fiat the men received a black alert that Slope was on the way to the private aeroporto just outside Ostuni. Intelligence sources had expressed concerns about this private airport for many years. It was small, difficult to find and likely to be used by hostile groups for entering and leaving Italy with minimum fuss. The car carrying Slope and two companions apart from the driver was currently hammering along the coast road heading for the point at which the road climbed into the surrounding mountains. It was almost out of sight of the two agents before Thrust managed to switch on the Fiat's ignition.

"Get your foot down Thrust or the bastard will be on the plane before we even reach the bloody airport."

Working together did not mean that the two were bosom buddies. They were opposites and regularly argued. This was not the time for argument and Wapping was not in the mood.

"I don't give a hummingbird's foreskin whether Slope flies out of Puglia. I don't care where he is going. And if you had the common sense of a cheeseboard neither would you. This is the cushiest posting I've ever had and I'm not about to blow it by getting too close to that mad bastard. You know what he's capable of. Anyway, we'll never catch up with him in this tin can. I'll drive along in the general direction of the airport, then we'll report that we followed him but he gave us the slip."

"I always knew you were an idiot Wapping. You can't ignore a black alert. They'll want to know chapter and verse. What plane, how many were with him, what direction the plane took off in. They'll know that we haven't done a proper job."

"Ah, but we will have done exactly that my little doubter. There were three men in the car. If one of them is Slope then we need to follow them. If they gave us a decent bloody car, like an Alfa Romeo or something we could have caught him easily. If we had what do you think would have happened. That bastard kills for fun and I'd like to see my pension in a few years. All we have to do is drive along for a few miles and arrive when the plane is well aloft then report that we tried but couldn't get there in time. If it makes you happier I'll speed up a bit."

Wapping duly did and started throwing the Fiat around bends at a respectable speed. This did little to placate Thrust who feared his own masters as much as the psychopaths he was occasionally forced to follow.

"There it is. That's the car, look they've pulled over. For fuck's sake keep driving. Don't look just drive past. With a bit of luck they'll think we're holiday makers or something."

"You'd better pray that they do," Wapping said doing his best to look like a Brit abroad. "I have a very bad feeling about this." That feeling got a lot worse as the car hit the rumble strips neatly laid across the road bursting three of the four tyres. Wapping struggled with the steering as the car lurched to the right.

Desperate to avoid the vertiginous drop with which the car was currently flirting he aimed for one of the boulders strategically placed to prevent such accidents. Sheer luck meant the car bounced off one of the boulders coming to a stop on the brink of the 200 metres drop."

Wapping and Thrust had both been stunned by the crash and were trying to clear their heads. They sensed rather than saw the three men they had been following casually strolling towards the hovering car. Thrust was trying to open his door which had jammed in the impact. Panic was taking hold as the car rocked their erstwhile targets putting their weight behind destabilising the Fiat. There had to be a tipping point and there was to be no escape.

Gradually the car lost any balance it had and began to slip on the gravel at the edge of the drop. In a matter of seconds they realised this was it. As Wapping regained consciousness he had a split second to admire the beauty of the view before the motion sent the car and agents plunging towards the valley floor. They had not even thought of drawing their weapons. The three men responsible clapped their hands as if to distance themselves from the murder. Two were hired thugs. The third man was Slope's double. The man himself had taken a night flight to Britain from Brindisi two days earlier. Wapping and Thrust would not live to draw their pensions. Slope, however would soon embark on his plan to recover his fortune and finally choreograph the deaths of Bones and Prideaux.

While Wapping and Thrust were breathing their last Slope was engaged on the research that was to lead him to the restoration of his fortunes. He was not getting any younger. He could not wait for convoluted schemes to pay off. If he were to recover his position of strength it would need to be quickly done. What he really needed was to recover his stolen treasure from wherever Cornelius had hidden it along with the priceless artefacts the stolen documents hinted at. His own basic research had convinced him that his treasure could well be hidden somewhere beneath a Norman castle in Wales. There are always stories of such hidden treasures. Mostly that is just what they are, stories. Slope's interest in history, he had lectured in the subject before his elevation to Master at an Oxford College. His particular interest in mediaeval history was leading him towards something of more substance.

Which is why he was ensconced in the Research Library of Wales poring over a range of mediaeval documents dating back to the early part of the 14th century. Shorn of much of his arrogance Slope had reverted to the academic world partly as a place to pass unnoticed and partly as he needed to confirm details to the story that he had known for many years.

He was in Wales to research the background to a major event in the history of the relationship between one of the Norman lords and the king of England at the time. That could well be the answer to his search for his own fortune as well as the priceless mediaeval treasure. As in all mediaeval stories detail surrounding the event was hazy and contradictory. But Slope was convinced he had teased out the mystery. The answer lay in the small fishing village of Oystermouth in west Wales the story had been told and retold for centuries. If it had achieved the status of myth then that was hardly a surprise. The story had most of the elements that focus human interest as fully today as in the 14th century. Unimaginable wealth, betrayal, cruelty and mystery tangled together inextricably to fascinate and appal. Such stories have equal appeal in the modern day. The attraction for Slope was that if he could verify the original truth and trace the treasure then he could re-establish himself as a threat to governments and an enormously wealthy man. It would take effort but there seemed no alternative if he was to live the life he thought was his right.

In the village of Skenfrith where they had rebooted their lives following the death of their friends Mark and Ginny, Bones and Prideaux were busy settling back into running The Hand of God. The time spent away in Puglia had not harmed the popularity of the famous old inn. The existing staff had seen to that. There was plenty to keep the pair busy even in late august. Summer was fading as the early autumn winds began to tune up. August was notorious for its fickle weather. It still looked like summer, at times it still felt like summer but there was the ominous threat of high winds and vicious rain storms. This was what heralded autumn and the bleak midwinter days just waiting in the wings. There would be shoots to organise, Bones's famous wine tastings to arrange and the necessary changeover from summer to autumn that all pubs and hotels needed to complete at the change of the seasons.

"Good to be back in God's country eh Bonesie?" muttered Prideaux as he worked his way through the changes to the menu. The inn had a reputation to maintain and at this time of year changes to the menu were essential. Geoff the chef prided himself on his use of locally grown vegetables and the finest organic meat available in the area. Complemented by Bones's extensive wine knowledge this ensured that The Hand of God retained its popularity and status as the finest inn for miles around.

"I have high hopes that this coming season of 'seeds and mellow fruitfulness' will be a splendid autumn. Plenty of good food, good wine and with a bit of luck some fine female companionship." Bones drifted off into a reverie as he imagined his ideal lifestyle.

It was early on a Monday morning and the weather was muggy. Hints of thunder could be heard over the Black Mountains but the sky over Skenfrith was clear and the signs are that it would be a good day. The two friends were slowly easing themselves back into their main roles. Their unwanted conscription into the intelligence services had yielded little. They had enjoyed Italian cuisine and particularly wine but Slope remained like smoke on the mountain. He was always just out of reach. If only Marco had pulled the trigger that time in the grotto Slope would already have met his maker. There was less dangerous excitement on the horizon for Bones and Prideaux.

"You don't have to come if you don't want to but I'm having to go down to Oystermouth for a few days. Don't expect you fancy it?" said Prideaux.

"I fancy it very much old chap. I've had many a merry old time down there where the tide rushes in and the girls rush about. I could tell you a tale or two about my dalliances. At least I could if it were not for the fact that I am a gentleman. Great idea and for once it will be what we want to do rather than what we are told to do."

"It's not exactly that sort of visit, more of a duty thing really. But I suppose we could stay for a few days after the funeral."

"What funeral is this? First I've heard of a funeral. I didn't know you had people down in that area Piers. Anyone I know?"

"You remember my granddad used to go on about one of his old comrades he was close to during the war. It appears he has died. I've had a letter to say that Granddad is not well enough to attend the funeral and wants me to represent him. Least I can do in the circumstances."

"Absolutely Piers old chap. Respect in all things. I should be happy to accompany you to the seaside."

"Right, that's settled then. I'll ring his son and let him know that we are coming. Plenty of room for us to stay in his castle." Prideaux allowed his words to float in the air as he walked through to the bar to telephone Harvey Williams to confirm that both men would be in attendance to represent Granddad and the Mumbles chums of whom there were very few remaining.

It took several seconds for Prideaux's words to register with Bones. "Piers, Piers. What is all this rot about you knowing someone who owns a castle?"

"As a matter of fact I don't. Simply that the son of William Williams, Granddad's pal from the war, owns one. I've never met him although he seems a bit of a strange chap if Granddad's letter is anything to go by."

"I bloody knew it. I failed to understand how a pleb like you could know anybody who owned a castle unless he stole it?"

"Repossessed it actually you twat. It's a Norman castle. 14th century if you're interested. And when the particularly unpleasant Norman who built the bloody place dropped his guard it was Harvey Williams's ancestors who nipped in and returned the place to Welsh ownership. Been in the family ever since. Damn great limestone edifice towering over the village. I'm told he has a great cellar there. However that does not mean that you'll be getting the key to it. I'm not even sure if we can stay there. He's a weird old buffer. Calls himself a herb whisperer apparently. Acts as if he's king of the village. Even wears a crown sometimes. Some say he's possessed by the spirit of the family de Breos who were Norman owners in the 14th century."

"That's more like it Piers. A man with his own castle would have to be a little strange. Since I don't believe in ghoulies and ghosties and things that go bang in the night it wouldn't bother me one way or the other. Mind you if he has a good wine cellar I'd be happy to give it the once over," smiled Bones. "Purely professional curiosity of course. I might well offer to take a few bottles off his hands if he can stretch to a tasting?"

"Speaking of wine cellars isn't it about time you got yourself down to ours to give it the benefit of your expertise?"

"Splendid idea old horse. Here's a good idea though. I'll go down to look after my charges. You stay on board here. No reason, just that whenever both of us are in the cellar it strikes me that several horses of the Apocalypse seem to tie up outside the front door. I could do without any more of that bloody nonsense thank you."

"You do what you want Bonesie. We've put all that nonsense behind us. Plain sailing from now on and a nice seaside holiday to look forward to after the funeral."

The man who exposed the flaw in the good guys as winners theory was getting much closer to his goal. This time he was more focused on one specific thing. Any collateral damage would be a bonus to Slope who was homing in on the information he needed. His sharp mind had pierced the fog surrounding the story of the royal fortune and its current resting place.

Sebastian Slope, murderer, and sociopath finally had the scent of something that would restore him to what he believed to be his rightful place in the world. There was more than a story as Slope's research had confirmed. There was documentation verifying that in 1326 King Edward II and his court had decamped wholesale to west Wales. They carried with them important documentation of the court as well as the bulk of the king's wealth.

Edward was hoping to stay safe enough in Wales to organise an army with the support of the Despensers. This plan failed. Edward was captured at Neath but not before he had sent his baggage train including court documentation, treasure and the crown of England on to a castle in Swansea. Logic dictates that Swansea Castle would be the natural home for such valuables. However, it was also known that the Black Castle was strategically important at that time. And that the two castles had been linked by an underground passage running from Swansea to Oystermouth. This was enough to convince Slope that the treasure lay somewhere in the unexplored passageways for which the Black Castle was famous.

14

FESTIVAL OF THE OYSTER

The build-up to the unofficial Oyster Festival was the biggest thing to hit Oystermouth for years. It was continuing at a bewildering pace. It seemed that every day brought new demands to the small subcommittee tasked with ensuring smooth running on the day. The committee held no powers but received orders from a whole range of bodies on what was expected of them. Everything they received was subject to long debate and discussion. Committee members had been carefully chosen for their tact and patience.

Cornelius had typically inveigled his way in as head of a security company. It was as good a cover as any. His 'company' was tasked with looking after security within the village, on the castle green and inside the castle itself. Local police had been informed that Cornelius and his men would be supporting them in ensuring that the festival passed without a hitch. Senior officers had also informed them that Cornelius outranked them all in any unusual activity that occurred.

Intelligence sources meant that Cornelius was aware that the two Swansea castles, Swansea Castle itself and the Black Castle would prove the focus of Slope's attention. Consequently the trap was set. All it would take was for Slope to walk into it. Cornelius was under orders to take the man alive. This would not have been his first choice but he was under orders. However, if something happened where taking Slope alive proved impossible then who could blame him if he ordered termination? In a confrontation with Slope anything could happen. On the day of the funeral of Harvey Williams Cornelius and the Job twins were wandering along the promenade in Oystermouth. Using the pretence of being visitors and dressed accordingly in reality they were ensuring that once the trap was sprung Slope would have nowhere to run.

Walking through the village at around the same time Bones and Prideaux were on their way to attend the Williams funeral.

"This is bound to be a fairly sombre affair Piers. What say you we nip across to the esplanade and get a few lungfuls of good sea air?"

"Great idea Bones. We have plenty of time and a chest full of clean air would be just the badger."

The two men crossed the main road though the village. The tide was in. It lapped lazily against the sea wall. Seagulls wheeled through a clear sky. The beauty of the view coincided poignantly with the service that the two men were soon to attend. For the moment all was well with the world. It did not last.

"Bones don't look now but those three men sitting outside Joe's Ice Cream Parlour, do they look familiar to you."

Bones couldn't resist and looked directly at what was the most familiar sight in the area, people sitting outside an ice cream parlour eating ice cream. "I do not fucking believe it. Piers those three trying for all the world to look inconspicuous are Cornelius and the Job twins. Now what in God's name are they doing here? Well we've two choices. We have to pass the café to get to the church. We can either turn around or carry on walking and ask what they are doing here. Not that we'll get a straight answer from Cornelius. Worth a try though."

With that in mind they continued to progress along the esplanade with the deliberate tread of men pretending not to have a care in the world.

"Well, well fancy seeing you here, this is a coincidence," teased Cornelius in his most practised sarcastic tone.

"Cut the crap Cornelius. It's nothing of the kind. There is no such thing as coincidence where you are involved. So what is going on?"

"Nothing is as you say going on. I'm here with two of my men to keep a general eye on things and to ensure the funeral you are attending goes off without a hitch. I was offered the opportunity to combine some work with a jaunt to the seaside. What's wrong with that?"

"Nothing at all," said Bones "except I don't believe a word you say. There must be more to it than that."

"You have me bang to rights guv," Cornelius answered in what he fondly imagined to be a Cockney accent. "I do have an ulterior motive. I have been asked to hold a watching brief over the festival coming up. Fertile ground for some lunatic to get up to something unspeakable. Too many people in a confined space always troubles the intelligence services. You'll appreciate that the latest government cuts mean that you have two coppers and a tandem to look after greater Swansea. That's where we come in. MI7 to the rescue. By the way you could help with the festival if you felt like it. We need a couple like you to help out on the catering committee. Ideal opportunity to advertise your little hideaway up there in Skenfrith. I'll get one of my chaps to give you the details. Up to you of course."

"Well Cornelius nice chatting to you. Piers and I are off to pay our respects to the war hero. See you around boys," he winked at the twins as he turned away to head for the church. Prideaux followed after nodding to the twins and both men crossed the road to the lane leading to the church.

The funeral took place without incident. It went smoothly as these things usually did. The war hero was buried with full military honours. Many ageing heroes attended the ceremony. It was a poignant rather than a sad affair as Williams had led an interesting and full life and death at the age of 89 was not unexpected. Prideaux and Bones had carried out their duty to the deceased and represented Prideaux's grandfather as he had wanted. Prideaux had also managed to establish that he and Bones could stay for as long as they chose as guests of The Black Castle. A week or two by the sea was a tempting prospect even with the dark cloud that always accompanied Cornelius hovering in the background. As soon as word spread that they were the proprietors of the legendary Hand of God the two were seconded onto the catering committee of the nascent festival. Appointed as advisers on the grounds that they ran one of the best pub/restaurants in the country seemed to make perfect sense. It did not mean that the two men believed a word Cornelius had told them. Experience had taught them better. Cornelius in turn had discovered to his cost that nothing made much sense where these two were concerned. At least it was a good cover story if nothing more than that.

The presence of the Job twins gave the two the confidence that allowed them to swan around the castle as if 'to the manner born'. They had mightily pissed off officers from just about every organisation present. They knew that they were just about untouchable and they behaved accordingly. They were aware that there would be very few, only the craziest, who would ever dream of challenging the Job twins.

Bob and Robert Job had the same sense of mischief as Bones and Prideaux with the added advantage of being the most effective killing machines within MI7.

The Black Castle having once been a neglected monument to Norman power had been renovated over the years and turned into a completely self contained building.

Harvey Williams had made his fortune in the digital industry. He had worked in London for many years before returning to the village of his birth. Among many changes to the village he was appalled to see the Black Castle almost a ruin. Like all the other village youngsters he had played in the ruins as a boy. To see the sad state that the castle had come to gave him an idea. He had the money. If he could persuade the government to sell the castle to him he could restore the place to something like its former glory.

The castle had for long been ignored by its owners. It was unsafe. However, a combination of grants and Williams's own fortune sustained a long-term building programme. There were plenty of battles with heritage organisations and local interests over the years but eventually the castle provided the family with a home and the security that a paranoid Harvey Williams had always craved.

Security inside the building was absolute and it had added benefits that became clear during renovation. The Normans were superb engineers. They had built the castle high on a rocky outcrop giving a perfect 360 degree view of the surrounding village and countryside. Inside the castle the main buildings to be expected in a Norman castle remained intact. They had been given security doors, windows and restructured and reinforced roofing had turned the romantic ruin into an impregnable fortress. The warren of corridors that ran throughout the castle had been mapped as far as possible. They were designed to confuse anyone but those living in the castle. Intruders if they got that far would soon become lost in a maze of passageways exactly as the Normans intended.

There was something else that gave the castle more than usual importance. Experts had calculated based on precise measurements that had been taken during renovation that only something like 30% of the connecting passageways had been identified. It was this anomaly that helped to preserve the local legend that untold wealth in the form of royal treasure lay somewhere in the castle and had done so since the 14th century. There was certainly enough documentation to suggest that such a thing was a possibility. Bones and Prideaux spoke of little else once the evening lubrications had taken place.

On a cool evening in September Bones and Prideaux were idling their evening away drinking their favourite wine, Domaine Laborie. Bones regarded it as a corner shop wine but its honesty was appreciated by Prideaux. Preparations for the Oyster Festival were continuing as well as could be expected with so many different bodies involved. Bones and Prideaux were merely figureheads anyway. The real work was left to experts with occasional contributions from the co-owners of The Hand of God.

"Piers old chap, I am prepared to drink this wine for your sake, but one of these days I shall take that unfeasibly large key," he indicated a mediaeval looking key lying on a faux dining table, "and open that wine cellar that they are so proud of. I might even do it tonight. Then we'll see what vintage wines are lurking there."

"Good plan my old tutti frutti. I'll come with you and hold your coat. I'd prefer to look for the royal treasure trove though. Now wouldn't it be a hoot if we could locate that little lot?"

"You don't believe that old tosh, do you? If there was that much loot swilling around in this place someone would have found it by now."

"You've changed your tune. You were practically convinced after speaking with Cornelius."

"I think you were right and the old duck was pulling my udder," blustered Bones. "I'd like to pick his brains on the subject, he seems very well informed, but he's buggered off back to London for a meeting with his superiors."

"Anyway maybe someone has Bonesie. For all we know it could be in a safe room down one of these endless bloody passages. Bloody Normans were obsessed with them. Anyway if someone had found it what would they do with it? It's all recorded. The documents still exist. It wasn't any old fortune it was the king's treasure."

"Well, I'll give you this he was a bloody useless king. Too busy playing around with his boyfriends to look after the country and its wealth. No wonder his father had no time for him."

"Right then my old reactionary let's give the cellar a go. Never mind if we hit on the treasure instead. Though it will take a bit of carrying mind."

"Knowing you I'll bet you have a cousin who has a few spare mules knocking about down in the village. Shall we need some of those burning brands you see in the films when the peasants go chasing after Frankenstein's monster?"

"You can be a tit sometimes Bonesie. You know full well there's a lighting system that runs throughout the passageways. Well the ones that they know about anyway."

It did not take long for the police to identify the corpses found in Snatch Alley. They were generally known to the police as low level criminals and local to the area. All three had police records for theft, and various degrees of assault. None had been thought to have been involved in activity that would invite this level of violence. There were rumours of gang activity linked to drug dealing but nothing emerged to link the three to international criminals of the standing of Slope and Bennett.

It was Bones who spotted the report in the evening edition of the Post.

"Hey Piers. Have you seen this report on those three lads that were murdered near the station? It says here that they looked as if they had been ripped apart by wild animals. You don't think, do you…?"

"You can stop that right away, Bonesie. I know exactly what you're thinking. If Slope was involved you don't think he'd be careless enough to leave bodies where they could easily be found.

They'd have ended up somewhere off Knab Rock if he'd had anything to do with it."

"How do we know that he's still in Italy? It would go some way to explaining Cornelius's presence in Swansea. I don't buy that load of old tosh about MI7 being drafted in to help with police cuts for a moment."

Piers nodded his head in agreement.

"There's a lot of publicity about this festival you know," continued Bones. "And Swansea is in the news all the time these days. What with new university campuses, offshore lagoons, the brand new airport project and the new research into the lost treasure of Edward II. They report that sort of thing abroad as well as over here you know. I realise that this is not London but if Slope got to hear that we may be sleeping over the top of countless millions in gold then he might well direct his feet to the sunny side of the street."

"Bonesie you are a 21 carat twat. I'd just about consigned that nightmare to the further recesses of my mind and there you go raking it all up again. Fat chance of me getting any sleep tonight. Look I'll talk to Cornelius. If there's even half a chance that Slope is anywhere around then he'll know. In the meanwhile please do not mention the bastard's name in polite company. Least said soonest forgotten and all that. I'm off down to the beach for a stroll. You coming?"

"OK Piers. Just one though. I've heard they've brewed a fine pint of stout at the microbrewery down at the Crippled Cabbage. Apparently they've found a way of adding essence of oyster to the mash. What a conundrum. Beer to make the old gentleman lie down and oysters to make him wake up and misbehave. You have to love this country!"

"Stroll first then perhaps a pint or two to lubricate the little grey cells. The few that are left that is." A bracing six mile circular walk during which the two old friends spoke barely a word to one another brought them back to the back door of the Crippled Cabbage. The outside tables were empty although inside the bar was rammed. "If it's OK with you Piers I think I'd prefer to sit here rather than join that scrum."

"That'll be two pints of Oyster Catcher then Bonesie. Your round next."

Prideaux pushed his way into the crowd at the bar. He was known to quite a few of the locals through his involvement with the food and wine festival. He nodded to several acquaintances as he snaked his way to the bar to order two pints of the latest locally brewed beer. It was pointless trying to talk to anyone as the decibel level had passed lethal some time ago. He handed over the cash and gradually managed to ease his way through the crowds and into the blessed peace of the pub garden. Carefully balancing the pints he negotiated the step down into the garden looking up towards the table where Bones had decided to sit. Bones wasn't there. A figure lay on the grass near the table where he had left Bones. There was someone bending over him. With the respect of the hardened drinker Prideaux placed both glasses on the low garden wall before running across the lawn yelling at a sound level that would have made him heard even to those within the nosy bar. He was a metre off the figure and without a clue of what to do next when the man turned his head.

"Shut the fuck up Prideaux. I'm doing my best to revive your oppo here."

"Cornelius. What the hell are you doing here? I thought you had returned to London."

"Bloody good job I'm not then otherwise Bones here would have joined the other heavenly boozers at The Gates of Heaven pub where they wait to be judged before being sent off to the other place. I've managed to get a pulse and there's an air ambulance on the way. He'll probably be OK."

Prideaux resembled a startled plover. He opened and closed his mouth. Sounds came out, none of them making any sense. The clatter of an approaching helicopter brought him to his senses as the pilot expertly hovered as he found a clear place to land in the pub garden. By now the entire complement of topers was watching through the bar window. For once the racket outside outweighed the usual cacophony coming from the bar. As the air ambulance touched down the doors flew open two paramedics hit the ground running and were on their knees either side of the prone figure of Bones. Prideaux picked himself up from where he had been bundled to the ground and out of the way by one of the burly paramedics who had no time for the niceties. "We'll take over now," he shouted as the two men did exactly that.

Prideaux looked at his old friend as they worked to stabilise his condition. Despite the confidence they exuded Bones looked in a really bad way. He looked as if he had been drained of blood. He looked more like a shop floor mannequin than the third Earl of Mount Charles. In brief minutes he was loaded onto a stretcher and was about to become airborne cargo.

"Hang on. I'll come with you," he shouted his words drowned out by the whine of the rotor. "He's my pal. I'm not letting him go on his own."

"I'm afraid you are Piers. He's in good hands and will shortly be receiving the best medical attention possible. He will be in a private ward I have already authorised. You will come with me and you will listen to what I have to tell you. None of your Oxford arguments."

Despite the authority in his voice Cornelius put his arm around Prideaux's shoulder leading him gently away from the helicopter that was rapidly building to take off mode. Prideaux allowed himself to be led to a quiet corner. Only then did he remember he was terrified of flying, especially in helicopters. Still if Bonesie didn't die in the helicopter the thing would probably crash anyway. Stupid means of transport. No back up plan at all. If the rotor went then it was curtains. Not for nothing had he been president of the Cynics' Society when at Oxford. Still Bonesie was his best friend and he needed to know what had happened.

"Come on then Cornelius. What was it? Heart attack, stroke or did he swallow a massive choking wasp? And what are you doing here? You never frequent this place. Far too low level for you. You are more likely to be found in one of your poncey wine bars than a good old fashioned pub. I can't believe you are here by accident. Far too much of a coincidence. Come on what the hell is going on and why is my best friend at death's door in a death trap flying over Swansea Bay? I think I have a right to know."

"How about thanks for saving my friend's life, Cornelius? Because that is what I have just done. But you are right I would not normally mix with your assorted working chums in this den of antiquity. Talk of hip transplants, dementia and hearing aids isn't really my glass of claret. As it happens I was looking for you and Bones. The news is not good. Don't look at me like that. I don't mean he's going to die. I mean that he wasn't laid low by any natural event. He's lucky. I drove down and just happened to have a fully charged defibrillator in the boot of my car. Did enough to get him back and stabilise him before the cavalry arrived. Never go anywhere without it. Departmental policy although I'm the only one who abides by it. Lucky for you and him that I do."

"Well it must have been something."

"Of course it was something. That something was the Canadian. He doesn't usually fail. Bones was very fortunate. The Canadian has a 98% kill rate when he takes on a job. If I hadn't been here then it would have been curtains. I suppose I should give some credit to those two lunatics you count amongst your circle. The Job twins were with me. We got here just too late to stop the bastard. He must have followed you here. We managed to scare him off before he finished the job. The twins chased him but he got away. Pity really. I'd love to have seen the twins take on that monster. In fact I'd pay good money to see it."

"What are you on about Cornelius? Who the hell is the Canadian and why would he want to harm Bonesie? He may be a pisshead but surely that's no reason to try and kill him. If that was the case there wouldn't be an MP left alive."

"The Canadian, my forgetful friend, is one of the best killers to have ever joined the AF. After that bastard Slope arranged the murder of Lola I wanted him dead. First I wanted him to suffer. He doesn't give a shit for any living creature so I knew I couldn't hurt him there. He does care a hell of a lot for the good living that a lot of money can provide. So I used my insider knowledge to drain his multifarious bank accounts. That left him short of cash. Unfortunately, I didn't count on him declaring open season on me and by association you two and the Job twins. Clearly the Canadian decided to take the job on. I have it on good advice he has also taken on the job of disposing of Slope. Playing both sides of the street. Quite how he thinks he's to be paid his bounty is beyond me. I mean if he kills me, my associates, you reprobates and Slope, whoever the hell is left to cough up any money? These AF fellows are a pretty crazy bunch. And I wouldn't mind betting there are others in the fellowship preparing to chance their arms."

"I bloody knew it. Whenever you appear hell is never far behind. What did that bastard do to Bonesie?"

"An attempted garrotting Piers. His preferred method of despatch as it happens. Bit mediaeval really but he doesn't usually make a mess of things. And I don't know why you're blaming me for everything. If I hadn't intervened Bones would be no longer with us."

"Well you're the expert Cornelius. What do we do now?"

"You can cut the sarcasm Piers. I was about to suggest that the Canadian's presence in these parts and his attempt on Bones's life may not be the end of it."

"I know that you twat. You put a price on Slope's head He always said he'd get both of us and the twins. And if memory serves he's not best pleased with you either…." Prideaux paused as he realised what Cornelius was getting to.

"It's as plain as a pikestaff Piers. The Canadian and God knows how many other professional killers are on Slope's trail. Slope, is pretty certain to be on our trail as he has a massive score to settle with me and by association you and all your chums. It's a pretty pickle when you look at it like that."

"Probably the understatement of the last three centuries. I still don't understand why the Canadian should try to see off Bonesie. He's pretty harmless."

"It's not obvious to me either Piers, but who can read the mind of a professional assassin. He is not a conviction killer. If the reward is great enough he'll kill anyone. I shouldn't be surprised if he tried to knock over Bones just for the fun of it. They're not like us you know."

"They're not like me I know that for certain. I'm not sure that they're not like you Cornelius my old fruit pie. Anyway the best idea is for us to get back to the castle. I'm not sure I'll feel safe anywhere now but at least there are some great big locks and bloody thick doors we can cower behind."

"Stiff upper lip Prideaux. Things may look bleak but we've got some good men on our side. You won't be abandoned and we will lay this ghost to rest for good. The Canadian might even do us a favour and take Slope out before we do. We're not exactly beginners at this lark, you know."

"You're not much bloody good at it either Cornelius. Still in the absence of anything better I suppose I'm stuck with you." The two men made their way back to the castle. Cornelius to contact his masters, and inform them of the Canadians appearance, Prideaux to contact the hospital on the priority number he had been given. His overriding thought was for the health of the best friend he had ever had.

15

THE SECRET UNDERGROUND

Three miles away from the castle that was now becoming the focus for the newly minted festival was the city of Swansea. The castle there had been the administrative base in Norman times. It had been rescued from decay in recent years and was now regarded as a tourist attraction. Its position in the centre of the city made it a favourite landmark for locals and visitors alike.

As darkness fell three figures approached the castle from the bottom end of Wind Street. Two of them were dressed in jeans and bomber jackets and did not look the sort you would wish to meet on a dark night in Swansea or anywhere else. They looked exactly what they were, killers. The man who walked slightly in front of the group was dressed in a suit and wore a Crombie overcoat topped off with a dark blue fedora. He walked with an obvious limp. Body language told that he was the man in charge. Slope was making an early reconnoitre of the castle that could just give him the edge he needed to beat the security cordon already tightening around the village those few miles to the west.

"Pick your feet up Gog and Magog. I have plenty to do and I don't want to waste all evening with you two dummies. I've an appointment with a lively young prostitute so let's get this over and done with."

The two men Slope referred to as Gog and Magog looked at each other. Neither could stand Slope but he paid well and promised much more. They had nothing else to do on this particular evening anyway. If Slope was true to his word this could be the job they had looked for all their lives. Their acquaintance with Slope was brief, the result of an interview at the Institute for Criminal Employment (ICE) near the marina. Run by a local gangster the institute kept a low profile but if you were of the criminal persuasion then they could be helpful in finding lucrative jobs for those with the necessary skills. Bert Crust and Ernie Moot had been petty criminals for years. They were both on the books of ICE as they searched for that big hit that would solve all their problems. They had answered Slope's advertisement at the ICE offices. Slope had not interviewed them as he was not the type to soil his hands with petty criminals. He had, after all headed what had been a virtual army when he was the Mr Rainbow of the Spriggans. Crust and Moot had been interviewed by an ex safe cracker who had subsequently become an employment guidance expert. At interview he tested the men on their competence in mindless thuggery before contacting Slope to say he had his men.

Swanning in to the office Slope read the report and nodded, "you'll do," to the men as they sat in the waiting room. "I'm afraid gentlemen, you'll have to do. Stick with me and I'll make you rich, cross me and I'll cut your throats before you can say knife. Understood?" The men nodded. Their adviser had outlined what their duties would be but was unable to tell them what the job was. Money was money to them and if they could indulge in some light violence along the way then that would be all to the good.

"Come on then. Follow me you likely lads. Get a bloody move on."

Crust and Moot followed Slope to the lift. They'd have preferred the stairs and there was something about their new employer that unsettled them. The lift arrived after what seemed like an ice age. Neither thug took to whistling but it was a close run thing. As the lift door opened Slope stood back indicating that the men should step into the lift. Bert Crust stepped into the lift closely followed by Ernie Moot. As Moot raised his right foot to step into the lift Slope pushed him heavily and unable to stop himself he cannoned into Crust. Both men fell heavily. Slope stepped in as the lift doors began closing. The men looked like the corner of the sales floor in Primark on a Saturday afternoon. Before the bundle of limbs and clothing could react Slope was holding a stiletto under the ear of each man.

"Now then my brave boys. Listen carefully, I am not given to repeating myself. I am employing you for your muscle power and callous disregard for human life. Both of you scored highly in your ICE aptitude tests. To me you are expendable. In fact if I chose I can send you spinning off into the void right now just for the sheer hell of it, but you could be useful so I shall postpone that pleasure. You will tell no one that you have met me and I shall contact you when I need your services. Understand?"

The men did their best to nod fearful that that the slim blade was a mere whisker away from the brain.

"I'll take that as a yes then." The lift doors opened and Slope was gone in seconds, two very rueful thugs regained their feet. Crust felt gingerly behind this ear. "The bastard's drawn blood. Look." He held out his hand to Moot who was engaged on the very same action.

"What do you think then Ernie? I've never met anyone like that. What did he say we had to call him?"

"Mr Rainbow or something, I think. But then he said that he was not Mr Rainbow. Of course he could be some sort of nutter. Bloody sounded like it anyway. He's not from around here, that's for sure. What's with the outfit? It's a bit Mafia like isn't it? None of those around these parts, though we aren't short of Italians."

"The thing is that he said he'd contact us. He might never do that. Best to just carry on and see what happens if he ever does get in touch. Plenty of opportunities for skilled lads like us to keep us going like."

"You're right Bert. Best lie low for a bit then get back to what we do best." The two men left the building in search of a quiet backstreet pub. They had made a pact to never talk of this experience just to be on the safe side. Normal life continued and they received no contact from the madman who for the immediate future was their employer. The memory of the experience in the lift had begun to fade for both men.

It was early evening in The Lugger. Crust and Moot sat at the bar staring down the blouse of the busty waitress who was the newest addition to this rundown pub. It had seen better days, so had its customers. Its saving grace was that the booze was cheap and the landlord was a good source of information of where the latest opportunities for casual criminals lay.

"Hey Ernie. I don't want to worry you but I've just seen a blue fedora walking past the front window." He nodded in the direction of the window that looked out onto the boats moored in the marina.

"I can't see anything," muttered Crust, tearing his eyes away from the barmaid's decoupage. "You must be getting old. You should have gone to Specsavers you tired twat."

The men thought no more of it and both returned to their new favourite occupation of ogling the barmaid's breasts. This pleasurable activity lasted only seconds as both men jerked to attention on their bar stools.

A low voice whispered in the left ear of Bert Crust, "I told you I'd be in touch when I needed your services. This is me getting in touch. Meet me outside in five minutes. Tell nobody and if you are followed then you will feel the force of my irritation. Now tell your little friend. Do not turn around. You will get your instructions once you have left this place.

Gog and Magog did exactly as they were told and ten minutes later all three men were walking up Wind Street towards the castle.

Recent works were evident in and around the castle. There was some fencing around the area mostly to deter vandals but it was the work of a moment for the three men to slip through a gap and into the shadows of the Great Hall.

At the far end of the Great Hall was an opening from where a spiral staircase led down to a large chamber. The lower the men got the darker it became.

"Here. Take a torch each and watch your steps. This staircase goes down a hell of a way and if either of you falls then you are on your own." Slope was demonstrating his usual concern for his employees. Health and Safety to him was nothing but a joke. With three powerful torches in operation the chamber was well illuminated. Walking through the chamber the torches alighted on a rusty old gate with an old fashioned padlock in place. At the side of the gate a crow bar had been left in place by one of Slope's men working with the construction company.

"Grab that bar Gog and smash the lock. I have a copy of an old document here that will give you an idea of the way the tunnel behind the gate runs. There should be enough light from the torches I gave you for you to do a recce." Crust picked up the crowbar and did as he had been told. Smashing the lock was relatively easy, opening a centuries old iron gate was not. Much heaving and cursing later the gate creaked open wide enough to allow Slope's employees to squeeze through.

"Right, off you go, quick as you can. I don't want to stand around here all night. What I need from you two is an idea of how far the tunnel runs and how negotiable it is. You don't need to know any more than that. I know what I hope you will find but the document is not that clear." The two men set off on their quest to find the course of the tunnel.

"I'm not happy about this," moaned Crust as he and Moot trudged along the tunnel flashing their torches randomly. Underfoot the stone floor was uneven and a broken ankle was a real threat. "Clever bastards those Normans Crusty," said Moot. "Look at the quality of this stonework. Goes back to the 14th century and it still looks bloody strong."

"You'd better hope that it is" Moot answered as he did his best to ignore all the horrible possibilities that were crowding in on him. They walked warily but quickly hoping to get the job over with as soon as possible.

"You don't think it goes all the way to Oystermouth, do you Moot? They were buggers for their tunnels those Normans. Perhaps they linked the castles. Although I heard that the Black Castle in Oystermouth is on top of about thirty metres of bedrock. That's why they couldn't undermine the walls."

"Thanks for that Crusty. Like bloody QI listening to you. You'd better hope we run into a rock fall before long then we can get back to him and report. Perhaps we can get back to the pub for last orders."

With this in mind the two quickened their steps until they came to a place where the tunnel took a very sharp turn to the right. They walked more slowly then as the stone floor felt more uneven. Around twenty metres later they came up against a wall. It was clearly built of brick and cut off the tunnel completely.

"Hey Crusty. I didn't know the Normans built in brick."

"Of course they didn't you prawn. That's old brick but not as old as all that. It's covered in dust, mould and what looks a lot like shit. And look there's some sort of metal plaque screwed to the wall. Clear off the dirt and shit so we can see what it says."

"Fuck off. I'm not touching it. It's probably rat shit. You know how many diseases those bastards drag around with them. I could get the plague doing that. You do it. You seem to be more interested in all this cack than me."

"Crusty, you clown you're about as much use as a chocolate condom," Moot opined as he took an ancient clasp knife from his back pocket. "Look, I'll scrape off some of the shit so we can read what's on the plaque. I bet it'll be something like, 'sod off you Welsh bastards', and signed Will de Breos the Third."

"Yeah I'm sure it will. Great sense of humour the Norman barons had. Just like one of them to come all the way down here for a joke. You just get scraping while I shine my torch so you can see what you are doing. Be sharp about it. The last thing we want to do is to wind that bastard Slope up."

"Keep the bloody torch still will you? I can't see a bloody thing with you waving it around like that."

"That's better. Well I'll be damned. It says SWANSEA UNDERGROUND STATION (sealed 1946)."

"Very funny Moot. You trying to tell me that Swansea had a tube system. A likely story. Now stop pissing about and tell me what it really says. We haven't got the time to prat about."

"I'm not joking Crusty. It looks like Swansea once had some sort of underground system. I wouldn't have believed it either. But what else can it be. Whatever it is it cuts the tunnel off. If Slope is thinking of getting all the way to Oystermouth under the ground well he's had that. I just don't fancy telling him though. He'll go bonkers."

"He'll go bonkers anyway if we don't get back there and let him know what we've found."

The men turned to retrace their journey. This time they hurried back as fast as they could in order to break the bad news to a man who would like as not shoot the messenger but the messenger's entire family, dog and canary included. A lovely example of being trapped between a rock and a hard place.

Slope was impatiently waiting for his two patsies. "Took you bloody long enough. I thought you might have found some sort of emergency exit and run off. You do, of course, know that I would have hunted you down and killed you most unpleasantly if you had tried such a thing. Well?"

The two men looked at each other and gabbled their answer. In a welter of terrified non sentences they managed to convey the basic fact that not only was there a brick wall blocking the tunnel but it looked as if there was an underground rail system directly behind it. The silence was palpable. Crusty turned away and vomited against the tunnel wall. Moot looked like the condemned man who wasn't a bit hungry. Slope's face creased as he let out a huge guffaw and laughed until the tears ran down his face. That rarest of things, a laughing Slope.

"I knew it. I knew I was right. Swansea did build an underground rail system. And it runs all the way to Oystermouth. To the quarry next to the castle to be precise. It is everything I wanted to hear and it completes plan A. What a pity for you two useless bastards that it means you both have to die. I could have some fun if I wasn't so busy. So this is for you Gog. Crust staggered backwards and fell as the bullet tore through his throat exiting through the back of his neck.

"Drag your dead friend through the gate and into the tunnel. There's a good boy Magog." Moot was rooted to the spot but knew there was no hope. His shoulders drooped as he dragged his late accomplice back into the tunnel they had both so recently vacated. He expected a bullet every second as he dragged the dead weight through the gate.

"By then Magog," Slope said still smiling as the next bullet caught Moot in the eye. My aim is definitely improving, he said to himself as he closed and locked the gate. "We'll sort that lot out tomorrow. For now I feel a celebration coming on."

There would be two empty barstools and one relieved busty barmaid in The Lugger that night.

16

THE ITALIAN CONNECTION

Zebedee was becoming concerned. Disturbing information was beginning to filter through the intelligence gathering system. Such heightened activity was usual when so much was wrong in the world. Syria and Iraq were in crisis. World War III looked to be tuning up centred on events in Ukraine. None of the Western powers seemed to have a clue how to tackle any of these nightmares. None of these fell under his direct jurisdiction but with the intelligence services at full stretch there was no possibility of drafting in extra bodies it meant that his operatives were under enormous pressure. A thorough analysis of the current situation did not serve to lift his unease. Under current arrangements his strength in the field comprised:

> Cornelius
> Bob Job
> Robert Job

It was not an encouraging list. Zebedee had no illusions at the paucity of his resources. He would need to strengthen them considerably to ensure that this was one trap Slope did not escape from. Intelligence sources confirmed he was now in Britain, possibly Wales. What resources he had gathered around him were hard to determine. As usual Slope had a tightly controlled agenda. Item one was to replenish his finances, item two was the final solution to the Prideaux/Bones problem. There was little indication as to how he intended to manage either eventuality. Because of the uncertainty around Slope there was no intention in Zebedee's mind of promoting his problems to the level of the current high security alert that held most of Europe in thrall. MI7 just needed Slope to come to them and trigger the trap.

After the exposure and disposal of Gabriel Zebedee had retaken command of the group within MI7. This meant dealing directly with agents in the field through Cornelius. Best guess as to Slope's intentions revolved around something that was probably mere legend anyway. Although Cornelius had frequently dropped hints suggesting that there was some truth in the legend. If Slope really intended to infiltrate the castle in search of the legendary millions as well as his stolen fortune then it should be relatively easy to deal with.

It was Bones who had originally propounded the theory to Prideaux. Bones claimed kinship with the original lords of Gower and gave some substance to the legend of the King's millions as a story that had been told in families and passed down through the ages. If it were true then resources would need to be focused on the Black Castle until more solid intelligence surfaced. Cornelius was the man on the spot and since he was no longer dead then it would be up to him to organise a disparate group of characters. He knew where the buck would end up if it all went pear-shaped but in the circumstances he had little choice. If harder information surfaced then he would have to flood the village and the castle with lower level operatives and hope for the best. Hardly meticulous planning but the bastard Slope was a slippery customer at the best of times.

The slippery customer currently ensuring Zebedee's sleepless nights sat on the balcony of his tenth floor apartment and watched the tide roll in on Swansea Bay. He was aware that the enemy suspected he was in the area but had been careful to ensure that he had not been spotted. On the principle of hiding in plain sight he simply went about his business. He even wore his trademark blue fedora but favoured the part of the city which was among the less salubrious. He ate in his apartment where he spent most of his time studying the documents he had copied from the research library in Oystermouth. There nobody gave him a second glance as he ploughed through the 14th century documents covering all aspects of the local castle. He had registered under the name of Obadiah Seed and produced the documentation to prove it. Slope was hot on the trail of the truth about what happened in those dark November days in when Edward II made his desperate run for safety in Wales.

A recovered and newly discharged Bones and a happy Prideaux were on the trail of their favourite Italian restaurant 'Fasta Pasta' near the harbour. The weather was dry though the wind off the sea was beginning to pick up. It was not a day for hats. This was a fascinating stretch of the coast and abounded with quality restaurants as well as the kiss me quick fare that all seaside villages provided.

"I don't know whether you've noticed Piers but there seems to be an awful lot of Italians in the village.

"No surprise there Bonesie. Italians have been settling in Wales for generations. Nothing new in that."

"I know that. That's not what I meant. I have a vague memory of you telling me that most Italians in the catering business came from northern Italy. Some place or other called Bardi if I remember correctly."

"You do remember correctly old chum. My grandfather used to tell me that lots of Italians came over way back and settled all over Wales. Quite a number of them came from Bardi."

"It's just that I notice that quite a lot of the dishes on offer around here seem to come from the south. You know turnip tops and that sort of trade. Now I yield to nobody in my love of Italian food but I also know that there are huge regional differences. So why, I ask, are there so many that offer dishes from the south rather than what you would expect. Law of averages and all that?"

"Never given it a thought really but clearly it is occupying that sock drawer that you call your mind. So come on. Let's have it."

"Well, just for fun let's try a what if… What if Slope is in this area? Presumably somewhere under cover and is planning some form of atrocity. Isn't it just possible that he might have imported some of his associates from the Olive Pickers? Rather a good trick is it not? They would blend in a treat. Nobody would think anything of Italians in Wales. They have been here for generations so they wouldn't arouse suspicion. Bloody clever I call it."

"Trust you to find something else to worry about. I would have thought your brush with the deadly Canadian enough to worry about. Surely somebody would have twigged if Slope was really over here. You and I both know that Cornelius being in the area was not about ice cream. I don't buy his story about policing the festival either. If Cornelius is here especially with the twins in tow they must know that Slope is around too. All we knew when we were over in Puglia is that we flushed the bastard out and he's mixed up with some Olive Pickers and untold nefarious activities. The fact we've heard nothing since would indicate he's eluded our cack handed security services, yet again," groaned Piers.

"Apparently he took off from Puglia in a light aeroplane. Nobody seems to know where it was heading. That's what I hear from Cornelius. He paid me a visit in hospital, bloody life-saver even smuggled in my favourite malt to keep me going, priceless. I'll always remember that." Bones starred meaningfully at Piers.

"The matron gave me strict instructions not to bring in any unsavoury foods or liquor. Hell's Bells you were at deaths door. I had your welfare at heart old chum, nil by mouth and all that," lamented Piers.

"You wound me sorely Piers," said Bones, "Cornelius is a little baffled by the whole Slope issue. They have him recorded as flying off to whereabouts unknown. But strangely they also have a satellite capturing his every movement in Italy. They also have plenty of witnesses who reckon that they have seen him out and about in Puglia. I can't see how even that tricksy bastard can be in two places at the same time."

"Well Bones I reckon that where Slope is concerned anything is possible. I'm inclined to see if we can have a chat with Cornelius and see what the latest is. Anyway I've lost my appetite all of a sudden. Let's get back to the castle. I can feel the grim reaper breathing down the back of my neck all of a sudden."

Three hours later and replete after a hearty repast the two sat in the castle kitchens waiting for the promised arrival of Cornelius.

Between them on the oak refectory table was a half empty bottle of Hermitage Blanc, Domaine Jean-Louis Chave.

"I say Piers, this 2009 is a remarkable vintage. We must get some for our cellar when we get back to The Hand of God. What thinkest thou old chap?"

"What I thinkest old chap is that you are gradually getting pissed on a wine that costs around £200 a bottle. Cornelius is likely to be extremely dischuffed when he rocks up to hear you singing See the little piskey or some such ditty."

"See your point you old bludger. Sounds a bit like his size twelves coming down the corridor at the moment doesn't it?"

The kitchen door swung open and Cornelius walked in. He had dark circles under his eyes and looked dead beat.

"Bloody hell Cornelius. You look a lot worse than I do. I'd say that you looked like death warmed up if I weren't such a sensitive soul. But I wouldn't start watching any serials on the old idiot box if I were you."

"Thanks for your touching concern Bonesie you have spotted that I am having very little sleep these days and that is hardly surprising. Now what, exactly, do you two lollygaggers want? I gather you would like to talk to me. Make it quick; I am a busy little bee."

"It's just a theory," began Bones.

"I'll stop you there Bonesie. Your theories are generally as mad as wasps. I'm not sure that there is any room in my mind to entertain yet another ghost story from you."

Piers intervened before a bout of name calling took place possibly descending into a full scale argument. "It's nothing like that Cornelius. Bonesie was just concerned that Slope might be in the area. If that is the case then I think we all have a right to know. You know how that bastard feels about us and that you left us well in the lurch by nicking his money. Least you owe us is to tell us whether we are about to be horribly murdered."

"OK. You're right. I've just been talking to Zebedee on the closed network. He is sure that Slope is in this part of the world. His intelligence suggests that Slope has also arranged for some of those blasted Olive Pickers to follow him over. Our speculation is that they must have some specialised skill that he needs and can't recruit over here.

"Doesn't take a genius to work that out," was Bones's reply. "Probably just as well because we don't have many of those knocking about. Government cuts again I suppose."

"Bonesie if you are merely going to be rude I can have you slapped in irons you know. It is not as if we are short of dungeons in this place after all. More dungeons than you can shake a manacle at in fact. OK, it's cards on the table time. This is the truth as far as I'm able to divulge. As you know I have personally relieved Slope of his millions. Because I have contacts I have had the lot turned into gold ingots which I have had hidden within the Black Castle. We're sure that Slope is already after the 15th century treasure reported to be hidden here. The plan has been to entice him in and spring the trap. It seemed a sensible plan at the time. Nobody was counting on the level of coalition cuts and the fact that we are having to cover for the decimation of the police forces of the country. It's not looking so clever now. Add in a veritable army of Olive Pickers and it looks as if we will be outmanned and outgunned. It will be bad enough if the bastard Slope is able to get away with recovering the bullion that now represents his fortune. If he also manages to acquire Edward's treasure to boot then he will have the wherewithal to finance God knows what sort of mayhem. There's one final problem that outranks the previous two. There are almost certainly original documents together with the royal hoard that could jeopardise the Windsor entitlement to the throne. Now if you let that particular problem out of the bag then I shall be obliged to have you killed. One more thing, you or Prideaux mention government cuts one more time and I'll kick you both from here to Margam along the drovers' road even if the bloody tide is in."

"OK. Keep your trousers on there's a good tadpole. Look or perhaps listen. The last thing we know about Slope is that he was involved with those murderous Olive Pickers. Now apart from occasionally slicing people up, what else were they doing? Well, I'll tell you. They were running some sort of bonkers scam shipping mature olive trees around the coast and up to northern Italy. That should tell you that they must have had some sort of expertise in sea going activities. Simple."

"That may well be the case. But there are plenty of people around here with that sort of expertise. Why not use them?"

"That's bloody obvious. They are not members of an organised crime set up that can give the Mafia a run for its money. And anyway Slope is and has been a leading figure. He's accepted by them."

"Again," said Bones with just the right cutting edge of sarcasm, "I have a theory that fits the case. He knows that you stole his money and probably knows by now that you are back from beyond the grave. He will therefore be after you. You dropped us right in the shit ergo he will be after us."

"That much is bloody obvious, Bonesie. It's hardly rocket surgery, now is it?"

"You are a snarky little badger Cornelius. Why don't you listen for a change? I'll make it easy for you. Three targets in one place. Too tempting for a start. If he is not already holed up around here somewhere the he is on his way here. Secondly there are more southern Italians in the village than usual. The Olive Pickers are based in Puglia so it is not much of a jump to believe they might have followed Slope over here. And finally we are currently sitting in a castle which for hundreds of years has been believed to be the last resting place of a king's ransom. I rest my case." Bones mimed the act of putting down a heavy case as he glowered at Cornelius.

"That's all fine and dandy but how on earth is he to do anything about it. This place is better protected than when the bloody Normans ran the place. Nobody gets in or out without identification. The place is tighter than a budgie's chuff."

Before Bonesie could say a word Prideaux jumped in to interrupt, "not now Bonesie. Let me have a go. Look Cornelius I accept what you are saying but you must know that Slope is not the type to give up on anything. What we need to do is come up with some idea of how we can magic up another plan now that yours is unravelling faster than a toilet roll tied to a dog's tail."

"We're already on that Piers. We are trying to be discreet about it. The last thing we want to do is warn them off. We need to nail this bastard once and for all.

"But you're right. Not thinking straight at the moment. Too much pressure. It's probably time I packed it all in. This will be the last of it. I want to leave under my own steam though before it's too late. I'll organise a meeting in the morning and we'll rough out a general approach. In the meantime it's probably best if we all keep a low profile."

"At last. Her Majesty's servants grind small and they grind exceedingly slowly but thank God they get there in the end. Now let's finish off this delightful wine before taking ourselves off to our various bed chambers. If the ghost of the White Lady walks tonight then I'm afraid I shall tell her to jog on if she starts rattling my door knob. I'm in no mood for ethereal sex. I'd much prefer a nice cup of cocoa and a jolly good night's sleep."

"Comes to us all in the end Bonesie," grinned Prideaux. "And just to help you to toddle off swiftly to the Land of Nod let nobody forget that there is the little matter of the AF like hell hounds on our trail. At least the bastards are after Slope too."

"Thanks for that Piers," chorused Bones and Cornelius, "what a lovely note on which to end a lovely evening."

17

PROFESSOR GURNARD SPINK

Slope rose in good humour the day after executing two of his untrained monkeys. Such is the way that he regarded those who worked for him once they had fulfilled their purpose. No loss to anyone, Crust and Moot were petty criminals who had taken his plan one step further along the road.

An old man who had the misfortune of meeting Slope in the Inn with No Name had started the ball rolling. An unfrocked solicitor and one time university professor Gurnard Spink was one of those inveterate conversation starters to be found in any pub or bar in the land. His fatal mistake was to assume that Sebastian Slope was the type of man keen to listen to his reminiscences of something that had dominated his life for so many years. Spink had spent most of his sixty years researching the story of the Swansea Underground Railway. Local folklore insisted that there was such a construction though prevailing opinion held that it had been destroyed many years past. Research had convinced him otherwise and despite his diligence he was not taken seriously however hard he tried to persuade anyone who would listen.

Slope was prepared to ignore the wreck of a man who sat right next to him in the cellar bar of one of the oldest taverns in Swansea. It was clear that he had fallen on hard times. He dressed in the clothes that charity shops put out for the bin men to collect. He was unshaven, stooped and had only one tooth in the centre of his upper jaw. It made him look like a goofy rodent. He was not a pretty sight. He was however keenly attuned to anyone who had not been subjected at length to his theories about the underground railway and its route.

"You're not from round here, are you?" The question was aimed at Slope as the old professor sat down far too close to him for comfort, and if he only knew it far too close for safety. "Take a look at this. From an old Waitrose carrier bag he pulled out a sheaf of stained and torn papers. "This is my research. I'd like to tell you about it."

"And I'd like to tell you about your imminent death which approaches closer by every second you inflict your loathsome stench on me. Now fuck off while you still can."

"Miserable bastard," was the reply. "Just thought you'd like to know that we once had an underground railway here that could have been better than that one in London, if only the money hadn't run out. Still could be if they got their act together…"

The words tailed off as he nursed the single Scotch an old acquaintance had bought him to ensure he went away to bother someone else. Slope's antennae were suddenly on full alert. He looked like a defeated old fool, ripe for the culling. But the mention of anything underground always caught Slope's attention. It would be too much to hope that the derelict knew whereof he spoke but there was just an outside chance.

"Listen to me you old goat. You have five minutes to convince me that you have anything of value to tell me. After that I suggest you remove yourself from my presence. I mean five minutes so do not give me a résumé of your life or I'll be forced to show you exactly where that life will end."

Spink was not one to miss the opportunity and in his deluded and clouded mind he was convinced he could make his case to this sharply dressed and obviously intelligent stranger.

"Look I've made a drawing of the original line. There's a map too. The only thing is that nobody has ever found the entrance to the railway. It's something to do with the rerouting of the river which changed everything in the city. But there are too many references to the whole thing for it not to have been built and to still be there. It's probably one of those mothballed projects that are in every city. That doesn't mean that the project couldn't be resurrected though. It was never intended as a passenger railway anyway. Just part of the industrial heritage." He turned to ensure that nobody could overhear him. Slope smiled at the theatrical gesture. His voice was only a fraction above a whisper anyway. It was all he could do to hear him in the first place.

"I'm pretty sure that this old document is the last piece in the jigsaw. It's only a scrap and pretty faded but it does show the area where the entrance was originally. Look."

A glance was enough to convince Slope that there was enough here to ensure that the old man would speak to nobody else. He would need time to pore over the document and whatever else was in the bundle of papers.

"Tell you what," he said in what he thought his most reassuring voice, let's go somewhere a bit quieter and you can tell me all about it. I'll buy you a drink in one of the harbour bars and you can tell me all you know."

Spink was too far down the road of his life to have any idea of the danger he was in. The thought of a free drink or two was enough to energise him to scoop up the papers into his carrier bag and follow Slope as he swept out through the bar's back door.

"Come on man. Keep up; I have things to do even if you haven't." Spink scuttled along limping on festering feet as he did his best to keep up with the man who seemed to be a sort of saviour. They walked across the boulevard and passed through the old beach tunnel working their way around to the quietest part of the harbour.

"Hold up, hold up," he gasped. "This bag is heavy. I'm out of breath."

"You soon will be," Slope muttered under his breath. "Give me the bag, I'll carry it for you."

Slope stood at the harbour's edge as a grateful old soak reached up to hand over the bag. As he did so Slope slid the blade into his right hand. Grasping the bag in his left hand his right hand shot forward. Spink gave a world-weary sigh as the stiletto did its work and he slumped to the floor at the harbour's edge. "Ah well. Fair exchange is no robbery. You have given me a bag full of old documents; I have given you the gift of eternal peace." So saying he rolled the man over with his foot until he dropped into the harbour. "Give my regards to the fishes," he said as he walked away licking blood from the stiletto as he walked.

An old man would not be missed and Sebastian Slope was that step closer to his goal.

As the sun streamed through the window of his rented flat Slope sat at this desk to look again at the documents he had so effortlessly inherited from Gurnard Spink. He had spent hours in research since the evening he had fortuitously met Spink in the Inn with No Name. The old man's corpse must have been discovered by now. There had been no mention of it in the local press. Perhaps the body had caught on the tide and been washed out to sea. Either way it didn't matter.

The documents were a ragbag of interesting information and wild speculation. Their major use had been to confirm Slope's general idea of a line that went from somewhere near the castle to Oystermouth all entirely underground. That had led to his discovery of the entrance in the bowels of the castle and to the deaths of two of his dispensable henchmen. That discovery had led to the more important recognition of the fact that once there existed an underground line of some kind. The two men who had paid for their efforts with their lives had been instrumental in confirming where the line had been walled off. Their bodies had already been disposed of by men working for Slope. New properties where being erected hard by the castle and an early morning cement pour for the foundations conveniently swallowed up two disposables.

Slope was beginning to establish the type of network he had once over lorded as the man who was not Mr Rainbow. That time seemed an age ago to him and he found his latest project a stimulating one. The untold riches that had been his once would be his again. Then the world could stand up and take notice. The flamboyant gene that was in Slope was looking for recognition. Once his fortune was assured he would go about cultivating the sort of people he yearned to be with. He wanted to associate with bankers, with lawyers, with academics, with media moguls. In short anyone who came near to him in terms of intellect. There was only one other quality such people needed and that was ruthless criminality of instinct. With such people he could move mountains and destroy nations.

For now his mind needed to focus on establishing exactly what was behind the wall that Crust and Moot had discovered when exploring the Norman tunnel in the centre of the city. Instead of being a chore the work involved took Slope back to his early days in the academic world. Research pleased him and he was good at it. The rewards of getting this right would be markedly greater than a degree or PhD award and that cried out to his materialistic drive.

In Puglia the only woman Slope had ever made any connection with was becoming jaded. It had taken Elizabeth Bennett a long time to get over being ordered to stay in Italy by Slope. She was envious of his latest involvement and wanted to be party to it. His double who had initially proved exciting, if nothing else for his flexibility had none of the imagination or basic cruelty of Slope. His pain threshold was far too low for her satisfaction. He would begin to scream well before she was anywhere near to orgasm in one of her regular sessions. Then he would crawl off to his room and stay there moaning for hours. It was beginning to annoy her and she was looking for an out. It was long weeks since she had killed anyone and the urge was beginning to surface too strongly to control. Something would need to be done before she exploded.

Following Slope to Britain was not an option. She knew roughly where Slope was but turning up unannounced could lead to one of his famous rages and likely death. She needed a plan that would place her back at the heart of things, something she liked best of all. Unless… what if she could get word to Slope that his double was a sleeper and she had caught him passing information to the Italian intelligence services? That might just work. To bring it off she would need to contact one of the Italian agents who frequented the bars of Ostuni.

Early evening found Bennett in a small bar in the labyrinthine back streets of the white city. Soft rain was falling. Bennett sat just inside the door of a bar well off the tourist trail. It was busy but not noisy. Bennett had her eye on a tall Italian who sat at the bar. Occasionally he would turn to look at her. She would pretend not to notice. He was drinking Moretti. At last he walked over and sat down at her table.

"Do you speak Italian," he began in a goofy sort of way.

"Not as such," she replied, stifling a giggle. "If this idiot is an agent then it will be easier than I imagined," she thought to herself. "This is no sort of challenge at all. Still what's the worst that can happen? I can always kill the stupid bastard if he bores me. It'll be up to him really."

Three drinks later and Bennett had total control of the Italian. She wondered why they employed such folk. Surely the point of an agent was that there was some sort of secrecy involved. This clown thought that his status as an agent would give him the right to ferret about in her knickers on the strength of a couple of bottles of Moretti. The tricky bit would be to plant the information that would inevitably lead to the death of Slope's double. The Italians were fairly liberal but were becoming increasingly pissed off with various Intelligence services using Italy as a playground. They had enough problems dealing with their home-grown organisations without people like Slope getting involved.

That was the gist of the message Bennett managed to convey to Mario Rossi before he ended up face down in the beer spilt all over their table.

She had run out of patience with the arrogance of the man. Slipping a mickey into his drink was the work of a second. He would have one hell of a headache when he eventually came round. He would, however, retain enough of the information she had passed to him to ensure that the Italians would carry out a full investigation. She had sealed Nerval's fate and Slope would hear about it soon enough from the contacts he retained among the Olive Pickers.

Bennett left the bar without a backward look. Slope would be in touch sooner rather than later. Slope never admitted need in any of its forms but if he thought things in Italy were crumbling then he would appreciate the value of Bennett's presence. He was at least predictable in that way. Having someone capable of murder without a second thought could only strengthen his hand in his latest scheme. Whether Bennett would appreciate the extent of Slope's Welsh adventure was a moot point. However, life had begun to pall in Puglia. Life with Slope was as dangerous as hell but it could be described as boring by nobody. She needed the rush. It was the only reason for being alive.

18

A DEADLY NUN

Blissfully unaware of the presence of Slope a bare few miles from the castle and without an idea of the scope of his plan Bones and Prideaux continued to help with the planning for the Oyster Festival. The Great Hall of the castle was to host a festival feast for the great and the good of the area. Williams had been persuaded to leave the castle for the build up to the festival. He happily accepted the offer of accommodation at The Hand of God. He did not like crowds at the best of times and the indications were that the planned festival would attract thousands to the small village. His absence was exactly the key to galvanise Bones into some form of action. Bones had been strangely absent-minded in recent weeks. Something was eating away and distracting him to such an extent that he was close to becoming a liability. Piers suspected his brush with death at the hands of the Canadian had unhinged him. Attempts to get him to focus had failed and Prideaux was becoming lost as to what to do. Even a trip to the newly opened Ale House in the village had failed to do the trick. This was a Bones that Prideaux had rarely experienced and it was becoming a real concern. The departure of Williams changed that overnight.

"I couldn't take to that bugger at all Piers. Don't know what it was he just made me uneasy. I'm glad he's gone. Gives us a free rein now. I shall apply the old Bones intellect to advising these sea jockeys just how to run a food and wine festival. Absolutely tickety-boo and a half. We'll search for buried treasure once we've whipped this lot into shape. Get it right and it won't do the old Hand of God any harm either. Best publicity we could get really."

The return of Bones to midseason form energised the old partnership as the pair applied themselves to showing the village in its best possible light. Wine was Bones's passion and his contacts were legion. He was able to source wines no one else had even heard of. He had used his and Marco's contacts to import a large quantity of the legendary black wine of Puglia. This wine was generally regarded as the preserve of connoisseurs. Some judicious bargaining had meant that the wine could be made affordable to the general public. It was, in wine terms, a major coup and produced a very smug Bones.

Prideaux was far too busy arranging the entertainment to allow himself to be irritated by Bones's nuclear smugness. He had called in favours from his artistic contacts to construct a stellar literary festival to wrap around the feast arranged for the castle green. He had managed something of a coup himself. The village was closely associated with local poet Dylan Thomas. The previous year had seen a plethora of events associated with the internationally famous writer in a year-long celebration.

Following that successfully would be a hard thing to achieve. Prideaux was convinced that he had hit the target with the invitation to the poet Silas Whinberry also known as the hermit poet. Whinberry lived on Gower in an old army tent and was seldom seen in public. He had been a successful poet in the eighties but disillusioned with the way the world was turning had removed himself from the public gaze to write his magnum opus. His manager Toby Grasper kept Whinberry in the public consciousness with judicious reissues of some of his most important poetry collections. Works such as 'All the people I have Ever Hated', 'Reflections in an Ice Cream Dream', and 'The Lonesome Death of Benny's Hat," sold steadily if not spectacularly. It certainly kept Grasper in cigars and the originator of the works in roll ups. Grasper was aware that Whinberry had rejected materialism but the agent had certainly not. Coupled with regular releases of recordings of readings of his most popular poems Grasper was doing very nicely. He occasionally visited Whinberry in his tent mainly to check he was still alive. He was ambivalent about this as a dead Whinberry would almost certainly add to the myth and the income. Grasper had long ago sewn up the legal situation governing royalties to his own advantage. Poets after all were rarely the most worldly of individuals. This particular poet was noted for his truculence and it had taken Prideaux many hours of persuasion before he agreed to headline the literary section of the festival. The festival was beginning to take shape.

Bennett had managed her return to Britain and was already on her way to meeting with Slope again. Her return had been without incident. Though not an adherent of the shoemaker's son, later magician Eliphas Levi she certainly adopted his advice on hiding in plain sight.

As she and Slope knew mimicking one's gait to that of the very old was an almost guarantee of anonymity. As a result her return to Britain went without a hitch. Her search for Slope was less straightforward. She had some hesitancy in any case as Slope was not predictable. He might be pleased to see her equally he could just as easily commit her to a watery grave. Perhaps it was the unknowing that attracted her. For now she sat on the Paddington train with a ticket that would lead her to Swansea. It was a reasonable bet as something certainly was stirring there. Taking few chances she had disguised herself as a nun. Staring out of the window as the train raced through the Welsh countryside Bennett gradually became aware of three dog-faced boys two seats in front of her on the other side of the aisle. All three were wearing tracksuits topped off with black baseball caps. They looked feral. They looked dangerous. They would have been dangerous but this was not their lucky day. She did her best to ignore them until it became clear that she was the focus of their attention. The three kneeled on their seat and stared at what they believed to be an elderly nun.

"Oi! Sister. Is that right what they say about you lot doing press-ups in the cucumber patch?"

The largest of the three youths made some sort of twisted sex face as he turned to look at his giggling companions. He was clearly the leader of this little band of losers. The other two giggled on cue as he continued with what he clearly felt to be wit and repartee.

"I've never shagged a nun. Even an old nun. How about it sister? Only me and my boys here. I won't tell your mother superior if you don't. Just being polite in asking like."

Bennett was conflicted. She could do without drawing attention to herself. But if these pathetic excuses for humans approached her she knew exactly how things would play out. Perhaps it would be best to move carriages. On the other hand the pleasure of watching the morons now gurning at her suffer in extreme ways could be very enjoyable. Good sense prevailed and she left her seat to move to the following carriage. Through the glass she could see that it was fairly busy. This would be the sensible option. She moved surprisingly quickly for an elderly nun and was through the door before the youths could respond. She settled comfortably into a seat near the centre of the carriage. That should be the end of the matter she thought to herself.

There was no sign of the youths. They must have gone off after someone else. Something niggled at her though. Bennett was not one to cut and run. She was one to cut though and her blood was up. If the opportunity presented itself she would ensure that the three would never bother anyone again. For now it looked as if it was over and she began to relax. Bennett had many secrets. One of these was her ability to appear completely relaxed whilst remaining fully alert. It was a very useful skill for a part time psychopath who was also a card carrying nymphomaniac.

She was in that heightened state as the rain rattled its way towards Swansea High Street Station. As the train passed the Liberty Stadium Bennett slipped into the toilet. She swiftly replaced the nun's habit with a pair of jeans and a T-shirt emblazoned with the words, 'Every Hour Shortens Life.' Topped off with a leather biker jacket she bore little resemblance to the pious sister of mercy she had so recently been. It was a favourite of hers and although it might have drawn attention to her many of those who saw it never saw anything else. Bennett did not do mercy. It was not in her canon. Her righteous anger was mounting but still under the cold control of the accomplished killer. Those lads on the train had insulted her sense of self-worth. Pushing the now redundant habit through the train window she regained her seat as the train pulled into a rapidly darkening station. She would wait in the shadows before following them. It would be a distraction from her main purpose of tracking down Slope, but t would be an enjoyable one. The enfeebled, ageing nun was in effect now the righteous destroyer. At least that was how she rationalised what she was about to do.

Bennett shrank into the shadows as the three walked past her. They were too intent on tripping and jostling weary passengers to even notice her. Scum of the earth she thought to herself as she watched them clearly searching for their next victim. They resembled nothing more than Alex and his droogs from her favourite book, A Clockwork Orange. They had the same swagger. The same disregard for others. The same obvious attraction to mindless violence. They were her sort of people. What they didn't know is that they were the hunted not the hunters they imagined themselves. This was going to be fun.

Their attention was drawn to a tall blonde woman. She was expensively dressed and obviously in a hurry as she tottered out of the station on unfeasibly high heels. She headed for the taxi rank completely oblivious to the three young men who had adjusted their pace to stay in touch. It was a busy area so they were taking no chances. She had almost reached the sanctuary of the one available taxi when the three caught up with her. The leader moved in front of her while the other two moved to either side of her lifting her off her feet and rushing her down the nearby alley. The action was so swift and efficient that the woman had no time even to shout for help. The abduction was witnessed by no one except Bennett who licked her lips with anticipation. She followed the group down the alley.

The woman had been half carried half dragged deep into the alley which was not a salubrious place for anyone to end up. Bennett could hear her whimpers as she worked her way through the semi-darkness to where the group had stopped.

"Got a live one here, boys," shouted the one that Bennett assumed to be the leader. Sniggers followed from the others. The woman struggled but was unable to free herself.

"Ever thought of killing anyone? Only if we did kill her nobody would find out. I wonder what it would be like?" The leader of the droog-alikes was on the cusp of taking that step too far. The voice from the darkness put paid to the little tableau. It was recognisably female but deep and confident. "I could help you find out if you would like me to."

The sentence changed the atmosphere instantly. Confidence oozed from the three as the lieutenants looked to their leader for guidance. He was as confused as they were.

"Who the fuck are you?" He shouted into the darkness. The immediate reply caused him to loosen his grip on the intended victim.

"You might say that I'm the sister without mercy. Now be good little boys and let her go. I have some business to finish with you three. She is no part of this so I suggest you let her go now. I can help you understand what it's like to kill someone. There is a snag though. You three clowns will be doing the dying. You didn't expect that now did you?" As she emerged from the gloom Bennett did not immediately register as a threat.

"You have got to be joking. There you go Killer," he smiled at the smallest of the gang. "There's your chance. Go and shank that bitch. It'll be good practice for you. You can manage that, eh?"

"Course I can Johnny. I'll split the bitch right down the middle." Killer's voice betrayed the fact that he was in reality a coward but losing face was never an option in this nasty little gang so he walked towards Bennett with as much swagger as he could manage.

"I think I told you to let her go," Bennett repeated, fixing her eyes on the leader. It won't do you any good but I might kill you a bit quicker than this clown. But I wouldn't count on it."

"Who are you calling a clown?" Killer felt his dignity despite the fear that was beginning to take over.

"You Krusty. Who else? Now stop waving that knife about and be a man. I can see that's a lot to ask but I'm getting bored with you lot." It was more than Killer could take and he ran yelling at the place he was convinced Bennett was standing. He missed his target but felt an excruciating pain in his groin as he staggered and dropped to one knee.

"You will find that I have severed a major artery and that you will take a little while to bleed to death. I have two more likely lads to despatch to their own hell. If you are still alive when I finish with them I might just pop back and cut your throat. That should aid your journey to the promised land."

It was too much for Johnny and Gimp. They let their intended victim loose and ran for their lives further down the alley. This was their patch. The woman was mad. It was Killer's fault for not getting rid of her. They knew there was a high wall across some waste ground that they could climb. Once over it they would be in the labyrinth of their estate where there were a hundred hiding places. The alleyway was starting to lighten as they approached the last hundred yards before they hit the waste ground. Johnny saw it first. It was a figure wearing a long dark coat and fedora. He limped towards them. They slowed down as he approached both still glancing behind them though there was no sign that they were being chased.

"Hold on there lads. What's all the rush? Is there a problem?" The man was well spoken and seemed friendly. They poured out details of what they had just witnessed. In reply the man assured them that he was a doctor and that they ought to try and do what they could to save their friend. He spoke so reassuringly that they felt brave enough to follow him back up the alleyway. The man had a powerful torch he had taken from his Crombie pocket. In the light of the torch things did not seem so threatening. They had no difficulty in finding the place where they had left the third gang member. They simply followed the moans that had become weaker as they came closer. There was the woman standing in the pool of light emanating from the man's torch.

"Well, well. What a happy coincidence. Sebastian Slope. I must say I wasn't expecting to see you so soon."

"Hello Elizabeth. I am informed of all new arrivals that might be of interest by the station guard. I'm pleased to see you too. Seems that you have been frightening the natives. We must do something about that mustn't we?"

"I have missed you Sebastian. I hope you have an hour or so to spare."

The extent to which Slope and Bennett enjoyed themselves that particular evening can be found in the report by local newspaper journalist Anselm Briouze:

'Local resident Levi Samways ran into more than he bargained for when he took a popular short cut through an alleyway near Swansea's newly refurbished High Street Railway Station. Samways, a solicitor with a local practice had failed to get a taxi at the rank outside the station and given the unseasonably fine weather decided to take the short walk to his home in the east of the city. Mr Samways told our reporter that he saw nothing untoward until he was almost halfway down the shortcut known locally as Snatch Alley. What happened next is in Mr Samways's own words.

"I've used that alley as a short cut many times in the past. It is not a particularly salubrious place but enables me to get home much quicker than taking the long way around. Wednesday was a particularly fine evening and I decided to walk that way. It is close to the station and the sound of the trains reverberates quite a lot. But I was sure I could hear a low moaning noise coming from a little further along. I know that on occasions this area is used for, what I call, illicit liaisons, so I walked on warily. What I saw made me instantly physically sick. There were three men lying tangled together in a heap. Two of them were dead and the third had lost almost all his blood and breathed his last as I looked at the horror. It was like a charnel house. The whole place stank of death. I don't know who they were but they had been tortured and mutilated over a long period. I ran back up the alley and when I got a signal on my phone I called the police. I've been having counselling ever since. I have seen nothing like it in my life. It couldn't have been worse if they had been ripped apart by wolves."

Police sources reveal the three men are local but have not released any other information. Animal experts have confirmed that there are no reports of wolves running wild in the Swansea city area.'

19

SLOPE'S MASTER PLAN

In Slope's seaside apartment a mere few miles from the City centre Slope and Bennett stood on the balcony admiring the view. The old axis now renewed and celebrated with a pleasant blood fest to revitalise the relationship Bennett was keen to know Slope's latest master plan. He was after all a master of master plans. This one could be a doozy. "I'm assuming you have a plan Sebastian. After all you have been here for long enough. Am I to be informed or do I just come along for the ride?"

"Of course I have a plan. Don't I always? Not much point in being a master criminal without a master plan. This evening I'll let you see how far we have progressed. I have men, Olive Pickers currently working on breaking through to an underground station that will allow us access to Oystermouth quarry. They are men I can trust and in any case I shall dispose of them once they have served their purpose. Essentially we are going underground until we reach the quarry that once served the Black Castle of Oystermouth. That will then allow us to access the underground network of caves lying beneath the Black Castle."

"That sounds lovely Sebastian. Why not just pay the entrance fee. Be a lot easier wouldn't' it?"

"I suppose that's what passes for humour in your twisted little mind. One more crack like that and you'll be tasting the local sea water at first hand. You are either in or you're dead. You know how it works so stop pissing about."

There was just enough lightness of tone in Slope's voice to reassure her that he hadn't decided to commit her to the deep just yet. Still not much point in antagonising the old bastard. And she was genuinely interested in what had brought him to this part of the world. He had always hated Wales. Anything that brought him here must be a major undertaking.

"Sorry Sebastian. I'm really interested in what has brought you here and I'd like to be involved. You know that I can offer plenty to whatever scheme you have lined up. I'll bet that it's something to do with restoring your fortune. I'd enjoy being involved in that."

"You will Liz, you will. You need to take a bit of a wild leap of faith to begin with. I think that writers call it 'a willing suspension of disbelief'. I am pretty sure that I know the whereabouts of a major forgotten fortune as well as being on the cusp of recovering a few millions of my own. Even better I am already a long way along the road to pinpointing it prior to its removal. Not only will I be able to live as I want again but I can get assorted assassins off my trail. The AF has been spotted in the area and apparently I am voted off the board and now fair game. The pièce de résistance will be the elimination of Cornelius."

"But he's already dead?' said Bennett

"Apparently not, the slippery old goat threw us a dummy."

"Well we shall just have to kill him all over again, what fun Sebastian," chortled Bennett.

"And of course Prideaux, and his mate Bones are in town. I really couldn't have planned it any better. I shall take immense pleasure in despatching them."

"Now that sounds more like the old Slope. Plenty of money and some very old scores settled. I'm in."

"Absolutely, you are in and remember there is no out. If it all goes to fuck you will have to take the consequences. Don't forget if it all goes horribly wrong it's every killer for himself. Herself in your case of course. There is a slight cloud on the horizon. You need to be aware that the AF as well as replacing us on the committee. They held a snap meeting notifying only those we had upset over the years. They were careful to ensure a quorum and voted us out. I always thought there was honour amongst killers. Looks like I was wrong. What's worse is that there is now an 'open kill order' on not just me but you as well."

"That doesn't matter all that much, does it, Sebastian? It's not as if we went to many meetings. It was always a fairly loose association, wasn't it?"

"The problem my optimistic little friend is that it has now become difficult to know who is in the field. There was only one constant. I remember it was rule 13 in the constitution. It was designed to protect members from becoming the target of other members. Never much more than a gentleman's agreement but members were always notified if they had become targets. They were also told who had applied to carry out the hit. I've been pulling in as many favours as I can and all I know is that the Canadian and God knows who else is on my case. It seems to be a free for all. I don't know about you."

"I can see where that might put a crimp in any complex scheme you are setting up. And I suppose the Canadian is still on the trail of Cornelius, now that he is resurrected and that shower, presumably hoping to collect the bounty you put on their heads in the first place. This is all getting nicely complex Sebastian. It's great to be back. I'm looking forward to all this. Those thugs we ripped up near the station. They aren't anything to do with all this are they?"

"Just thugs. Wrong place, wrong time. I'm only telling you all this so that you are aware that you will have to be on guard at all times. For now let's take a walk down to the beach and get some fresh air. It'll be around four hours before we can go and check on progress with the logistics. Just keep your wits about you that's all."

The two left the flat via the stairs. Slope would never use a lift. It was too easy for an assassin to either trap the target inside having tampered with the controls. Staircases gave at least a fighting chance. Recent events were beginning to work through and what had been originally a leisurely project was becoming much more urgent. Emerging into bright sunlight tempered by a cool wind the couple began to walk along the promenade towards Oystermouth. Passers by would have seen an anonymous looking couple. There was nothing to mark out two of the coldest killers in existence.

As the evening air began to cool, Slope and Bennett retraced their steps passing Slope's apartment building and on towards the castle. Slope had filled Bennett in as they walked on the basic plan to locate the treasure that he was convinced lay hidden in the Black Castle of Oystermouth.

She seemed less convinced than he but the survival instinct persuaded her to an outward show of enthusiasm. Slope was not a man to be baulked or even disappointed when he had the bit between his teeth. Given the nature of their relationship the bit would normally be between her teeth in any case. She proved successful as Slope walked towards Swansea castle with a discernible spring in his step. In double quick time they had reached the lower recesses and were making their way along the underground passageway towards the brick wall that was the only barrier between them and the forgotten underground station. Sharp metallic echoes could be heard just around the corner where the passage way branched to the right.

"It sounds as if the men are hard at it Liz. Good for them. We are deep enough here to be unheard by anybody above."

A loud crash of falling masonry told them that a breakthrough of some kind had been effected. Choking dust came billowing towards them as they covered their faces with handkerchiefs. It took minutes to clear. Gradually, they were able to walk further forward without fear of falling. Turning the corner they were met with a group of very dusty men and a station platform complete with a pristine steam engine. The Spirit of Swansea was waiting in the station with seven wagons attached. Everything was to scale though the train and wagons were half size. It looked for all the world as if it was waiting for the night shift to arrive. This was far better than Slope had ever imagined. Here was the means to access the flooded underground cave system that led to the bowels of the Black Castle. He motioned to one of the men in the group as he and Bennett stepped through the gaping hole made by the diggers. The man followed as Slope and Bennett hauled themselves up onto the platform to approach the engine.

"Get into the engine and have a look at the state of the controls," he ordered. The man obeyed instantly. He busied himself within the cab for some time before eventually poking his head out and shouting to the two, "all it needs is some coal and water and it'll be ready to roll. I'd suggest some general greasing of the more important moving parts but she'll be ready to run then. If we work overnight we could have her ready for you by first thing tomorrow morning."

"Make sure you do then or I shall be very disappointed," replied Slope with his usual tone of menace. The man knew exactly what he meant. He jumped down from the platform and returned to what was left of the old dividing wall. A quick chat with the rest of the gang and the appropriate arrangements were in place.

"6.30am tomorrow and not a minute later or you will understand what the word wrath really means. Have a good night now."

Slope and Bennett left without a backward look at the work gang he had assembled. He had managed to put together a handful of ex-Spriggans and current Olive Pickers. Always a chancer he had relied on the fearsome reputation he had established over years to enforce his rule over them. His record was devastating. People died around Slope. He and Bennett had always been equal opportunities killers and people seemed to die just as often around her. When the pair were in tandem the mayhem could become almost biblical. The sum of both killers was much more than when there were two individuals. A mutual psychopath's appreciation society was close to the mark. These workers were making the mistake many make when faced with real tyranny.

"Keep your heads down boys was the mantra. Never look them in the eyes, they'll turn you to stone or mince possibly."

The rationale behind this misguided policy was the reputation that Slope had for paying for results when times were good for him. They did not know that at this point times were not good for him. He was used to being the hunter not the hunted and there was a Canadian on his trail. There was a price on his head and he had no intention of paying the railway gang a penny. Oblivious to all this the men worked through the night hoping for a decent payoff when the miniature train had proved its worth. They hoped that would be the last they would ever see of Slope and Bennett. On such false hopes many people fall. The men worked on.

It was 6.30 on a Swansea morning. Slope and Bennett turned up according to the previous night's arrangement. There was a sense of vague satisfaction amongst the men as they put the finishing touches to the miniature train. The self-elected ganger was an ex-Spriggan who thought his membership would give him some protection. He took it on himself to greet the couple as if they were royalty on one of their interminable tours of industrial Britain.

"Morning Mr Slope and Ms Bennett. Everything is shipshape and Swansea fashion. The engine is fully fuelled. The wagons are coupled and everything is ready to go. All ready just as you said, sir."

"Good," replied a businesslike Slope. "Good for you anyway. All you have to hope now is that this contraption will get us as far as Oystermouth. Remember, breaking down is not an option. You," Slope pointed at the ganger, "Up there in the cab with me. I want you to show me how to drive this thing. It won't take long to learn how to handle it. If you can manage it…." He didn't even bother to complete the sentence.

Slope was in his element. He was in complete control and the men he was now treating as if they were school kids were so cowed by his fearsome reputation that they never questioned the orders he barked at them. It was if he carried a touch of winter with him. Things seemed to get colder around him especially when he was engaged in moving a plan forward. If the train behaved as he was confident it would then he would be able to drive it himself. He would need allies in the event that he located the treasure but he would be able to ditch the four men who had done so much to prepare the train. Slope had no concept of loyalty, foot soldiers were disposable. He had always been an adherent to the old adage one that could almost stand as a mission statement supposing he believed in such New Age tosh: a secret between three people can only be kept as long as two of them are dead. For Slope the number was almost infinitely expendable. He only allowed Bennett to live out of habit and perhaps a sense that she was the only human he had met who shared his complete contempt for the rest of mankind. A match made in hell if there ever was one. For now engine driving was to be his newly acquired skill set. Woe betide his instructor if he did not carry out his instructional task effectively.

The small engine was a tight fit for Slope who was much trimmer than he had been. With the ganger on board there was little room for manoeuvre. Thankfully for all concerned the motive power of the engine was provided by an unknown petrol distillation. The distillation had been hailed as the new fuel when it had been first used for the journey to and from the limestone quarries of Oystermouth. It had been efficient and quiet with none of the problems of diesel. At a stroke it had eliminated the need for coal at a time when coal was king. This was one of the reasons that it had been kept under wraps in a sensitive period after the last war. Another reason had been the effects of two fatal explosions that tarnished the reputation of the new wonder fuel. It still rejoiced in the mundane working title of Pet645, it never did merit a name and the train that might explode weaved its merry way on the underground run to the limestone quarries of Oystermouth.

20

CORNELIUS RETURNS

Overlooking those quarries on a fresh cool morning were Prideaux, Bones and the Job twins Bob and Robert. They had a perfect view of the lakes that had formed over the years that the quarries had lain disused. Their vantage point was the battlements of the Norman castle that glowered at the surrounding village from its motte.

Bones was still recovering from the murderous attack on him by the Canadian. He wore a silk cravat over the medical gauze still covering the scar left on his neck by the attempted garrotting. As those who knew him expected he was milking the situation to the last tiny little drop. His account of the attack bore little relation to the reality but showed him in a better light as someone who fought with all the strength and tenacity of a mightily pissed off leopard.

"As I was saying chaps." The words filled his companions with dread.

"For the love of laverbread Bonesie, please not again. I just can't stand it. We know you made a valiant attempt to fight off a giant assassin. We are pleased that you are recovering. We do not want to hear the story for the nth time. We have at least two hellhounds on our trail, our part of a food festival to arrange and several million pounds worth of treasure to unearth. I think that's enough to be going on with for now. Don't you?"

"I'm not sure I like your tone old chap. After all I very nearly died. I glimpsed the grim reaper in all his seedy glory and it wasn't a pretty sight. He reminded me a bit of old Petroc Trethewey. You remember the drunken don that ended up despoiling the hallowed waters of the Cherwell at Parsons' Pleasure swimming hole."

"I remember the old bastard very well." Prideaux had spent many years attempting to bury such memories. "I came a lot closer to losing my life than you have Bonesie. Remember that Trethewey's membership of the Spriggans did for him in the end. And please also remember that it was Slope who sent the old bastard to a watery grave. Now it might have slipped your notice but that very accomplished killer is once more on our trail. Personally I'd prefer to concentrate on matters in hand rather than rake up that unsavoury business."

"Take your point old fruit. Water under Folly Bridge and all that. Job in hand. That's the badger. Loud and clear my old darling. Let's talk wine then. I've admired the view and a very bucolic one it is. However, this far above sea level always tends to make the old pins a little wobbly, don't you know. Time to descend to ground level I think. What about you chaps?"

Bones's words were addressed to the Job twins. Bob and Robert Job were becoming a little skittish. They were not the most reflective of men. In fact their default mode tended to be severe violence. They were still festering over their inability to catch the Canadian following the attack on Bones. They knew that but for their intervention Bones would now be pushing up daisies in the nearby cemetery. Capturing the Canadian would have been the type of workout the overactive Cornish brothers required. The Canadian would have provided real opposition for two men who liked nothing better than a good old fashioned tear up. In its absence they were heatedly disagreeing over the possibility of leaping from the battlements to land in the surrounding moat. Only a fool or madmen would attempt such a stunt. The twins were neither; they were just a little bored.

The arrival of Cornelius was the incentive the four men required. Things had been unpredictable of late and predictability was one thing on which Cornelius insisted. "I know you lot have little time for me," he began "but things are finally coming to a head. I want the four of you to follow me down from here where you are as a matter of some interest sitting ducks. I have not been wasting my time since the attack on Bones."

"Bloody pleased to hear it. I like to know where my taxes are going. Don't want you civil servant types swanning around blowing my tax dollars on three hour lunches and the like."

"If you paid your taxes that ancient pile of yours down there in the dark heart of Cornwall wouldn't be about to be sold to the highest bidder. Your family have been poncing off the taxpayer and everyone else for generations."

"You wound me sorely, Cornelius. I thought at least we had a truce these days. After all you are supposed to be bloody well dead and you have sunk enough of our finest malt whisky free and gratis back at The Hand of God to float a trawler, you and your deceased doppelganger. Are here no standards left these days?"

"I have no intention of asking twice. You and Prideaux are only wasting litres of good Welsh air courtesy of the government through the good offices of those two madmen who seem to have a soft spot for you. I know all this alma mater stuff but don't forget they act on my orders and the balloon is about to go up. Now we can discuss it here where a half decent sniper could pop any one of us like a badly inflated balloon or you can follow me to the great hall to listen to the latest intelligence I have been able to gather.'

"Since you ask so nicely," smirked Prideaux "we will follow you to the ends of the earth, well the great hall anyway. And I have a feeling that the sun is more or less over the yardarm. Perhaps you could find your way to breaking out some of the special stuff you enjoy courtesy of the taxpayer. Bonesie and I think much more clearly when fortified with a decent slug or two of the good stuff."

The group descended the spiral staircase from the battlements and crossed the courtyard to the great hall. Prideaux was aware that there seemed to be much more activity going on than had been the case of late. What struck him was the fact that the activity seemed to have a more concentrated focus than was usually the case. Cornelius led the way into the vast chamber that was the great hall. Little had changed since the 14th century. The massive fireplaces still served to heat the building though it didn't do to be too far from a heat source. One of the many things impossible to eliminate in such an ancient building is the draughts that come piling in through any available interstice. Internally the hall had been fitted out with the usual necessities for modern communications. Nothing, however, was fixed. The castle was still under the guardianship of the government through its heritage arm. In extremis it could be used as a centre when events demanded but it could never be allowed to be altered to fit a 21st century sensibility. Ghosts of the 14th century abounded and any concessions to modern life had to be removable.

When Cornelius managed to get his group seated and relatively quiet he passed each of them a folder. "I want you to look at page three...." He began. Prideaux interrupted before he had finished his sentence. "If you even mouth the words role play then I'm off. For fuck's sake. Just tell us what's going on. You bloody intelligence wallahs are never happy unless you are playing silly buggers. All we want to know is what is going on and when we can go home. Yes I know we've got a food festival to organise but we've done most of the work. It's this weekend anyway so once that is done can we get back to running our pub or not?"

"I'm not going to lie to you. You are not here against your will but from now on you will go nowhere without my permission." Cornelius had taken sufficient teasing from Prideaux and Bones to last a lifetime and was not prepared to take any more. Things had moved to a stage where Slope's plan was beginning to become penetrable. It was bound to include the usual leavening of mayhem and murder. He dared not allow two reluctant souls to swan about as if all were right with the world. It was not.

"This is how it is. You two are in protective custody from now on. You will be armed however much you disagree because the threat is a real one. We know that Slope is in Swansea. We are not sure where but there is clear evidence that he is here. His DNA and that of the harpy Bennett has been found on those lads that were found butchered in the alleyway near the main station."

"I don't want to appear smug Piers, but I told you as much," Bones preened.

"Our man is due to report back to me tomorrow so I will know more then. Make no mistake. If you try to wander off you will be in extreme danger. The Canadian has already shown his hand and he is also after Slope don't forget, as well as us. All I ask is some more grown up behaviour from you two."

Bones was looking agitated at Cornelius yet again displaying his customary arrogance. Only Prideaux was aware that something was bothering him. The Canadian's attempt at throttling Bones had shaken him badly. He was strictly a non-combatant. He held strong views but apart from Prideaux his closest friend was John Barleycorn and his natural habitat the bar. Any bar. Of late he had spent a fair chunk of time recuperating from the attack in the local hospital. A strict no alcohol policy had given him the chance to try sobriety for the first time in years. His response was to find another all absorbing hobby. This time he was able to focus on the area's local history. Bones had never been a man for the academic approach. If you really wanted to research an area with which you were not familiar then it was local history and local people you turned to. Following that belief in the enforced environment of a local hospital was most revealing. His captive audience was more than informative and Bones found himself enjoying himself sans alcohol for the first time in years. His findings were responsible for his current impression of a man sitting on a particularly virulent nest of fire ants.

Prideaux's intervention took the sting out of the occasion. "Cornelius, if you don't let Bonesie explain what is on his mind then I think he will very likely explode. You never know, he's been sober for a few weeks now. He might even have something valuable to contribute."

A frustrated Cornelius nodded his assent. He knew Bones wasn't stupid and with a clear head he might genuinely have something to contribute. There was nothing to lose. He hadn't told the group but his faith in his man within Slope's latest grouping was very weak. He had made no progress at all in finding out where Slope had his base and kept promising things he failed to deliver. Either Slope was keeping him very close or his cover was already blown. "This had better be good. I have better things to do than listen to your rambling."

"Bollocks to you Cornelius and double bollocks to you Piers. I can function just as well pissed or sober. However, come closer to me my little inklings I have things to reveal. Don't worry this is not an extended rant. My research reveals that the story about Edward II and the treasure being hidden somewhere in a Swansea castle has local support. It's one of those stories that has survived the generations. Here's the rub. With all the digital gadgets available to penetrate the ground and the popularity of that Time Team programme you would expect anything of value here to have been already dug up."

"That seems more than likely," interjected Cornelius. "And are you seriously saying that a few locals in the hospital have provided you with more information in a couple of weeks than the massed ranks of British academia over the generations." Cornelius found it difficult to keep his face straight as he enjoyed himself by pretending ignorance. He knew the mystery of the castle and had cracked it many years since. His stance was merely to humour Bones and in the process to see how far the old blusterer had got in his research.

"That's exactly what I am saying. This is why. The academics have come at this from completely the wrong direction. They have looked at historical documentation and nothing else. As a consequence the castle has never been properly searched. They have never taken into account the two key elements that make almost anything possible within this particular castle."

"Please, O wise one, enlighten your followers with your industrial wisdom."

"Certainly Cornelius. You have hit the nail rather appropriately on the head. Industry is the key to this whole thing. I hope you two are listening," Bones turned his attention to the Job twins who shared a general inability to stay still or quiet for any more than minutes.

"Absolutely fascinated Bonesie old fruit," the brothers trilled in unison.

"Park the sarcasm you two and pin back your cauliflower ears for a couple more minutes. Most people see this village as a fishing village. Obviously in the past oysters have played a major part in its development. These days it's looked on mainly as a holiday village playing host to beach and water sports lovers from around the world. The old industry that flourished here is now neglected and basically hidden."

"I didn't know there was any industry here Bonesie," Prideaux interrupted. "Are you going to tell us what the industry was?"

"What you don't know would fill a very large tome Piers old chum. And if you blighters keep interrupting I'll never get this story out. Where do you think the limestone came from to build a massive bloody Norman castle in the first place? I suppose you," he looked at Cornelius, "suppose that the Normans who built the castle sent an order off to Robert Price's for enough stone to build a lovely big castle to be delivered to one William de Breos, CoD."

"Now who's being sarcastic," mumbled Cornelius.

Ignoring him Bones continued. "To the south west of the castle not even a mile away is an interlinked series of quarries. That's where all the stone came from. Over the years they have flooded forming a series of natural swimming holes. Some of them are apparently bottomless. Years ago local kids used to swim in them. Everything is off limits these days. Even the grounds around the castle have changed over the centuries. But and it's a thundering great but, there is a watergate that leads to the caverns directly under the castle."

"How does that help us Bonesie?" The twins had at last found their interest awakened. So kids could swim in natural pools. So what? Bob and I spent most of our childhood in Cornwall doing the same."

"Perfectly reasonable thing to do Robert. The point is that once the castle had been built they kept one quarry drained so they could access any stone they needed for repairs. They let the others flood so that supplies could be brought into the underwater caverns and from there directly up into the castle."

"There's a very obvious flaw in all this Bones. I doubt you will have noticed it but if the quarries were accessible then they would also be accessible to anyone bringing in supplies either from Swansea by road or by sea. Any attacking army would easily be cut off. I thought the Normans were supposed to be clever." Cornelius was becoming irritated with the way in which Bones was holding the floor. He was delighted to have spotted a major flaw. Perhaps this would silence the old buffer, for the time being at least.

"A bloody sight clever than you are supposed to be Cornelius my old honky tonk. They didn't bring in supplies by road or sea." Bones was in his element now. He milked his finale for all it was worth. Deep at heart he was an old ham. If he could have conjured a drum roll, he would have. "The Normans brought in supplies through the tunnel that their engineers had built from Swansea Castle to one of the flooded quarries that led directly to the watergate. Good God man they even built specialised skiffs to transport supplies and men directly from the tunnel's end through the watergate and into the system of caverns. That way no attacking army got a look in."

"Well I've heard everything now. I suppose they were little motor boats they used. Did they take out day trippers around the bay?" Cornelius was on the back foot now. At last Bones was making some sense but it was not something Cornelius could admit to himself and certainly not to Bones. The piss taking would be too painful.

"British Intelligence used to have quite a good reputation Cornelius. You are doing it no favours. The Normans designed slim boats that could easily slide though the often narrow passageways through the caver system. They also had extended narrow prows that resembled the neck of a swan. In later years the skiffs came to be called swans. That was because one of De Breos's closest allies was a man called Guillame de Blanchefort. His coat of arms featured a black swan with blue and yellow wavy things. That's not where Swansea got its name though, that's another story."

"OK. I'll admit there might be something in what you say. But how does that help us?" Cornelius was fishing now. Bones was in his element.

"I'm amazed how quickly you forget the important things Cornelius. Surely you remember our first encounter with the bastard Slope. Remember how he used the Norman tunnel from Garway Church to the cellar of The Hand of God. Remember how the bastard engineered the deaths of Mark and Ginny Williams? He could never have got to us without the tunnel. That was a Norman speciality. They did exactly the same thing between the two major castles in this area. And to conclude, the way this can help us is in the knowledge that the tunnel from Swansea to the quarry is still usable."

"Now come on Bones. I know that you and your pal Prideaux operate in a fantasy world a lot of the time but you are not telling me that a mediaeval tunnel covering that distance is still possible to navigate."

"That's exactly what I'm telling you. It has had some help to survive as long as this however. The other thing I found out on my little hospital sojourn is that the Norman tunnel was the inspiration for a short lived company to lay a railway line along its length. That was the basis for what was to eventually be an underground rail system between Swansea and Oystermouth. Even back in the forties it was obvious that the popularity of cars and buses would eventually choke up the sea road between the town and the village. They put a lot of money into strengthening and repairing the tunnel which is apparently perfectly usable. Local wisdom says that there is even one of the original trains down there. They just walled it up and left it. Shame it didn't work out. Would have been a boon in the modern age. Anyway that's it. I have no idea whether Slope is aware of any of this but if he is you can bet he is working on using it to his advantage."

Bones's revelations had managed the desired effect. The silence was positively palpable as those present absorbed the magnitude of what they had just heard. It wasn't as if Slope didn't have form in such things. He was comfortable underground and fully aware of the advantage of surprise that such features could provide. All of a sudden the castle fortifications seemed a lot less reassuring.

"Thanks Bonesie I'll never sleep easily in my bed again but forewarned and all that. At least we are aware that we have a weak spot. Well, Cornelius what do you intend to do with Bonesie's information? Even if it's all conjecture it certainly needs looking at."

"And that's exactly what I intend to do Prideaux. I'm hoping that my man on the inside of Slope's latest organisation will report back this evening. If he does so and we are able to locate Slope then we'll make a pre-emptive strike and take him out once and for all. In the meantime this is all sub judice. It goes no further than these four walls. I shall be in touch with Zebedee and strengthen our resources on the ground immediately. There are men at Brecon waiting to be deployed. I'd like you all to behave as naturally as possible until we have investigated further."

Cornelius turned to the Job twins. "Under no circumstances are you two to go anywhere near that quarry complex. Do I make myself clear?"

"As clear as a Cornish stream boss," they chorused in reply both wearing the most angelic of smiles.

21

DOWN AMONGST THE DEAD MEN

The Slope express had made its subterranean way from Swansea to Oystermouth. Slope quickly learned enough about the engine to feel confident about taking charge on his own. His erstwhile instructor has been banished to one of the following carriages. For the first time for some years Slope is enjoying himself without having killed or having someone to kill immediately. The accompanying foot soldiers though cowed by his reputation will prove useful should he meet with opposition. Driving the train for once provides the simple pleasure of motion and blots out some of the more unsavoury aspects of an unsavoury life. Reverting to childhood helps lift some of the pressure. The plan does not have the usual Slope hallmark of organisation. Since the demise of the Spriggans he has been forced to operate on a shoestring and with untested muscle to carry out his preparations. The powerful amongst the great and the good have melted away and he is left to his own devices. He knows that the current plan has massive flaws. There are too many unknowns for him to exude his usual confidence levels. Driving a miniature train under Swansea streets allows him to bury all that for a short time.

That time gets shorter as he hears a warning shout behind him. "Lookout there's something on the track. Slow down or you'll derail the bloody thing." Roused from his reverie Slope looks up. Through the gloom he sees a large sleeper part way across the narrow gauge line. He snatches at the brake handle and applies it with all the force he can muster. There is a high pitched screaming noise as steel bites on steel. Gradually the train slows but it is touch and go as to whether the engine hits the sleeper with enough force to result in a derailment. In the event the brake does its job as the train slows to a gentle stop nudging the offending sleeper as it does so.

Slope's instincts are immediately sharpened. This is not the action of nature. A sleeper that heavy has not simply slipped across the line. This is human action and to a man used to violence in all its forms that means enemy action. The lighting in the tunnel is adequate but no more than that. Up ahead there is a glimmer of light. It shows that the train is almost at its destination and the sun is penetrating the darkness to allow the men to assess the situation.

"You two, get down and shift that bloody thing," he shouts to his instructor and the man sitting next to him. "Watch yourselves. This is no accident. The rest of you I hope are armed. I'm guessing you have your stilettos with you. It would be handy if you had some firepower too."

Some quick-fire Italian confirmed that the men were armed with handguns in addition to the ubiquitous stilettos. There was a great deal of grunting coming from the front of the train as two of the Olive Pickers heaved and twisted in a desperate effort to shift the sleeper from the track.

It was instinct that made Slope turn. He had been desperately willing the men labouring to remove the sleeper to get on with it. It was that feeling everyone gets when they are in a gloomy place and something moves. Sometimes there is no sound but it is obvious that something is there. Slope turned to face back down the tunnel. Two of the three remaining men were in the penultimate. There was no sign of the fifth man. A familiar choking sound was the sign that the fifth man would no longer be of any use or ornament to the current project. A shadow filled the side of the tunnel as Slope did his best to make out what was happening. There didn't appear to be a struggle. It was a quick death and almost silent. There was a soft noise as a lifeless body hit the floor of the tunnel. The fifth man had been garrotted.

The Canadian stepped over his victim and approached the front of the train. He had not uttered a word. This was business. There is always collateral damage in any business. Assassination had more than its fair share. The efficiency of the Canadian had frightened the other two into immobility. They were men of the world. They knew they would be next. And given the size and brutality of the Canadian neither expected to see another dawn.

The height of the tunnel forced the assassin to stoop more than a little as he approached Slope and the two toilers on the railway line. They too had gone very quiet and were out of view beneath the level of the carriages. They had realised what was happening and crouching made their way around to the opposite side of the train.

"Nothing personal Sebastian. I'll make it quick for you. You won't suffer, much. Honour amongst killers really. Once it becomes clear that I carried out the hit I'll be able to increase my fees substantially. I'm looking to retire and go home to Montreal in a year or two. One can get a bit tired of all this killing. Still a contract is a contract. Not something I normally do but for old times' sake, your preference. I can do you a garrotte, knife or if you'd like I could just break your neck. Unorthodox I know. I'll make sure that I leave one of these two alive to confirm who carried out the killing. Pays to advertise….."

Whatever the Canadian was about to say next was choked off as Slope fired his machine pistol from waist high. The burst caught his target in the throat almost decapitating the giant. He staggered falling to his knees. He looked almost comical as he swayed there for moments before Slope finished him with another burst to the head. Dust swirled around the tunnel as twenty stone of prime Canadian beef breathed its last. All dreams of a return home to a quiet life dissipated as one of the AF's most prolific killers expired on the filthy ground."

"First rule of assassination old chap, don't talk about it, do it. You got distracted. Even the best of us can make that mistake and in this business there is no room for mistakes. You can come out now. It's all over and none of you have seen a thing. You two, have you removed that bloody sleeper?"

"We've managed to swing it over the side. It's not affecting the track so the train will pass it easily."

"Right then you get those bodies up against the wall over there and we'll go on to see what is around the corner. I reckon we must be close. That stream of sunlight must be coming in through some sort of metal grill. Once we get to the end we can work out what to do next or rather I'll work it out you'll carry it out. Happy with that?"

The men were still in shock. They had all seen violent death in their time but the casual way in which Slope had carried out what was in fact an execution had unnerved them. They were deep beneath the city streets and in thrall to a cold killer. Nothing to be done but follow along to whatever conclusion lay around the corner. Clearly once they had outlived their usefulness they had a fair idea of what fate awaited them.

The train restarted without a hitch. Slope's driving was a little more circumspect as they approached the end of the line. None of the men were flat earthers but what if the end of the line was just that? What if there was a long drop into a flooded quarry? An ignominious end at the very least.

The light was improving rapidly. Weak sunshine became stronger to such an extent that the four remaining men and their leader began to shade their eyes. The train slowed to a crawl. The track ended in a buffer that the train eased up to and stopped. Behind the buffer was an iron gate. There did not appear to be a lock on it. It took all five of them to eventually open the gate. They had strained at pushing it then at pulling it. It was only when one noticed that the gate slid into recesses in the wall that they managed to shift it. Behind the gate and to the left was a chamber hewn from solid rock. Steps cut into the rock led down to a deep pool of water. There was a rock shelf just above water level on which were stored several Swan boats with the traditional swan neck that was the representation of the arms of Guillame de Blanchefort. It was beginning to look as if Slope was in business.

The way the steps were cut into the rock declared their Norman origins. The steps had been here for centuries and although worn were perfectly serviceable. Doubtless they would have passed a modern day health and safety check. More modern were the lights recessed in the rock that gave sufficient illumination for safe negotiation at any time of day and night. Slope and his cronies were down at water level and onto the shelf in a matter of minutes. A quick check on the boats revealed that they too were serviceable. Slope stood in the prow of the leading boat as they launched two of the strongest looking boats on to the tranquil waters of the largest of the flooded quarries. The quarry like all the others was completely hidden from view by a canopy of trees and bushes that had grown up over the years. By use of the outsize paddles designed to propel the boats they quickly crossed to the eastern side of the lagoon. In around twenty minutes they had reached the jetty that abutted the watergate. The massive gate that for centuries had barred access to the castle was badly rusted and had jammed in the open position. There was enough room for the slim boats to slip through easily.

Both boats were now in the interconnected series of caverns that time and the Normans had constructed running right under the castle and its grounds. Powerful torches shining from both boats lit up this underworld with reflections from the carved rock making it look like a place of magic. It was a masterpiece of engineering utilising the qualities of the rock to establish what amounted to a series of canals running through tunnels carved through solid bedrock. At two or three places either side of the main artery there were series of steps that obviously led up to the lower chambers of the castle.

All this was a bonus for Slope. He now had all he wanted. Access to the lower chambers of the castle was vital if he was to make a serious attempt at finding the treasure. He had his escape route and his method of transportation of any loot he was able to find all in place thanks to the efficiency of the small train and the tracks on which it ran. This was the reconnaissance that dreams were made of. He had four reasonably reliable men in his thrall and another dozen hardened members of the Puglian Olive Pickers waiting for his call. All it now needed was to cover his tracks until he had mobilised his troops and picked the best possible time to strike.

The return journey went without a hitch. The boats were returned to their original place on the natural rock shelf. The train returned them to the platform back in the city carrying the corpses of the Canadian and the unfortunate Olive Picker. On arrival back at the platform Slope issued his orders to the four remaining Olive Pickers. "I'm sorry about your friend but I'd like you to ensure that he finds a good home together with this big Canadian bastard in the next big pour of concrete. There are to be no witnesses. Do I make myself clear?" The four men nodded as one.

"Play your cards right and you lot will be able to go back to sunny Puglia with more money than you will ever be able to spend. Fuck it up and you'll be joining your friend and the Canadian. But I think you know that already."

Slope turned on his heel to leave the four to turn in yet another night shift making arrangements for two more disposables to disappear without trace. Such was the norm when Slope was on a mission.

22

THE JOB TWINS ON WATER

The Job twins were not known for their subtle approach to life. They held to an approach that went roughly, if hitting it hard doesn't work then hit it harder until it does. This had served them well as students and in their eventful careers within British Intelligence. Cornelius's instruction to lie low until a strategy had been agreed had fallen on stony ground where these two were concerned. Worst of all even suggesting that the flooded caverns possibly held a secret was very much a red rag to very eager bulls. In their teens the twins had snorkelled in abandoned china clay pits in mid Cornwall simply for the hell of it. Both of them swam like mackerel and a flooded quarry would be an opportunity rather than an obstacle. Best of all it would be the chance to blow off some steam. Forced inactivity did not sit well on the brawny shoulders of two burly Cornishmen.

"Come on Bob, let's get on with it." The two crept out of the castle early one morning through a passageway at the rear of the castle. "I thought that this lot would have discovered this passage by now Bob. Doesn't give a real sense of security when we've been using this exit for weeks. Nobody else seems to know it's here."

"Never mind that Janner, let's get wet." The two men made their way through the undergrowth and to the edge of the flooded quarry.

"What do you reckon to all this talk of treasure then Bob?"

"Same as you bro. Lot of old toffee I expect. But you never know. I know that Cornelius thinks it's a runner. I heard him going on about it back in Puglia. He was chatting to some Italian guy in that bar Bonesie liked so much in Ostuni. He couldn't see me and he was rabbiting on in Italian. He kept going on about Edward II and his boyfriends and how it was well known that he had visited the Black Castle in Oystermouth back in the 14th century. Don't know who the bloke was but I haven't seen Cornelius that animated for some time. He walked outside and I followed him just out of curiosity. He was on his mobile. It was pretty obvious that he was filling Zebedee in on this whole business of the Black Castle. Bit surprised really that he was on an open line. Anyone could have picked that conversation up."

"Might be something in it then. Can't see Cornelius putting himself out these days though. He's already nicked Slope's loot. He's more minted than if he'd won the European lottery."

The sun began to break through some low cloud to give sufficient light for the two men to find a safe place to enter the water. Their headlights gave them the extra illumination to see well enough to strike out towards the centre of the quarry. They reached the centre quickly thanks to powerful strokes and a confidence of swimming in all conditions in their native Cornwall.

"Hey Janner, focus your light over there, will you? It might be the early morning start but doesn't that look like a watergate to you? I didn't think this castle had anything like that. Surely they were strong enough in this area to stamp on any attacks."

"You know the Normans Bob: belt and braces bunch. Bit like supporting Millwall. Everybody hates them, they don't care. Except they liked nothing better than going underground. You know that. They always have escape tunnels. I know the Black Castle was well defended but you know what the consequences would have been if the Welsh attackers did break through. Be like a fox with piles in the henhouse. Sheer bloody murder. Hey, race you!"

Robert swam off towards the indicated spot closely pursued by his brother. The two were in their element. Physical exercise and fierce competition: the time when the brothers really came alive.

They reached the spot in short order. It might have been a tie, it was certainly close. What the brothers found was of such significance that it replaced the traditional squabble about who came first and who came nowhere.

"I was right. It is a bloody watergate. Who knew?" Robert was triumphant. Whoever had won the swimming race, this discovery trumped it. The twins knew all about the passage that allowed exit and entrance at the rear of the castle. It emerged into the woods and was protected inside by a heavy door that they had copied the key to. This was something else.

"Come on, we can get through the gate. Looks as if it's rusted open. I think I can see what looks like a boat right at the back. As far as I know nobody runs pleasure boats here in the quarries. Perhaps there's a local fishing club and it's their boat. Come on let's find out. Now we've come all this way it'd be rude not to."

What faced the twins was the unknown. Their danger antennae were vibrating mightily. Woe betide anybody who made the wrong move with the twins in this mood. They were not known for their forbearance at the best of times. What they saw changed everything. A line of swan skiffs drawn up on the natural rock shelf, steps leading up to a level spoke eloquently of secret access to the castle that nobody had ever mentioned. Nobody even knew. Now that the twins knew they realised how exposed the castle was. If Slope was involved then trouble was coming down the line like a juggernaut with faulty air brakes. Their joint train of thought was interrupted by a soft splash emanating from the stream that ran into the darkness of the cavern.

"A water rat," whispered Bob.

"I don't care if it's a rabid otter with a bellyful of Special Brew. Switch that lamp off and get back here behind the boats. Oh! Before you rip some fucker's head off let's try to find out who we're dealing with. And listen, if it happens to be Slope or one of his cronies please leave enough of them alive to find out what the fuck is going on."

"Certainly will old chap. I hope you don't mind my pointing this out but your language gets a bit bloody ripe when you get excited."

The splash was repeated. This time it was closer. The brothers huddled behind one of the upturned boats. It was definitely a boat.

It was clearly being piloted by a novice judging by the splashing that was going on.

"Can you see anything, Bob?"

"It's one of these boats with three blokes in it. They are all wearing balaclavas. Looks like a bank robbers' outing to me. They're just coasting in to moor against the shelf. We'll need to hit them pretty hard just as they are tying up. All for one and one for all bro. Trelawney's Army and all that."

The brothers were coiled like sprung steel. The boat made a soft sound as it nuzzled the rock shelf. Two of Trelawney's finest launched themselves at the two larger figures who were on the point of stepping from the boat onto the shelf. The force with which the brothers hit the figures knocked them off their feet. One fell back into the boat hitting his head as he fell, the other soared right over the boat crashing into the rock on the other side of the water. The third figure swung at Robert with an overlarge paddle catching him on the temple and knocking him sideways.

"Bastard," yelled Bob as he crashed a mighty fist into the covered face of the slim figure. It fell back into the boat as an enraged Job twin jumped in after it. Pulling the figure to its feet he ripped off the balaclava.

"I mean bitch," he grimaced as he viewed the features of Elizabeth Bennett. Her nose was broken and she was spouting blood from her mouth. But it was Elizabeth Bennett. No assailant turned his back on this creature and lived. Bob picked her up in his arms and threw her onto the rock shelf. The crack as she hit the shelf suggested that she would be out for some time. Bob was taking no chances as he leaped onto the shelf and tied her hands and legs with the ties he always carried with him.

He turned his brother onto his back. "What the hell happened? Bob what hit me?"

"You got decked by a girl. You got knocked out by Elizabeth Bennett. Don't worry though I got her for you."

"Stop pissing about Bob. I've got the headache from hell. I think I've lost a tooth as well. What are you on about?"

"Look if you don't believe me. That bundle next to you is the bitch Bennett. On your behalf I have rendered the beast unconscious. Her two pals are also unconscious. One of them is a bit waterlogged. Now see if you can get to your feet, get your knife out and do not take your eyes off Bennett. If she moves, cut her throat. I mean it. She's is a killer many times over and I prefer her unconscious to any other state. You sure you're OK?"

"Bit groggy but I'm fine."

"I'm just tying those other bastards up. I'm going to go out onto the lake to call backup. Where there's Bennett, Slope is sure to be. He must be close. There's no signal in here. Now I'll only be a couple of minutes. But please don't piss about. If any of them move knife them. It'll be good to take them in alive but these are not just local thugs and Bennett has killed more people than I've had proper pasties."

Bob rowed the skip back onto the surrounding lake. As soon as he got a signal he called in his information to Cornelius who despatched the undercover force newly arrived from Brecon. It meant lingering longer than he was comfortable on the lake. They took ten minutes to arrive but he was able to act as a reference point for them to cross the lake as quickly as possible. Once they set out towards his position he rowed the skiff back whence he had come.

"Don't blame me Bob. She was too quick. Her hands were turning blue so I loosened the ties a bit. I was holding my knife against her back, somehow she managed to trip me. I know her reputation and I thought my time had come. She grabbed my knife and killed her companions before I could get to my feet. Look!"

His twin was standing in a pool of blood. Both men were rapidly bleeding to death, their throats cut through to the bone.

"She just looked at me, smiled and said, 'good luck with getting anything out of those two,' and handed the knife back to me so I knocked her out again. I don't think she's dead but I'm not loosening any ties on her in the future."

The cavalry arrived and the twins instructed them to clean up the cave and dispose of the two bodies discreetly. It was clear now that serious preparation had gone into all this. Bennett was involved which meant that Slope wasn't far away. The boats were replaced as closely as possible to the arrangement that the twins had clocked when they first entered through the Watergate. Everything looked as it had done before the twins arrived. They were now determined to find out what lay at the top of the stone steps far above their heads.

Robert briefed Red Leader the undercover soldier in charge of the Brecon contingent. "Let Cornelius know what we are doing.

You better see what he wants doing with Bennett. She'll need interrogating. We have to know what lies above. I've a fair idea of what lies below and I don't like it. We need to know what we're up against. It's beginning to feel like a game of chess where we are playing against a grandmaster while wearing blindfolds. Tell him that the twins say that we need to go to black alert. I can already smell blood. Leave a couple of your men here and tell them to keep their eyes open for God's sake. This could get very messy."

The twins started up the stairway. At least their backs would be covered while they did a recce. They were not prepared for what they found when they reached the chamber above. "Bloody hell, Janner. I don't believe it. I didn't know the Normans had railways. That'll be a bit of a shock for old Portillo."

"I sometimes wonder about you Bob. Course it's not the Normans or the bloody Victorians. It's a lot more recent than that."

"And how, pray does the local historian know this little gobbet?"

"For a start it has Swansea Iron and Steel stamped on the rails. That means it's a 20th century line. You can bet your boots that the Normans built the tunnel. And I'll guarantee that if we follow it we'll end up in Swansea castle. The Normans weren't daft. They knew how hated they were. If a castle was overrun they knew it would be severed cocks all round and the devil take the hindmost. You can't go about oppressing a population and not get some form of kick back. It's a Norman bolthole for God's sake. At some stage it's been adapted to take a narrow gauge railway. Must be something industrial. We'll have a quick look about then get back to the castle. I don't like the feel of this at all."

The twins were interrupted by the sounds of automatic fire. "It's bloody started already. That's coming from below. Sounds like its Geronimo time. Let's go."

This was the twins in their element. In their heads they were playing cowboys and Indians just like they did as kids back on the family farm in Cornwall. The only difference was they now held Glock machine pistols rather than sticks pulled from the hedgerows. They took the stairs at a rush almost sliding down to the cavern below. The light was enough for them to see movement. The last echo of gunfire had died away and they could hear the splash of oars.

Hitting the ground with a thud both men fired off speculative bursts. Make sure the bastards keep their heads down Bob," shouted his twin.

"We're shooting at fuck all Janner," Bob shouted back. "Looks like they got the Brecon boys."

"How do you know that," came the shouted reply.

"I just fell over one of the poor bastards. Practically decapitated him they did. He never stood a chance. Looks as if they're making a break for it. The other one's over here too. Nothing we can do for them."

"Oh! I think we can do something for them. Let's get those bastards who killed them. If I'm going down I'm taking some of them with me."

Two steaming mad Job twins picked up one of the remaining skiffs and planted it in the water. Rowing like demons they burst back onto the lake. They had rowed pilot gigs in competition as young men in Cornwall and the killers out on the flooded quarry would need an outboard to escape the wrath of Jobs. There were three of them initially unaware that the hounds of hell were on their tail.

"Keep it steady, Bob. I'm going to put a bullet or three into that one at the back."

True to his word Robert Job's burst of fire hit the man in the rear of the skiff. It blew the back of his head off as he slumped forward showering blood and brains over the two men who were paddling. Realising the danger they were in they now started paddling like men possessed.

"Just a thought Janner; I wondered if we should try to take the other two alive. I know they don't deserve it but we might be able to get something out of them. It might be sometime before Bennett comes around, if she ever does, you gave her one hell of a lamping."

"Good point Bob. Perhaps I'll shoot them a little bit. Then we can have a go on those torture machines in the castle's Black museum. I've always fancied lengthening someone on the rack. There's an Iron Virgin in the display too."

"I can't see Cornelius sanctioning that. He's more likely to do it by the book. I suppose if we don't tell him it'll be job done if we can get them to talk. Come on then. Put your back into it or they'll be lost in the shrubbery before we can get at them."

The twins did exactly that. They were overtaking the fleeing skiff at pace. They were close enough to see one of the paddlers drop his paddle as he manhandled his dead companion over the side. The break in the rhythm caused by his action slowed the skiff and allowed the twins to get ever closer.

"Duck, Bob!" Bob threw himself to the bottom of the skiff letting off a burst of fire that took the man who had been manhandling the corpse in the chest. The force of the bullets knocked him off his feet and over the side of the skiff. The remaining killer slowed the skiff. He knew it was hopeless. "Watch the bastard Bob. He must be armed. Don't drop your guard."

The two slowed their own skiff as they cautiously approached. Both were perfectly prepared to shoot this man too. Although it would look a bit better for them if they were able to take in a prisoner. Their reputation for mayhem was well known and well deserved. The twins were never that keen on taking prisoners. The skiff in front of them rocked as the only man standing struggled to gain his feet. He was facing away from the twins. As he straightened Bob could see he held a handgun. He had one hand in the air as he raised the gun. Instead of turning to fire on the twins he stuck the gun in his mouth and blew off the top of his head.

"Just like taking the top off a breakfast duck egg," observed Bob. "I was going to shoot him anyway. He obviously couldn't wait to leave this vale of tears."

"Too bloody terrified of being taken alive more likely," observed his twin. This is really starting to bother me Bob. That bloke has just blown his brains out rather than allow himself to be captured. We're not in Syria; we're in Swansea for God's sake. What the hell was he thinking, he must think we're a bunch of animals. I wouldn't really have put him in the iron virgin. What makes me worry is that there are five men dead and we only came here for a bit of a looksee. I think this is going to get very dark before we're finished with it."

The twins towed the skiff containing what was left of the suicide to the edge of the lake and tied up both boats.

23

CASTLE SECRETS

Deep inside the castle Slope had found his goal. His research had paid dividends and the envelope that had seemed so innocuous had revealed its secrets. He had penetrated the locked room and was overwhelmed with the treasure stacked so high it almost filled the inner chamber.

His ace in the hole was Bennett. She was small enough and agile enough to gain access to the final piece in this whole jigsaw. It had been her idea to allow herself to be captured in the labyrinth underneath the castle. Her two accomplices had to be silenced as they had already questioned just what the hell they were doing there. She could take no chances and she hadn't. The twins weren't surprised that she had turned on the men with her. They were well aware of her penchant for violence. They knew it held a sexual force for her. To capture someone capable of such a threat to them needed no justification. They were action men anyway. It would never cross their minds that anyone could allow themselves to be captured. Once Bennett linked up with Slope then the die would be irrevocably cast. They were so close to the end that Slope could smell it.

At this moment Bennett lay on the flag floor of the castle torture room. Her hands remained held tightly behind her back by the ties that had become something of a trademark of the twins. Because they were so tight her fingers were already turning blue. She was barely conscious. The decision had been taken to leave her there for a time as part of the softening process. It would take a good deal of effort and guile to get anything from this most hardened adversary. Light never broke in the torture room. It was part of the design. There were no windows. The door fitted so perfectly that no light crept underneath. The Normans knew how to demoralise a prisoner. For practical purposes there was electric light available from a low voltage bulb that merely highlighted the gloom that helped to suck all hope from the imprisoned soul.

It would take Bennett all her considerable powers to remain upbeat. She would come round in an hour or two and would be at her lowest ebb. A good time to press her. The Normans would have used flat stones piled on her abdomen until her innards were eventually forced out of her mouth. Modern tortures were inclined to use psychological means. And ends can justify means when situations are serious enough.

It was a very gradual return to consciousness for Bennett. Her head throbbed as it might after a three day eventing on Special Brew. Her eyes flickered open as she struggled to force herself into conscious. "Some bastard is going to pay for this," she muttered to herself as she struggled to turn over on her side. She ached everywhere. Her brain felt as if someone had removed it through her nostrils and replaced it with last night's chip papers. This was a wild beast confined, not tamed. Stretching her right leg she realised that her legs were not tied.

"Fools," she thought. "I can do this."

She knew that the key was freeing her hands. Much longer and she would lose all feeling and they would be useless to her. The deliberate gloom meant that the room that held her gave no encouragement to her. She could only see a metre or so in the gloom. Nothing suggested itself as a weapon. She would not let the bastards break her will. She had been in worse places than this. There must be something. Sheer bloody determination got her to her feet. She promptly slumped back against the wall hurting her shoulder as she fell. The wall gave her the impetus to push herself upright once more. Things were getting bleaker. There was no higher power to which Bennett could or would appeal. Like Slope she was a confirmed atheist and had always believed that she was alone in a hostile universe. If the world was closing in on her now then, "what the hell". It was no more than she had expected. But one last shot at murder, mayhem and untold riches? What a beautiful way to go. Not a grubby end like this. Left to die in the dark. It wasn't what she had imagined.

A sharp metallic sound disturbed her melancholy imaginings and sharpened her instincts all at the same time. She couldn't quite place its origin. Her hearing had sharpened even after such a short time incarcerated in the windowless room. She focused on the sound desperately trying to identify its origin. It was definitely a key turning what sounded like an ancient lock. She was not ready for this. They must be coming to torture her in an attempt to find answers. "They'd have to get very inventive to get past my enjoyment of pain," she told herself. A sadomasochist by inclination her heightened pain threshold gave her advantages in many situations. If nothing else she would make it hard for them.

The ancient door creaked open. Bennett was conscious of a rush of cold air. She identified the direction but couldn't make out who had entered the room. She would use feet, teeth anything she could to get in a blow or two. But she couldn't hit what she couldn't see. The single bulb was useless. Somehow it made the room even darker. The door slammed. A bright light illuminated the room and temporarily blinded her. She blinked so hard that her eyes hurt. She could smell someone close to her then felt the prick of a dagger underneath her left ear. She knew what it meant. She had done this often enough herself since adopting the favoured weapon of the Olive Pickers. One false move and the stiletto would pierce the brain through her ear. No second chances. Dead on the ground. A trickle of blood and farewell to the vale of tears. She stood rigidly hoping for the opportunity of a blow before the lights went out for good. She was still blinking but couldn't clear her sight.

"Just who the hell are you? Do me a favour and just get on with it. If you are going to kill me then bloody well do it. You must know you'll regret it if I get a chance to get near you. I've killed plenty in my time. You'd be one more statistic. So bloody well get on with it."

"Sebastian sent me. Your diversion worked," whispered the Olive Picker.

The lights dimmed until they were at a level where Elizabeth could adjust her vision to see her collaborator clearly. She blinked incessantly gradually clearing the tears in her eyes until she was able to see who it was standing directly in front of her. Finally focusing on the figure she burst into peals of laughter that forced tears of a different kind to flow down both cheeks.

"That's perfect. I knew it would. I'm just surprised Sebastian bothered to have me released. He's a callous bastard and I had assumed he'd cut me out after I'd served my purpose."

Bennett managed to reduce her laughter to a controlled giggling as her rescuer cut the ties from her hands. She could not hold back her contempt as she gasped, "I suggest you move yourself. I imagine Cornelius is on his way to interrogate me as we speak. The sooner I get to see Sebastian the better."

"And I suggest you shut your mouth Bennett. Or I'll shut it for you," the Olive Picker nicked the skin beneath her ear drawing blood which aroused her. But she banished such thoughts to concentrate on the present and the need to make haste.

The message was clear and unequivocal. Bennett knew that the Olive Pickers could be dangerous and had no qualms about killing at the drop of a hat. Given who she was dealing with she had little choice other than to cooperate. Knowing Slope as well as she did she imagined their time on this earth was limited. As soon as they had served his purposes they would no doubt be dispatched.

The slightest of nods signalled acquiescence as the two figures left the torture room closing the door behind them. They disappeared into the darkness of the castle's lower chambers.

An hour's stumbling along uneven castle floors by the light of a hand torch led the two to one of the lowest of the castle rooms. Gradually the light improved which seemed unlikely. Clearly money had been spent in the hidden depths. They were now walking along much more even floors and well lit corridors. Gradually they emerged into a corridor where the taller of the two could stand up straight rather than walking bent backed. At the end of the corridor was a mediaeval door under which light pooled. As they approached the door opened and the two entered a large, well lit room with a large group of men poring over a series of maps placed on a massive table against the far wall. The room was dominated by a central pillar clearly the work of Norman builders. From behind the pillar stepped Sebastian Slope.

"Welcome to my operational hub Elizabeth. Your diversion worked a treat, well done. The pillar you see before you is known as the whipping post. It's where wrongdoers were whipped to within an inch of their lives and often several feet beyond that. This room has seen some blood in its time.

"I need you to keep some sort of order amongst this motley crew Elizabeth. They can be a lively lot at the best of times. However, we are near our goal. The maps and documents you see on the table there give a very good indication of where the royal treasure is secreted. Nobody knows we are here and we have a short time to do the necessary work. You Elizabeth are an essential part of the jigsaw we have in front of us."

"Thank you Sebastian," hissed `Bennett in the most sarcastic tone she could muster. "I'm glad you have further use of my services. That is very thoughtful of you. I have recently been knocked senseless, imprisoned and almost lost the use of my hands and have been lying on a filthy floor trussed like a chicken for hour after hour. Shall I start immediately or might I have the chance to clean up first."

"Don't be sore Elizabeth it was your plan after all. And there's no need to clean up at all since you are about to be up to your eyes in shit shortly in any case. I need you because you are small and slim. Just the shape and size to be able to crawl into a garderobe in search of the X that marks the spot. We've tried and none of these Olive Pickers will fit, too much pasta and fine wine. You do know what a garderobe is I assume."

"I now see why I was rescued," she smiled, "and of course I know what a bloody garderobe is you patronising bastard. It's a Norman shit chute, and I'm not doing it. Those places are bloody dangerous. If you're so sure that you're right then you bloody do it."

"That's the whole bloody point. You are the only one small enough to get into the damn thing. I believe that somewhere around half way down you should find some markings that will identify the resting place of the bulk of the treasure. And I'd advise you not to take that tone with me if you want to carry on walking when this is all over and done."

"Promises, promises. Typical man."

Slope permitted himself a smile knowing Bennett's preference for sex of the most violent kind. That time could come soon enough but for now there was work to do. The room that Slope had accessed from the flooded caverns underneath the castle had been discovered through a stroke of luck. The documents that Slope had acquired from Spink before he slipped the drunken old man into his watery grave were comprehensive. They contained detailed information on the city much of it classified as secret. The room had been built before the Second World War when invasion by Germany seemed not only possible but inevitable. The castle was chosen because of its relative obscurity and chaotic layout. It was relatively easy to disguise a room within the thickness of the massive walls constructed by the original Norman masons. Once constructed the room was provided with air conditioning, heating and lighting all supplied by an advanced generator. It was then used to house hundreds of Britain's most famous art treasures. The major city galleries of Britain were emptied and their treasures transferred to the seaside castle where they remained for the duration of the war stored in perfect conditions. The whole thing was conducted in secrecy. The men involved had the highest security clearance and it was made plain that anyone revealing the secret could expect immediate imprisonment followed by the opportunity of facing a firing squad under military regulations governing the entire country.

Many of those living in proximity to the castle had heard rumours. In villages there are always rumours but the secret was never revealed. The inevitable documentation in a nondigital age, however, was a different matter. Records were kept and British civil service were the best in the world at this. Somehow a letter from the castle custodian of the time to the War Office confirming receipt of art works worth hundreds of thousands of pounds had found its way into a collection of documents with which Gurnard Spink trawled the city pubs hoping to convince listeners of the knowledge he had obtained. Any of those who waved the old man away impatiently would not have believed the secrets he had managed to accumulate over the years. Slope had hit a major jackpot by the accident of listening to the old man against his better judgement and the discovery had proven crucial to what had previously been a half-formed plan.

Bennett's altercation with the Jobs had provided the necessary diversion to gain access to the now empty room. Slope had been able to install half a dozen of his best men to take the plan to its next stage. As all treasures had been returned to their respective galleries and museums at the end of the war the room had gradually been forgotten. Nobody came to this level within the castle as nobody knew there was such a level. The masons and their successors used by the original Norman baron who held the Black Castle were skilled at devising secret passageways and disguised rooms in the building.

William de Londres had much to fear from those surrounding the original castle and he had instructed his masons to be creative in the castle's interior design. The de Breos family who followed in his footsteps and that of the Conqueror's had even more reason to fear enemies. The last in the de Breos line was a cunning and manipulative schemer. He knew only too well that if the castle was ever breached then he could expect no mercy. He took the skills and deviousness of interior castle defences to heights never previously contemplated. As a result the castle was a warren of passages ending in blank walls. A mystery of floor levels that made no sense and a carefully constructed masterpiece of illusion that confounded castle residents never mind anyone who managed to penetrate its significant outer defences. It was this very deviousness that recommended the castle to the war office when the decision was made to move national treasures away from places they could be easily looted by the Nazis. It was the perfect place for one of the most devious criminals in history to plan his final coup.

For now Slope had the tricky task of persuading Bennett that her best interests lay in taking the considerable risk of confirming whether the document purporting to reveal the whereabouts of the royal treasure was genuine or not. Other documents in the bundle had proved their worth already. The details of the planned Swansea underground railway system, the existence of the very room they occupied and the layout of the canal system that penetrated the caverns beneath the castle. All these documents had proved authentic. Surely the treasure was authentic as well.

"Sebastian, I'm sure you have my best interests at heart but seriously how do you propose I climb down what is essentially a 30 foot chute that has been variously contaminated with centuries worth of waste of every possible kind?"

"It's not as difficult as you might think, Elizabeth. All that waste will have decomposed by now and in any case I don't need you to go all the way down. The secret, if it is there at all, will be found around halfway down. You will be lowered using a pulley system operated by two of my men who know exactly what they are doing. There is no way you can fall. You will be wearing a harness, so you see there is no danger at all."

"You show me the men operating the pulley and I'll decide. Never mind why, just bring them over here and let me have a few words with them, then I'll let you know."

Slope nodded and beckoned over two of the men at the table.

"This is Vincenzo and this is Federico. They will be cooperating your pulley system Elizabeth."

"That'll be all thank you Sebastian. You can return to your document table. I'll call you in a moment or two with my decision."

Slope did as he was asked but was unable to suppress a grin as he moved to the other side of the chamber. He knew exactly how Bennett operated. In seconds two of his men would be bent double with tears of real pain in their eyes.

"Now Vincenzo and Federico come closer and concentrate. Parliamo Inglese?" Both men nodded. "You look young and fit to me. Move closer if you will. I'd like to ask you one or two questions before we move into the next chamber. I'd like to check your equipment."

As she spoke Bennett grabbed at the crotch of both men. Her grip was like that of a mole wrench. She squeezed and twisted as the faces in front of her twisted in concert with their revolving testicles.

"Now that I have your undivided attention I'd like to make you a promise. You do the job you have been asked to me. That is lower me carefully until I instruct you to reverse the process. Complete both actions successfully and you will live long and happy lives. Fail in any sense and I shall come back to haunt you except it will not be in spiritual form. I shall find a way of tracking you down and I will kill you. Capisci?"

The men nodded frantically as her grip continued to tighten.

"Please, we have agreed. You are hurting me. I promise I will do whatever you want, only let me go." Federico was sobbing quietly as he spoke.

"You might regret that. Not many men do what I want and live to limp away. Don't worry I'll let my grip loosen gradually. Wouldn't want you two to go spiralling upwards and hit the ceiling now would we?"

This is what passed for humour in the twisted world of Elizabeth Bennett. She did as she said she would releasing her grip to the relief of two suffering Italians. They remained bent over as if the years had suddenly piled on their agonies. "Now follow me and let's have a look at the tackle in the next chamber. I've already had a damn good feel of your tackle in this one. Follow me."

The two did exactly as they were told walking bent double like two obedient chimpanzees as gradually the pain inflicted by Bennett subsided to a dull roar. Slope watched them go and couldn't stifle a guffaw as he imagined the discomfort the men would be feeling for the rest of the day. The men would do as they were told. He had already given them their orders. Later he would visit the chamber himself and confirm what he expected from them and most of all from Bennett.

The adjoining chamber was a massive contrast with the well appointed room the three had just left. One of the castle's original rooms it had been left in its original form. The room was dominated by a central column. It was the only touch of elegance in what was an overtly functional construction. It had been variously a dungeon, a prison for short term incarcerations and a room dedicated to torture. The Normans were no shrinking violets when it came to the use of torture to elicit information or confessions. The central column was a structural part of the room but had a much more sinister function as well. It was the feared and loathed whipping post. Hundreds had suffered agonies either in punishment or in encouragement to reveal secrets over the generations. It was the ultimate threat and nobody resisted its power. There was no need for an 'Abandon Hope All Ye Who Enter Here' sign over the studded wooden door that secured the room. Anyone brought all the way down to this level in the castle would already know their fate. There was no escape. Bennett felt very comfortable in such a room as she walked to the far corner where the garderobe was sited.

"Come on then you two gibbons. This is your chance to show me your tackle. I warn you. If I am not completely happy with what I see you will both feel my wrath. The old whipping post could find two new customers after all these years. It's up to you. And don't think that because there are two of you that you have any form of advantage. One false move and neither of you will see the sun again."

Vincenzo and Federico had absorbed enough stories of the killer that was Elizabeth Bennett during their time in Puglia when they first hooked up with Slope. They had never met her in those days but were aware of Slope's admiration for her ability to kill without a second's warning. They had heard the story of the death of the sailor in the harbour bar in Puglia. They had no illusions about how deadly she could be. The only hope for them was to do exactly what they were ordered to do and pray that the result was the one that Slope and Bennett were anticipating. In that spirit they walked over to the garderobe where the pulley system had been hastily erected. With the air of a couple of school kids showing their teacher a working model they had made they explained the working parts to a clearly bored Bennett. Eventually she had heard enough,

"You know Federico I'd like to know that the pulley has been put to a physical test. Here's the thing. You get into the basket there and we'll see if it will take your weight."

With the dull stare of a condemned man Federico lifted his leg over and climbed into the basket.

Two very nervous Olive Pickers took the greatest care in demonstrating the safety of the pulley system Bennett was so sceptical about. An hour later she appeared satisfied, at least in the safety of the system that could help to take them ever closer to a fortune that could yet be mythical rather than real. Having forced both men to take a turn in the basket she pronounced herself confident in the tackle in use.

"Now then you two let's see whether your personal tackle has made a full recovery from my outrageous attack earlier today. Let's see what you are made of and remember I call the shots. I think I'm going to enjoy this."

An hour later Slope entered the dark chamber to find both Olive Pickers held upright only by the tethers that tied them to the whipping post. They were both naked and dripping blood. In the corner a dishevelled Bennett lay with her back against the rough chamber wall.

"I've had a lovely day," was all she said grinning at Slope with an expression that was half victim and half predator.

24

THE VILLAGE TAKES A TRIP

The weekend of the festival had arrived. It had been so long in the planning that locals felt it would never be realised. The village had a reputation for dilatoriness. Things got done eventually. The place had a centuries-old connection with another Celtic outpost in Cornwall. There they did things 'dreckly', here it was now in a minute. In both cases it was shorthand for when we feel like it we'll get around to it. Locals here would not be hurried into anything. The festival, however, caught the prevailing mood.

Too many years of austerity had taken the shine off living in such a beautiful spot. A spell of enjoyment and to hell with the consequences was well on the cards. It showed in the willingness of locals to take part. It showed in the spring in the step of the oldest residents. Belying their years they organised, became organised, constructed stalls, manned stalls. They smiled at visitors even to the extent of helping them to find parking in a fishing village that was never designed for the 21st century. Old scores were buried, for now. For the time being this was all about the village. This was their opportunity to showcase one of the genuine jewels of the Welsh coast.

The theme for the festival had been decided at the first meeting of the organising committee. It was an obvious one but one that left plenty of scope for invention. After all, the stalls, pop-up shops and restaurants were clustered in the shadow of a Norman castle dating from the 14th century. There was scope for people to dress as lords, ladies, beggars and vagabonds. And of course as jesters. There was always a jester. Sometimes a whole nest of jesters infested such festivals. There would be displays of archery and of falconry. Re-enactment groups were engaged to stage mock versions of the real thing. There would be music from the past and the present. Modern day troubadours could battle it out with those who specialised in the music of the 14th century. What could possibly go wrong?

Bones and Prideaux were bustling around the castle fields putting the finishing touches to The Hand of God stand. Prideaux had brought in his young chef, Hartley Whitney. Whitney was a holder of the prestigious Croix de Bouche Paris, one of France's top gastronomic awards. He had torn up the books of culinary wisdom of generations to impose his own eclectic take on the business of dining. He would never refer to it as fine dining. To Whitney a well prepared dish of road kill squirrel could rank right up there with the freshest sea bass and samphire jus. For marketing purposes this most innovative of chefs had been persuaded to rein in his more leftfield dishes for a concentration on freshly cooked fish dishes.

This was the fishing village of Oystermouth and fresh fish and shellfish had been almost its raison d'être for centuries. And when the castle at its centre had undergone one of its periodic refurbishments excavations had revealed thousands of oyster shells in the detritus of centuries. Overfishing and pollution had changed the fortunes of the village. Now, at last the oyster was back in all its glory. The bay was clean again. The new oyster beds were already bearing their salty fruit and supplementary mussel beds were adding to the renaissance of what had been the staple food and industry for years.

In honour of the occasion chef Whitney had developed a new signature dish. Oysters six ways was already causing a stir in the culinary world. Food critics were being forced to respond to this upstart who was happy to crow about his skills and innovative imagination. Older more established chefs, especially those involved in the media, were inclined to be sniffy about this young man who cared not a fig for their views. He didn't need to. Gourmets, wannabes and the world's media were beating a path to his door. Better still for The Hand of God was gradually becoming the only destination for those who were serious about food. And of course this reputation did no harm to the inn which had fortuitously come into the hands of the two friends following the deaths of Mark and Ginny Williams by Slope and Bennett.

To complement the food offer Bones and Prideaux stood ready with one of the finest wine cellars available. As success built upon success the shadows of violent death were taking wing and allowing Bones and Prideaux to settle into a new way of living. Slope and Bennett could not be forgotten, certainly not forgiven but this was a time for living. Yet even now there was a nagging hollow feeling. It was almost like a subtle but unavoidable scent that wafted across the subconscious when it was least expected.

Prideaux was more prone than Bones to such doubts and worries. He could fake happy but that is mostly what it was. The Black Dog never strayed far from his side. He had suffered from a form of depression for most of his adult life. He had developed strategies to deal with it. He often likened himself to those unfortunates who had never learned to read.

"Unbelievable, Bones how illiterates are clever enough to reach middle age without anyone ever guessing that they can barely read a newspaper. It's just one of those things that they deal with through tricks and subterfuge. I knew two of my dad's friends who could hardly read a sentence even in their fifties. They would never admit it. Most of all they wouldn't admit it to themselves. They could even keep it from themselves. That's one of the reasons I did those voluntary reading classes for adults back in the old FE days at the college down at the Oxpens."

"Commendable old chap. Now I know you are a miserable bastard but at least you are consistent. Look, I am as conscious as you are that Slope is around. This is real, not like the Beast of Bodmin rumours on the moor down in Cornwall.

"I'm surprised you haven't sent young Whitney down to the moor. If anybody could find the beast it would be him. You'd have to be quick mind or he'd have the bastard in his oven and offering mythical beast with swamp water dressing on the menu. Don't tell him I said that. I don't think the boy has much of a sense of humour. He hasn't really spoken to me since I took the piss out of his lobster in lime lather with a corn biscuit accompaniment effort."

"Actually I'd appreciate it if you'd give him a chance. He's a young lad and already doing well, I'd hate to lose him."

"No sooner said than done old chap. Now come and give me a hand with this wine. This is the best of our cellar we are setting up here and it has to work. This is not wine for the pissheads, this is for the connoisseurs and we have to get it right. This'll take your mind off the bastard Slope. Don't forget there's a hell of a lot of cover around here. Slope's not going to come riding in on a white horse to rescue Bennett. She's just rough sex to him. He wouldn't risk his life for her. He doesn't have the Spriggans around him these days. No doubt he has a few nasty bastards to hand but he'll have to get past Cornelius and his men as well as the twins to do any damage."

"You're right of course Bonesie. You know that I can easily get depressed and it's times like this that are the worst. I should be full of beans, relaxed and happy. Truth is I'm wound up tight. It's just that I don't have the capacity to relax. I just feel that if I do the whole thing will come tumbling down. Something ghastly will happen is what I'm trying to say."

"I know the last thing to tell a depressive is cheer up you old buster. All will be well and all manner of things will be well. For fuck's sake cheer up you miserable old biscuit. Nothing's going to happen except we are going to have a jolly good time and I'm not letting anyone bringing me down."

"I'll do my best old pal. I think my problem is that I think too much. It's a bad habit I picked up in Oxford."

"You picked up more than one bad habit in Oxford my old buster. I could favour you with a complete list except that I am a busy man and an exposition on the strange habits, beliefs and superstitions of Piers Prideaux doesn't even make my lecture list at the moment. I repeat for the love of good wine cheer up and concentrate on helping me set this display up. You don't have to think, just do. I'll tell you what then we'll have a little drink or three and I'll listen to your whingeing into the wee small hours."

Bones was the best tonic that Prideaux had ever had. None of the mystery of the expert in curing psychological problems for the third earl of Mount Charles. Not a bit of it. The old practicality of:

"Mad? I'll knock a bit of sense into you" is what prevailed as far as he was concerned. Prideaux wasn't allowed any leeway either. Such tough love wouldn't work for everyone but it worked for Prideaux. They spent most of the remains of the day ensuring that the stall allocated to The Hand of God looked its very best.

On the castle green it looked as if the entire village had taken a trip back in time. A huge variety of stalls were decked out as if they were expecting the arrival of the knights to begin a jousting competition. There were knights. These knights were practising their choreographed battles in the lee of the castle. They were armed as they would have been in the century they were trying to recreate. Everything as realistic as possible. Swords were recreated down to the smallest detail except that edges were blunted. The same applied to bodkins. Despite the care taken a 14th century replica sword could still split a skull if the choreography went awry. A sharpened bodkin could easily split a stomach sack. For this reason practice sessions were always conducted in perfectly serious mode.

Bennett had managed to compose herself following her exertions. She was sated but excited at the sight of the gold bullion stacked in the chamber. Slope had ordered his men to excavate a bricked up passageway leading off the main corridor and there it was. It had to be the work of Cornelius, a quick approximation of the value of the bullion tallied with the amount he had stolen from Slope, the crafty intelligence man had converted the money to bullion to ensure it could never be tracked down through the labyrinth structures of modern financial institutions. Slope was impressed with the old buffer's wiles but could hardly bring himself to admit it. Surely the recovery of his fortune would be enough to satisfy Slope. There were his missing millions. But Bennett could plainly see that it was clear that this was not enough for Slope. He was an angry man. The fortune he had amassed had been siphoned off and transformed into gold ingots. It would take an absolute age to move the recovered fortune in its present form. That bastard Cornelius. It had been his work and was designed to royally piss Slope off. The action had worked. This was only part of Slope's revenge. Heads were going to roll. Slope felt violated and he would have his day.

Then there was the issue of the royal fortune. Perhaps even more important were the documents that Slope knew would cast doubt on the right of the current royal family to the throne of England. These would be absolute dynamite if used correctly and could bring the entire British state to heel. The bargaining potential was enormous and thrilled him to the marrow. He had done his research and finding his own treasure in the process was a bonus. He now had the means to add to that the documents Edward II had brought with him from the treasury on his flight from London. The landing of Queen Isabella and Roger Mortimer had persuaded Edward that he had no choice but to flee. Taking his favourite, Hugh Despenser and as much of the treasury gold with him he headed for West Wales via Caerphilly. It was known that half the treasure had been left at the well fortified castle in Caerphilly. That part of the treasure was recovered following the capture of the King and Despenser near Cardiff. It was generally assumed that the king had taken the rest of the fortune together with certain documentation to the west of Wales ending up in the castle at Oystermouth. That was the last that was seen of it. Rumours abounded concerning its whereabouts but Slope had the key to the recovery of this portion of the King's treasure including the original crown of England. It was within his grasp. Bennett would help him recover it.

"Well Elizabeth I am delighted to have recovered my fortune. Although it is going to take considerable efforts to move it via the underground canal and railway. But we must turn our attention to more pressing matters your time has come. Let's get on with things." Reluctantly Bennett climbed into the basket.

Slope handed her the handset of a two way radio. "You are looking for the Despenser coat of arms on the side of the garderobe. It is approximately half way down. When you find it report back and I'll bring the basket to a stop. The arms will be your access to that lower chamber. I know because I have the documents to confirm it. Be careful though. The Normans might well have booby trapped the chamber. Good luck and contact me once you are in the chamber."

The basket started to move. It shook just a little too much for Bennett's comfort. Too late she was in it now for good or ill. There could be no turning back. Gradually she descended the garderobe. It took an age but suddenly the basket slowed its descent. This must be it Bennett thought. The radio crackled into life. Slope's voice was distant. "Can you see anything yet Elizabeth. You should be at the right level."

Bennett looked around focussing her torch on anything that appeared out of the ordinary. The torch was powerful enough but the stone seemed uniform. Slope's voice came over the radio. "Elizabeth, you are looking for an anomaly. Anything that doesn't fit. Can you see anything?"

"Not yet, Sebastian. Hang on, there is something. Give me a second. I see it. There's a protruding stone and I can just make out a coat of arms alongside it. That must be it. I'm just leaning over to touch it. There's the outline of what must be a door next to it. It's small but I suppose they weren't very tall in those days."

Bennett swung the basket closer until by leaning over the side she was able to grasp the gargoyle. The coat of arms was clearly that of the Despenser family. She struggled to move the gargoyle. She felt some movement, then at last it began to turn slowly at first but once in motion it seemed to become easier. As she turned the figure clockwise there was a grating sound and the door began to open.

Once the dust of centuries had settled Bennett was able to see into the chamber. Better still the basket was slowly swinging closer to the open door. Bennett had always been athletic and had retained enough physical strength to stabilise the basket by holding on to the open mouth of the gargoyle. That gave her the chance to launch herself onto the lip of stone that marked the chamber entrance. She landed on her stomach with a force that winded her. She lay there for minutes as the basket swung wildly in the garderobe and she recovered her strength. The torch lay where she had thrown it. She picked it up and stepped through the door into the room. It wasn't what she was expecting. Scanning the room she became aware of any number of engines of torture. "You have to hand it to those Normans, first class torturers. I'd love to have been alive in those days. What fun," she thought to herself.

A whirring sound broke into her reverie. The basket was moving and it was moving upwards. Bennett rushed towards the door as she saw it disappear from view. "Bennett to Slope. Come in you bastard. What the hell are you up to? If this is a double cross I'll hunt you down. I'll pull out your eyeballs with my fingers and cook them in front of you. I'll sauté your bollocks with shallots and a balsamic vinegar jus. Then I'll force feed them to you. I'll…I'll…"

"Calm down Elizabeth. You have done exactly as I have asked. I needed someone I could trust to test out the lift. And ensure our Norman friends had not left any murderous booby traps behind. I'll be down just as soon as the basket reaches the top. I'll let you in on the secret as soon as I get down there. It'll take a little while. It's hardly an express lift after all."

"You'd better be down," snapped Bennett still angry but mightily relieved. She could tell when Slope was lying which was most of the time. This time he didn't sound like it. And it looked as if a long quest was at last coming to an end. There were still plenty of obstacles to overcome but the end was in sight. It occurred to her that among the obstacles could easily be some created by the Normans. It would be as well to take precautions. Accordingly she warily began to circle the chamber.

This was clearly something more than just a torture chamber. It was the Rolls Royce of torture chambers. The implements of torture were in surprisingly good condition. Somehow they had managed to seal the chamber so that damp had not penetrated here as it had in so many of the castle rooms. There in the corner was the iron virgin, a favourite engine of torture. It was constructed of a hardwood Bennett didn't recognise. In the form of a woman it looked like a tomb set on its end. Inside, the iron spikes were placed in strategic areas allowing the torturer to gradually close the door on his victim. As the spikes pierced various parts of the victim's anatomy he would offer amnesty in return for information. Bennett knew that whatever information was offered there was only one way that it could end. The door would be finally closed screening out the dying screams of yet another victim. There was even a groove running from the base of the iron virgin across the stone floor to the door leading to the garderobes. They were nothing if not efficient the Normans. There was no doubt that this was the killing floor. There were even rollers stacked in one corner to dispose of bodies with the minimum of effort. They would be rolled to the doorway and tipped into the abyss. No doubt on occasion there were men who still retained life so that they were aware that they were disposed of like so much waste.

"I'm glad that basket held firm or I could really have been in the shit," thought Bennett. The thought amused her as she checked out an array of racks, thumbscrews, ropes, and knives together with the flat stones used for pressing victims. It was altogether a torturer's dream. What fun she could have had in such a place. If only she had someone to practise on.

The sound of the basket being lowered brought Bennett back to the present day. She moved back into the shadows. She was taking no chances. She was expecting Slope but this was a bizarre situation even for her. Someone had made the same jump as she had. The gasp as they landed told her that they had achieved a similar result: winded. She moved to the shadow of the iron virgin which hid her completely from whoever it was entering the chamber.

"Elizabeth, I hope you are not playing silly games. We really don't have time. There is much we have to do if we are to get out of here with all that I deserve. Just show yourself."

"Just checking Sebastian. One never knows what to expect when lingering in a torture chamber. It really can attract the most unspeakable of people."

"This is much more than a mere torture chamber. It is also a mausoleum holding some quite significant remains. They weren't all tipped down the shit chute you know. Some of them rest here when by all the rules they should be in Westminster Abbey or somewhere similar. Now switch your torch back on and I'll make the introductions."

25

ONE LAST LOOK

In the clean fresh air of the village the festival went dreamily on. It was an occasion to relax and allow the world to flow on by itself. The surroundings were perfect; the weather too and there was an abundance of jesters. It was not only dream time it was mediaeval dream time. Troubadours, mediaeval dress, wooden swords for the children, real bows and arrows for the men and women. Mock battles and tableaux wherever the eye strayed. All of it fuelled by the gentle mead like drink concocted by the local brewer. The castle formed a background to the general bonhomie. Nobody thought of horrors happening elsewhere. Just for now nobody cared. Bones and Prideaux were doing a roaring trade on their stall. But there was something troubling both of them. They had enjoyed their break. Bones had even survived a murderous attack by the Canadian. He was relaxed despite something nagging at the back of his mind. Prideaux never relaxed. He had no capacity to relax. He was one of those who believed that the moment you relaxed that was when the hammer would fall. He wasn't so much highly strung as over tightened. Even he though felt the threat of relaxation creeping around his shoulders.

"OK Bonesie. Let's do it. You know you want to. One last look. What harm can it do? Soon we'll be home in The Hand of God and relaxing properly. We won't do that unless we make one last effort at finding the treasure. Be warned though we are likely to find nothing. Hundreds have searched for it and failed. I reckon it has to be one of two things. Either it is something hidden in plain sight or something completely unexpected.

One more thing. I'm going nowhere without the twins. I'm not dropping my guard."

"OK Piers. I'll get Italian Tony to mind the stall; you give the twins a call. They're around here somewhere along with half of MI7 and enough squaddies to sink a ship so I don't think there's much to be concerned about."

"I'll relax when I see Slope and Bennett lying stone dead and not before."

"Come on then you miserable old sod. The twins are up near the gatehouse. Little bit of bother with a couple of surfers with too much sun and cider. Picked on Bob apparently. Never mind they'll be out of hospital soon. Both the twins are in happy mode which is just as well, otherwise those surfers would have surfed their last."

The two walked up the steep incline to the castle gatehouse. The ambulance was just backing out having loaded up the senseless surfers.

"Bit of a wipeout," grinned Bob. "Just reminded them of their manners: What are you pair up to?"

"Just one last look for the treasure we thought before we return home," Bones answered. "And it'll be good to get out of the sun. Bad for the skin you know, causes wrinkles and such."

"It'll do you no good with the ladies if you get all wrinkled up Bonesie."

"Piss off Piers. Anyway the ladies like a man with a lived-in face."

"Depends who's lived in it I reckon," chimed Bob. "Come on then, if we're going let's go. Robert just pushed off somewhere in the castle to find Cornelius and see if he's managed to prize anything useful out of Bennett. I'm sure we'll catch up with him."

The three men set off in high spirits and began the long descent towards the castle's centre. The castle had been modified and added to for centuries and finding one's way around in it was problematic. Nothing necessarily made sense. Turning corners often led to a blank wall. One corridor could lead off another taking you back to the original spot. This was nothing to do with the original builders of the castle but subsequent owners who simply added rooms and corridors as the whim struck. In its own way it was tempting to forget logic and simply wander. That is exactly what they did. The only constant was that they were moving inexorably lower into the real bowels of the castle. Security lighting, whitewashed walls and the powerful torches carried by all three men made the descent a less dangerous one than it might have been. Even so they had only descended about halfway leaving a good ten metres beneath them. What they couldn't know is that they were unavoidably drawing closer to the torture chamber mausoleum where Slope and Bennett lurked.

High spirits persisted though Bob was on full alert. He was heavily armed and had insisted Bones and Prideaux had brought their pistols too. Protestations were swept aside. Bob summed it up neatly by reminding his recalcitrant companions of the days when all three had been at the mercy of Slope and Bennett. "I'd happily face those two any day of the week but not without a gun in my hand. Now let's concentrate shall we?"

His face left no doubt that he was serious. They walked along corridors they had never seen before and small talk dried as Bob's advice seeped into the brains of the two non-combatants. Somewhere in front of them a noise alerted them to the fact they were not alone. Bob instantly slipped into full combat mode indicating that Bones and Prideaux should stay back. They needed no second invitation and gratefully watched as he moved silently forward with his machine pistol at the ready. Minutes later a scream that could curdle milk echoed through the passageway.

"I sincerely hope that noise is a local ghost earning its performance fee," muttered Bones.

"You don't believe in ghosts, do you?" asked Prideaux.

"I'd prefer that it came from a ghost than anything of flesh and blood. If there is something up ahead that has upset Bob then we are in real trouble. I suggest a tactical retreat."

"Sound idea Bonesie," added Prideaux. "I think it's about time the professionals dealt with this." The two friends turned to make the hasty retreat that was a usual response to any form of physical danger. They hadn't managed to put one foot in front of the other when they were stopped dead by a shout.

"Stay exactly where you are my heroes," The voice, dripping with sarcasm, was that of Bob Job. Where do you think you are off too?"

"Off in search of reinforcements," answered Bones without a blush.

"I'll believe you Bonesie and it's not a bad idea. I don't think we have the time though. Some poor bastard is being tortured very close to here but there seems no way into the room. The walls are all blank. By the time we get anyone down here it'll be too late. And no, Bonesie it is not a ghost."

It was clear that whoever was suffering was close at hand but with no obvious entrance to a chamber in sight things looked bleak for the victim.

"This is a Norman castle for God's sake," Prideaux pointed out. "Look around, there will be some sort of door on a counterweight. The Normans always used some adaptation of that to hide a chamber or anything they wanted to keep secret. Search the walls. There will be some indication of where the hidden entrance is. Think Agatha Christie except with stone rather than dummy bookshelves."

"I wish it was bloody Agatha Christie," Bones muttered but grudgingly joined the others in the search.

"Over here," shouted Prideaux. "I'll bet this is it. The arms of Despenser are just here above that stone that juts out from the rest. Now I've not seen anything else like that in any of this plethora of passageways."

The combined strength of the three men started a movement that surprised them with its immediacy. Bones and Prideaux added their weight and the door suddenly gave way depositing all on the floor of what was evidently a room dedicated to the art of torture. There was a grating noise as the door swung back into place. Approached from the passageway there would be no indication that there had ever been a door. The room was like a sauna. Through thick steam the three could just make out those in front of them.

"Welcome to hell," said a smirking Slope. Don't bother to even reach for your pistols. I have other plans for you but move an inch and it might be necessary to shoot you a little bit. I welcome you to my favourite dream and to your worst nightmare."

Wearily the three got to their feet. This wasn't what they had expected. Slope, Bennett and four other armed men covered them. Disarming them Slope's men tied their arms behind them and pushed them back against the room's central pillar.

"You are now tied to the whipping post where you will wait your turn on whatever instrument of torture I choose. Just to put you in the mood you will be able to watch Elizabeth oversee the death of the bastard Cornelius. He's bubbling away nicely. Slope nodded towards a huge cauldron emitting clouds of steam that was positioned in the great fireplace.

"You mean that you are actually boiling Cornelius to death. You sick bastard Slope."

"Nonsense Prideaux. Standard practice back in the day. Any cook whose cooking did not make the grade could be boiled in his own cooking pot. Henry VIII did it all the time. He was more famous for that than for beheading his wives. I hadn't counted on anyone hearing the screams though. I think he's just about done now. And in any case we popped him in to cook when the water was just luke warm. Just as you do with a lobster. It's a lot less cruel.

"If you and your tiresome companion hadn't been bickering loud enough to wake the dead then you might even have caught us unawares. Sealed your own death warrants right there."

The three were forced to watch as a wild eyed Bennett stood on a chair to peer into the cauldron where Cornelius had met his end.

"Well done Elizabeth, we'll make a chef of you yet." Slope turned to address the four as if he were on the hustings addressing a hostile crowd.

"I have located the bullion that Cornelius translated my pension pot into. You will note the size of the gold bar," Sloped tossed the bar across the room to Piers. "They are much smaller than usual but due to a new process much denser. More valuable per bar. I'm not sure I can get it all out before the rest of MI7 descends. But I intend to try to move as much as I can. That's not the real prize though, this is." Slope held up the envelope that had been left at Garibaldi's Overcoat in Puglia.

"What is it with you psychos that you have to boast about your successes Slope? Is it inadequacy? I think that's probably it."

"Well done Prideaux. You've just earned yourself some additional exquisite pain. And it is not inadequacy. It is simple. I enjoy showing cockroaches like you and your useless pals how far below me you are in the food chain. You have no idea what this envelope holds but this is something people have searched for over centuries." Slope drew out a golden medallion and dangled it in front of the helpless three.

"This is what it was all about. You'll need to twist your necks to see the four tombs to your left. Those tombs contain the treasure Edward II hid here in the Black Castle. The first three tombs each holds a skeleton. Each of the skeletons are all that is left of three of Edward's closest allies. One of them was the official crown jeweller. Around the neck of those men there were three pieces of the medallion designed by him. The three were slaughtered then dumped in the tombs. In addition at least half the gold looted from the treasury before his flight to Wales is contained here. In the fourth tomb lies the crown of England and in a sealed box a parchment that clearly shows the illegitimacy of the current royal family.

"Now that is the prize. That parchment is worth more than all the gold currently resting in this room. All it took to get into the fourth tomb was to reassemble the three pieces into a single medallion. I found a jeweller capable of doing the job properly. He's probably floating off the coast of Puglia by now. The finished article when assembled gave the instructions to open the fourth tomb. It was in Latin of course. The benefits of a classical education, eh! Worked like a charm and slid open as if it was only closed yesterday."

"Bollocks. You have finally lost your mind Slope," Prideaux was unable to contain himself any longer. "You are surrounded by riches beyond the dreams of avarice. You'll never get this gold out without being discovered and how long do you think it will be before they come looking for us. You've blown it Slope. You'll never get out of here alive."

"Any volunteers to have a go on the rack? Bennett is something of an expert. Or there are the masks. You'll probably die quicker. Perhaps there is someone who would like to try out the iron maiden. It's stretching, spiking or some form of hot iron torture. Today's menu is a little limited. Come on Prideaux. I could warm you up with a little light whipping. You lot, he turned to the Olive Pickers, start loading that lot and get it up to the higher chamber."

The men did as they were ordered. They wanted out of this hell before it was too late. Slope and Bennett seemed to be more focused on torture than getting way with the gold and other valuables. They began to load the gold, a tricky prospect as it meant leaning out over the abyss to pull in the basket that always seemed just out of reach. It took a while to establish a system which enabled substantial numbers of gold bars to be hauled up to the mouth of the garderobe.

Behind them Slope had Prideaux tied down on the bed of the rack. Bennett began to turn the handle, slowly at first, then with more vigour. She too recognised that as exciting as the torture was they really needed to get out of this place. Prideaux screamed as the rack did its job. Bones was in tears as he was forced to watch his best friend in agony.

Bob Job was twitching. Odds weren't good but if only one of them could get free of the whipping post that the Olive Pickers had securely tied them to.

"Take a bellows to that brazier and put some torture irons in it to heat through," Slope ordered. "I'm going to make you wish you had never been born."

Job braced himself but it was Bones who Slope untied from the whipping post and dragged towards the now white-hot fire irons.

"I love the smell of burning flesh, at any time really," smirked Slope as he placed one of the branding irons close to Bones's face. He winced.

"Hold him," Slope ordered as Bones struggled. Ripping off his shirt there was a sizzle of burning flesh and a scream as the iron burned its mark onto Bones's forearm.

"Hold the bastard I said," Slope repeated as he fought to subdue his victim. Slowly Slope's man sank to the floor. The back of his head was missing. A sniper's bullet had ended his involvement in torturing Bones. Slope threw Bones to the floor and ducked back into the shadows. Bennett turned to see Robert Job running towards her. She practically cut him in half with her machine pistol.

"Good shots Elizabeth" Slope yelled as he emerged from the shadows. Cover the twin will you. Don't shoot yet we may need hostages." Slope ran to the exit to the garderobe. The three men who had been loading the gold lay dead. The sniper had taken them by surprise. All lay dead. He saw the rope swinging in the void. Robert Job had abseiled unseen down the garderobe. Returning to the chamber Slope grabbed the box in which the crown and incriminating documents rested.

"Stay there," he ordered Bennett. "I'll go up in the basket. They won't be expecting me. I'll neutralise any operatives in the higher chamber and send the basket back down for you."

He didn't wait for an answer but sprinted towards the basket. He managed to haul himself inside and lay curled with his machine pistol ready. At least he had the evidence of royal chicanery and the English crown in his possession. It was just possible he could shoot his way out.

The basket lurched as it reached the mouth of the garderobe. Slope sprang to his feet and let off a burst of fire. There was nobody there. The gold that had been stacked in the corner remained untouched otherwise the chamber was empty. Robert Job must have been acting alone. But where were his own men? Rats and sinking ships sprang to mind. He felt the basket shake and half turned to see what it was. A large Cornish fist crashed into the side of his head. The blow had forced him to drop his pistol. Bob Job picked it up and started to pistol whip an already dazed Slope.

"You killed my brother Slope. You shouldn't have done that." Job was icily calm as he administered a fierce beating to Slope now pleading for his life. Bob Job finally exhausted his hatred of Slope. Taking the pistol, box and medallion with him he jumped onto solid ground. Slope lay moaning curled on the floor of the basket. The horror of all that had happened suddenly hit home and Job fired several bursts at the supporting ropes. Slope was too far gone to realise that he was about to plunge sixty metres to a certain death.

"That's just me putting out the garbage," Job thought to himself as the basket plummeted towards the bottom of the garderobe.

His climb up the abseiling rope had taken its toll but he had to alert the rest of MI7's operatives to the whereabouts of Prideaux and Bones. He headed for the Great Hall to alert the troops.

Bennett had raced to the garderobe in pursuit of Job, missing him, but shouting to alert Slope that he was loose and in pursuit. She shouted again for Slope to send the basket back for her. And was surprised to see it hurtling past toward the bottom of the dark chamber. She had forgotten all about Prideaux who had managed to free himself from the rack. He had tried to calm down a screaming Bones. Bennet suspected that Slope had been in the free falling basket surely no one could survive that? Her immediate concern was flight things were unravelling. She did not expect to see Bob Job swinging back down the chamber, a man possessed. He would have killed her on the instant. She had to hide. There was only one place left to her. She opened the iron door carefully and stepped inside. Closing the door as quietly as possible she heard the raging bull run past. She was in luck. The metallic clunk of the contact plate informed her that her luck had just run out. It started the progress of the internal spikes towards her. Her screams were muffled as the spikes penetrated her major organs. Without a torturer to control the machine her death was quick. The machine then performed its final act automatically opening the door to the garderobe to send her body plunging to the garderobe floor. She was shortly to join a basketful of Slope. Two psychopaths united in death on the castle midden.

Job negotiated the spiral staircases that led to the Great Hall. He looked up as he began to climb the final steps leading to the Great Hall. Framed in the doorway above was the unmistakeable figure of Zebedee.

"Good job, Job," Zebedee had a smile like a cold razor. "You've saved us all quite a bit of time. Now I'll take that," he nodded at the box containing the crown. Job had no choice but to hand over the box.

"Haven't you forgotten something Job?" Job feigned ignorance. "The documents, the documents. Hand them over." Job glanced at the gorillas who had appeared on either side of Zebedee.

"Don't you think that the British people have a right to know that the established monarchy does not hold the throne by right. It is plain enough in the documents. Surely in a democracy…?"

"I suppose you're a constitutional expert now. And who told you this is a democracy? It is up to me and a few others to decide what is best for the British people. If they were to realise that the royal family holds the crown illegally it would only unsettle them.

Anyway, be a good chap and hand them over." It was with reluctance that he handed over the documents.

"Now run along and organise a search party to rescue your little friends. I take it that Slope and Bennett have come to a sticky end or you would not be standing in front of me as large as life and twice as ugly."

Job nodded. "And you are sure that there is no way back for those two? They are pretty resilient you know."

"If you want confirmation I suggest you will need a team of shit shovellers who double as skilled abseilers. I suppose eventually they may stink the place up. Much as they did in life really."

"Fair enough. And Cornelius?" Job shook his head. "Ah well I suppose you only die twice. Not a bad title for a spy thriller that, eh? Well carry on."

"What about the gold?" Job couldn't resist the question.

"Don't be worrying your pretty little head about that Job. We have a department to take care of such things. I'm sure that the chancellor will be doing a little jig, ghastly sight mind you, when he finally does the sums. I've also got a feeling that MI7 is soon to come into a substantial increase in funding. Very satisfying, don't you think. I'm sure that you will receive recognition in due course. Just don't forget the terms of your involvement. I'm sure you are aware that any breach would trigger immediate termination. We have that in common with the Mafia, you can join but there is only one way you can ever leave. You can return to your little lives in the countryside satisfied in a job well done. I think you get my drift."

Bob Job walked off to organise a rescue party for Bones and Prideaux. As he walked he shook his head in bewilderment at the state of his country. He knew that he could never tell anyone what he knew. Yet again the Establishment were the only winners. His twin brother had died for this? Nothing would ever be the same again. Losing his brother was like losing his right arm. A country run by people like Zebedee did not deserve the kind of loyalty shown by the Job twins and others. He could not know it now but it would be many years before the Establishment that sheltered such men as Zebedee and his like would finally be exposed to the full glare of a proper democratic examination. But that's another story.

EPILOGUE

Bob Job returned to Cornwall where he took up the running of the twin's natural woodland site. The brothers had established a thriving business following the murder of their friends Mark and Ginny Williams. Robert Job was buried at the woodland site the twins once ran together. His twin planted a white rose at the head of the grave. Bones and Prideaux were the only ones from outside Cornwall to attend the funeral. The flag of a Free Kernow was lowered to half mast to the strains of Trelawney played by a Cornish brass band as the body of a Cornish hero was lowered into his last resting place.

Bob Job is no longer an MI7 operative. Several years after the above events he received a letter of thanks from the palace. He burned it. He never talks of the past. These days all his energies go into representing the constituency of Mount Charles in the newly founded Cornish Assembly. He keeps a loaded machine pistol in easy reach. One day he will avenge the death of his brother. To date neither Zebedee nor his minions have discovered that Job walked away wearing the medallion that will open the fourth tomb. Opening the tomb and conducting DNA tests on the body buried there would finally establish whether the current royal family rule by right or whether the rumours are true. Bob Job wears the missing medallion around his neck.

The new government have launched an investigation into the whereabouts of the medallion on instructions and under orders communicated by the Palace. The committee charged with running the investigation is to be chaired by Zebedee. This committee meets on a regular basis and all minutes are communicated to the Palace and no other body or individual. Zebedee received a knighthood for services to the state. A month after these events his department, MI7 was given a substantial monetary boost. The chancellor did his little jig. It was awful.

Piers Prideaux and William Radleigh de Beaune are once again running their country pub and restaurant, The Hand of God, in Skenfrith. They too received a letter of thanks from the palace which they promptly burned on the pub's log fire. The two old friends never talk to each other about the past. The scar on Bones's arm has healed well but late at night he will regale regulars with tales of his heroism once upon a time in a castle near the sea. Prideaux has vowed to write the story of his experiences with Bonesie and is currently seeking a publisher.

Gawain Cornelius received a funeral with full honours. He is buried in an unmarked grave in the corner of one of the many sites in the UK now given over to the desperate search for onshore wind power.

Sebastian Slope and Elizabeth Bennett lie at the bottom of the garderobe. They are both still dead. It has not yet been decided when to cap that particular garderobe. No organisation has so far agreed to risk recovery of the bodies as it is too dangerous a task. Instead it has been suggested that a portion of the £12 billion earmarked to renovate both houses of parliament, the centre of democracy in the UK, could be used in order to seal off the final resting place of two of the most murderous individuals in history. Current thinking is that a committee be formed to discuss the best way forward.

The torture room in the Black Castle has been completely sealed and the lower passageways placed off limits to the visiting public. It was suggested that it could be opened as a Black Museum but local opposition was vocal and organised and for once local democracy prevailed.

Discussions continue on the possibility of resurrecting the idea of an underground railway to serve the city of Swansea and its outlying areas. This idea has received much support locally and nationally as a means of further enhancing the ongoing developments taking place in the area including the new university campuses, the Bay lagoon development and the return of the Mumbles Train. A committee has been formed to complete a feasibility study.

Marco Spinelli's gourmet restaurant in Puglia never did come to fruition. His bar 'Garibaldi's Overcoat' continues to prosper. As a man of mixed Cornish and Italian descent Marco chose to name his bar after a piece of Cornish folk lore. This is what gave the bar its name. The Italian patriot Giuseppe Garibaldi (born 4th July 1807, died 2nd June 1882) became friendly with a soldier called Colonel John Peard. The two men looked so alike that they could be taken for twins. They fought side by side through Garibaldi's Italian campaigns. They became such good friends that Garibaldi visited Colonel Peard at his home near Fowey in Cornwall. When Garibaldi said goodbye to his friend he left his cape, lined in red, with his friend. Peard is remembered as Garibaldi's Englishman although in effect he was Garibaldi's Cornishman. That cloak is now one of the main exhibits in a small museum in Fowey. Marco remembered seeing the cape as a child though in his memory it was an overcoat rather than a cape. He thought that Garibaldi's Overcoat would be a good way of marking his joint ancestry by using it for the name of his bar near Ostuni in Puglia. Colonel John Peard is buried in Fowey cemetery.

I am reminded that my habit of using real locations in a work of fiction could lead to some confusion among my readers. I should point out that some of the locations in this book exist in reality. However, my use of them is purely fictional. For example the Black Castle is not Oystermouth Castle, just as Oystermouth itself is fictional as part of this story. The same applies to Skenfrith and The Hand of God, the gourmet pub run so brilliantly by Piers Prideaux and William Radleigh de Beaune the third Earl of Mount Charles. I must say that there are times that I wish this pub really did exist as I should very much like to visit the place. But there we are. Reality and fiction are close neighbours, that is all they are.

In case you should wonder how much else in the book has an element of truth here is one more snippet. The Olive Tree thefts described were a genuine problem not that long ago. True they were organised by the Mafia rather than the Olive Pickers, but they happened. In the modern age particularly valuable examples of the trees that provide Puglia's most sought after product are tagged. The most valuable trees are tracked by their own individual satellite.

Although to my knowledge the Olive Pickers do not exist as an organised criminal group some of the other organisations most certainly do. I have no evidence of the existence of a criminal gang known as the Spriggans. The Spriggan, however, is a figure of Cornish folklore and much more can be read about its existence, fictitious or otherwise in the first novel in this trilogy of two. A Touch of Pigskin features some of the same characters and locations while taking time out to visit Paris.

And one last thing. It is a matter of record that Edward I stayed at Oystermouth Castle on 10th and 11th December 1284. It is also fact that his son Edward II and his favourite Hugh Despenser were on the run in Wales with a vast treasure in 1326. Parts of that treasure were left at Caerphilly Castle and according to records a significant amount of that loot was, "left at a castle in Swansea." A group of Kidwelly men are listed by name as having ridden off with some of that treasure. Of the rest there is no evidence to suggest that it has ever been found. Enjoy the stories.

Dai Blatchford
June 2015
Oystermouth.

WELL, DID YOU LIKE IT???

If you did, like it, please let everyone know and share the experience…Amazon is a good place to post your thoughts but any social media is a boon for getting great books into good hands. If you want to check out some more scintillating moonshine from the South Wales backwoods you can find us where we live at Jack Noir

www.iponymous.com

www.ingramcontent.com/pod-product-compliance
Lightning Source LLC
Chambersburg PA
CBHW020632260626
47157CB00008B/2699